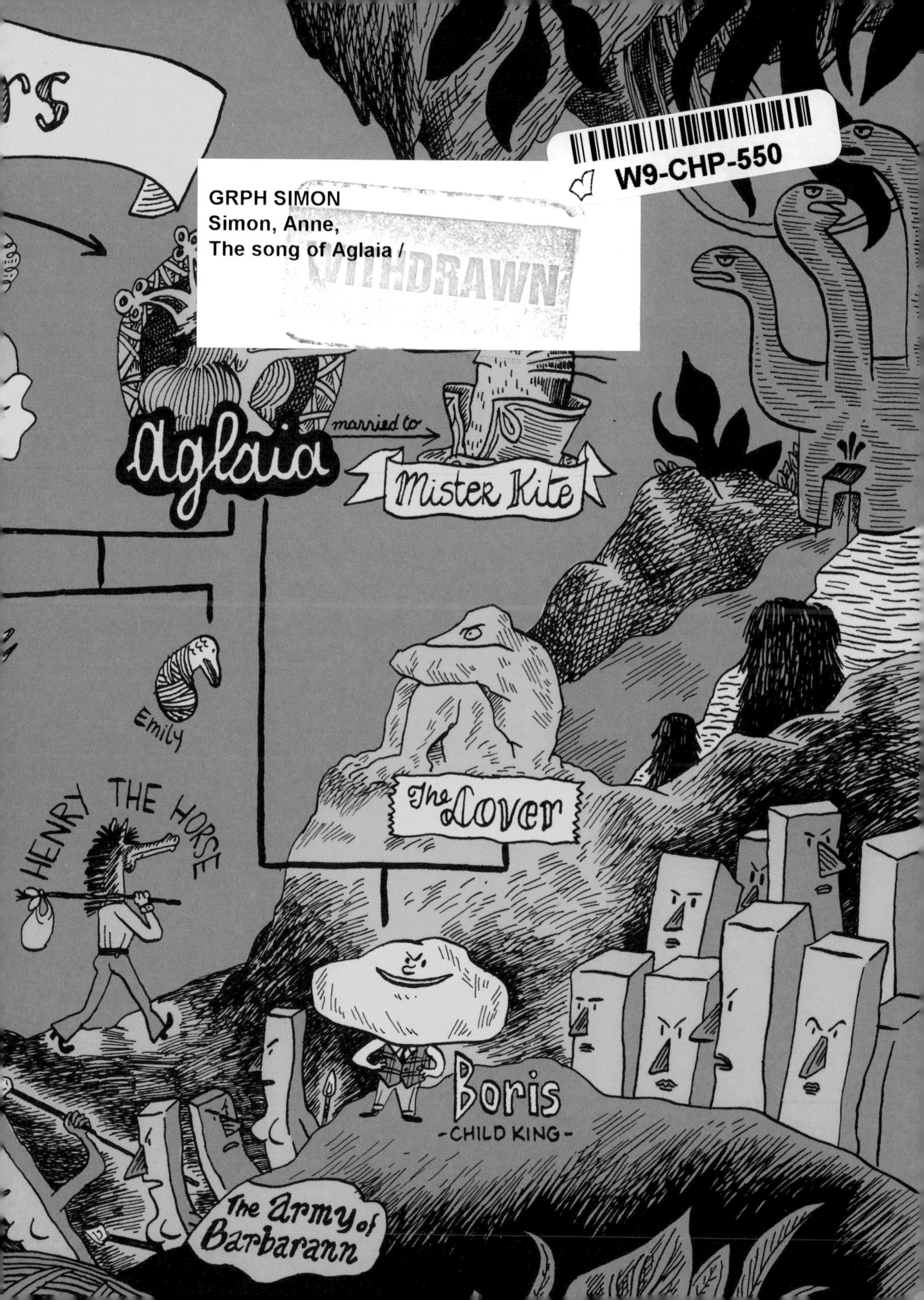
rs
Aglaia
married to
Mister Kite
Emily
HENRY THE HORSE
The Lover
Boris
-CHILD KING-
The Army of Barbarann

Anne Simon

THE SONG OF AGLAIA

Fantagraphics Books

FANTAGRAPHICS BOOKS INC.
7563 Lake City Way NE
Seattle, Washington 98115

Translated from French by Jenna Allen
Editor, Spot Letterer, and Associate Publisher:
Eric Reynolds
Book Design: Keeli McCarthy & Anne Simon
Production: Paul Baresh
Publisher: Gary Groth

ISBN 978-1-68396-107-9
Library of Congress Control Number: 2017957105

First printing: June 2018
Printed in China

Story 1, "The Oceanides," was pre-published in German in
Strapazin #99 (June 2010). Story 8, "Kite & Aglaia," appeared
previously in *Dopututto* #12 (January 2008). Part of Story 9,
"The Crown," was made June 28 2008, in Brussels, during the
24-Hour Comics event organized by the publisher l'Employé du Moi.

www.instagram.com/anne0simon/

Thanks to Guillaume, Damien, and Jacq Cohen. Thanks to
Delphine and Sandrine for their attentive editing.

CONTENTS

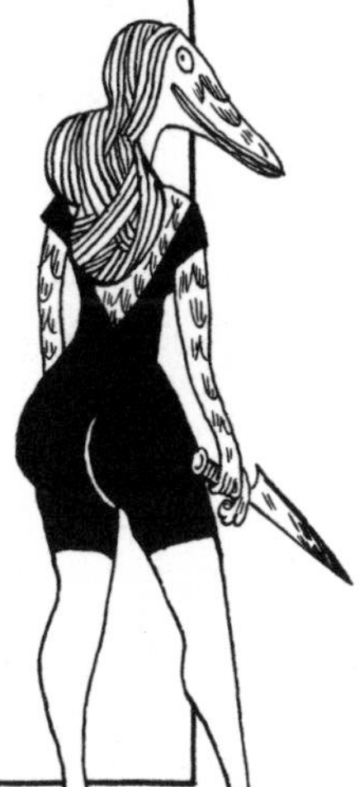

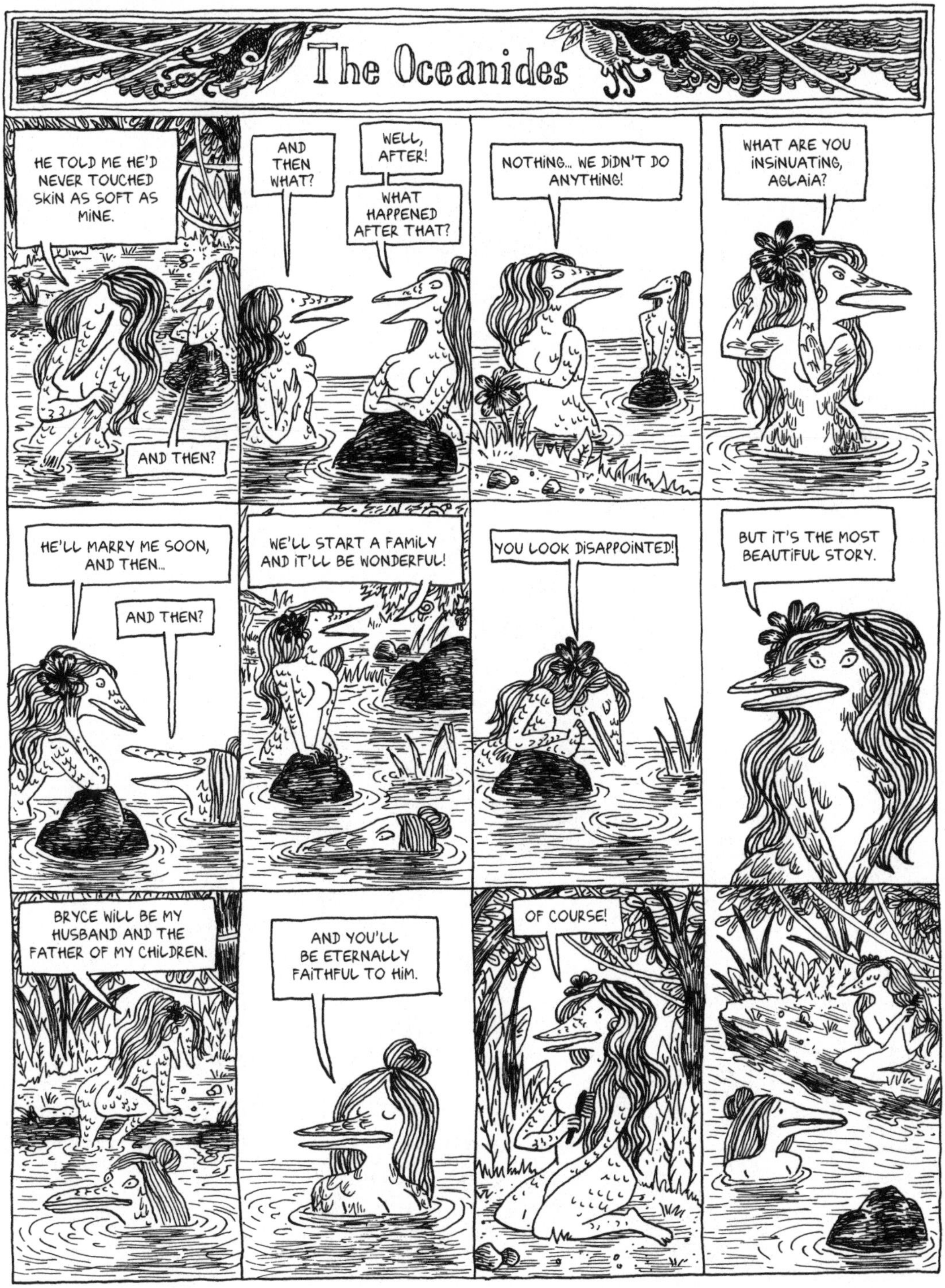
The Oceanides
HE TOLD ME HE'D NEVER TOUCHED SKIN AS SOFT AS MINE.
AND THEN?
AND THEN WHAT?
WELL, AFTER!
WHAT HAPPENED AFTER THAT?
NOTHING... WE DIDN'T DO ANYTHING!
WHAT ARE YOU INSINUATING, AGLAIA?
HE'LL MARRY ME SOON, AND THEN...
AND THEN?
WE'LL START A FAMILY AND IT'LL BE WONDERFUL!
YOU LOOK DISAPPOINTED!
BUT IT'S THE MOST BEAUTIFUL STORY.
BRYCE WILL BE MY HUSBAND AND THE FATHER OF MY CHILDREN.
AND YOU'LL BE ETERNALLY FAITHFUL TO HIM.
OF COURSE!

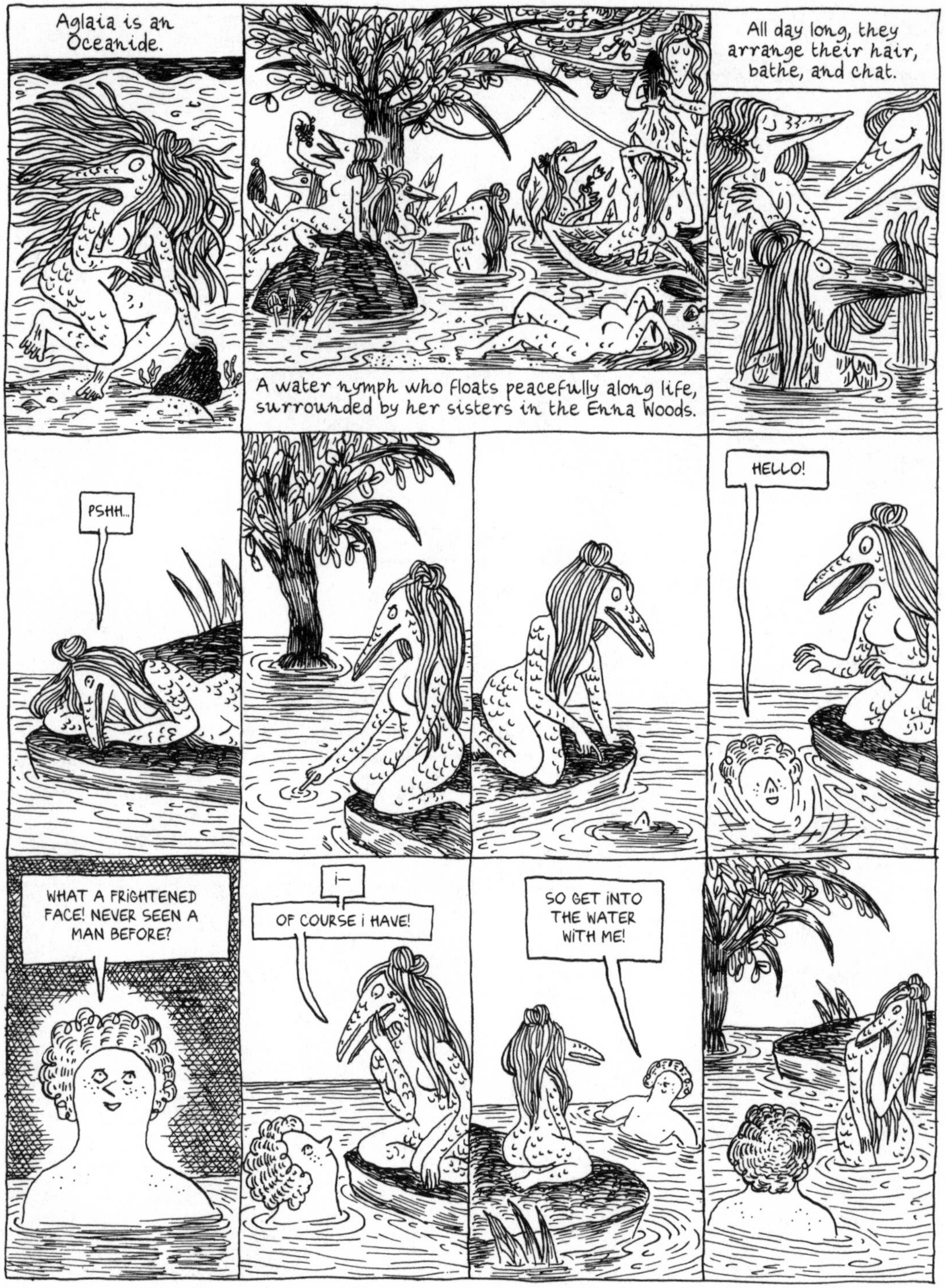

Aglaia is an Oceanide.
A water nymph who floats peacefully along life, surrounded by her sisters in the Enna Woods.
All day long, they arrange their hair, bathe, and chat.
PSHH...
HELLO!
WHAT A FRIGHTENED FACE! NEVER SEEN A MAN BEFORE?
I—
OF COURSE I HAVE!
SO GET INTO THE WATER WITH ME!

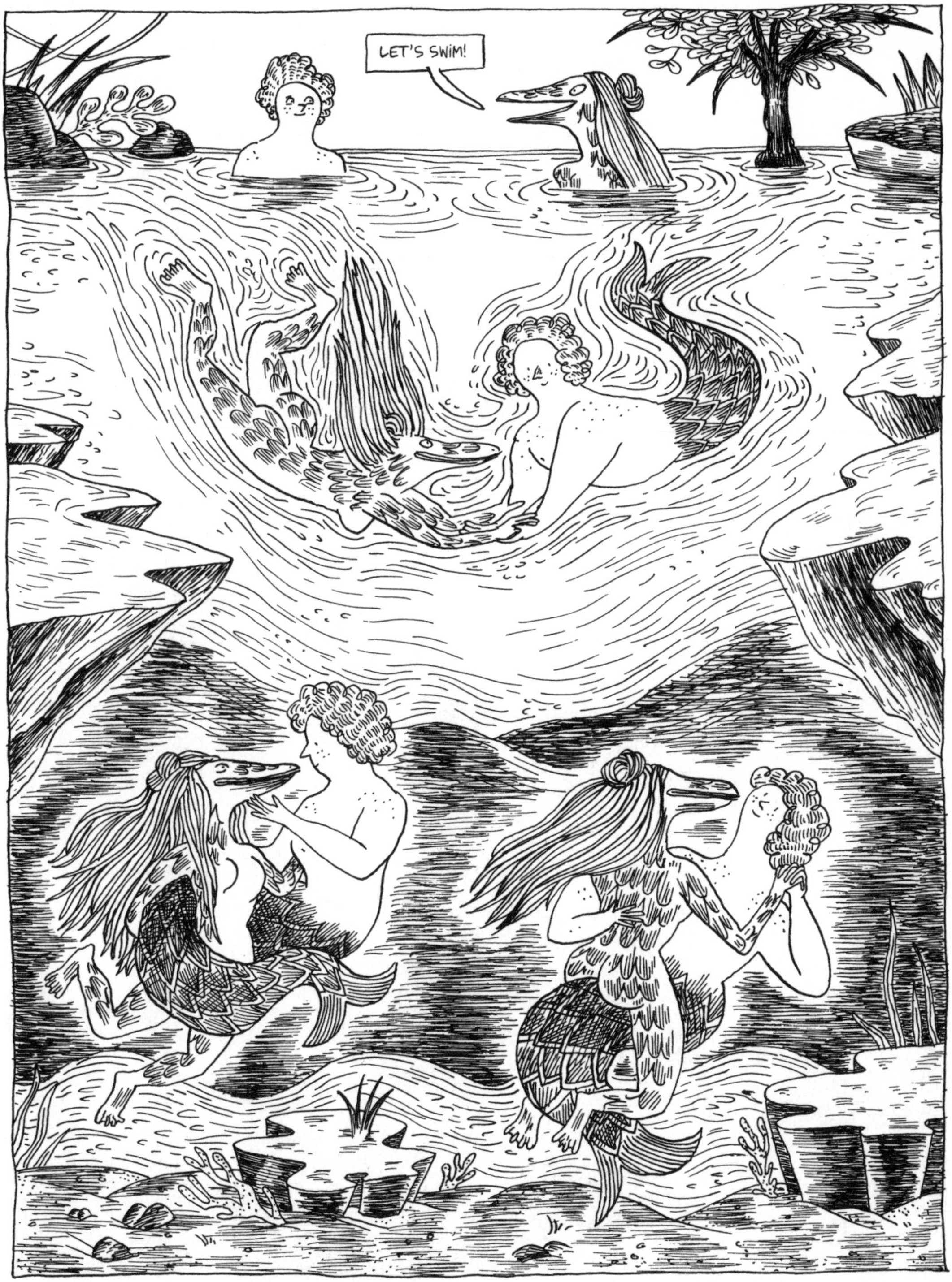
LET'S SWIM!

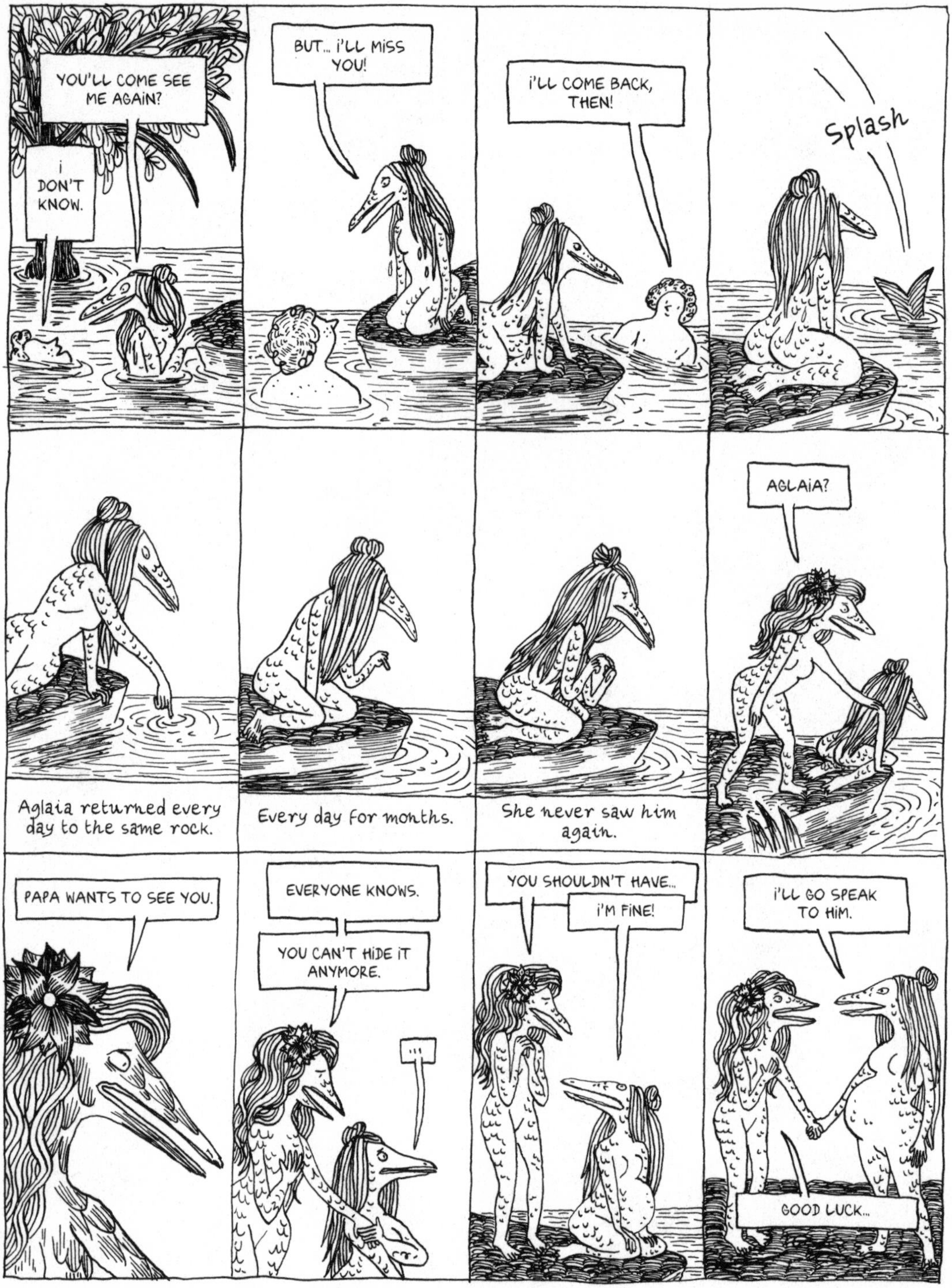
YOU'LL COME SEE ME AGAIN?
I DON'T KNOW.
BUT... I'LL MISS YOU!
I'LL COME BACK, THEN!
Splash
Aglaia returned every day to the same rock.
Every day for months.
She never saw him again.
AGLAIA?
PAPA WANTS TO SEE YOU.
EVERYONE KNOWS.
YOU CAN'T HIDE IT ANYMORE.
...
YOU SHOULDN'T HAVE...
I'M FINE!
I'LL GO SPEAK TO HIM.
GOOD LUCK...

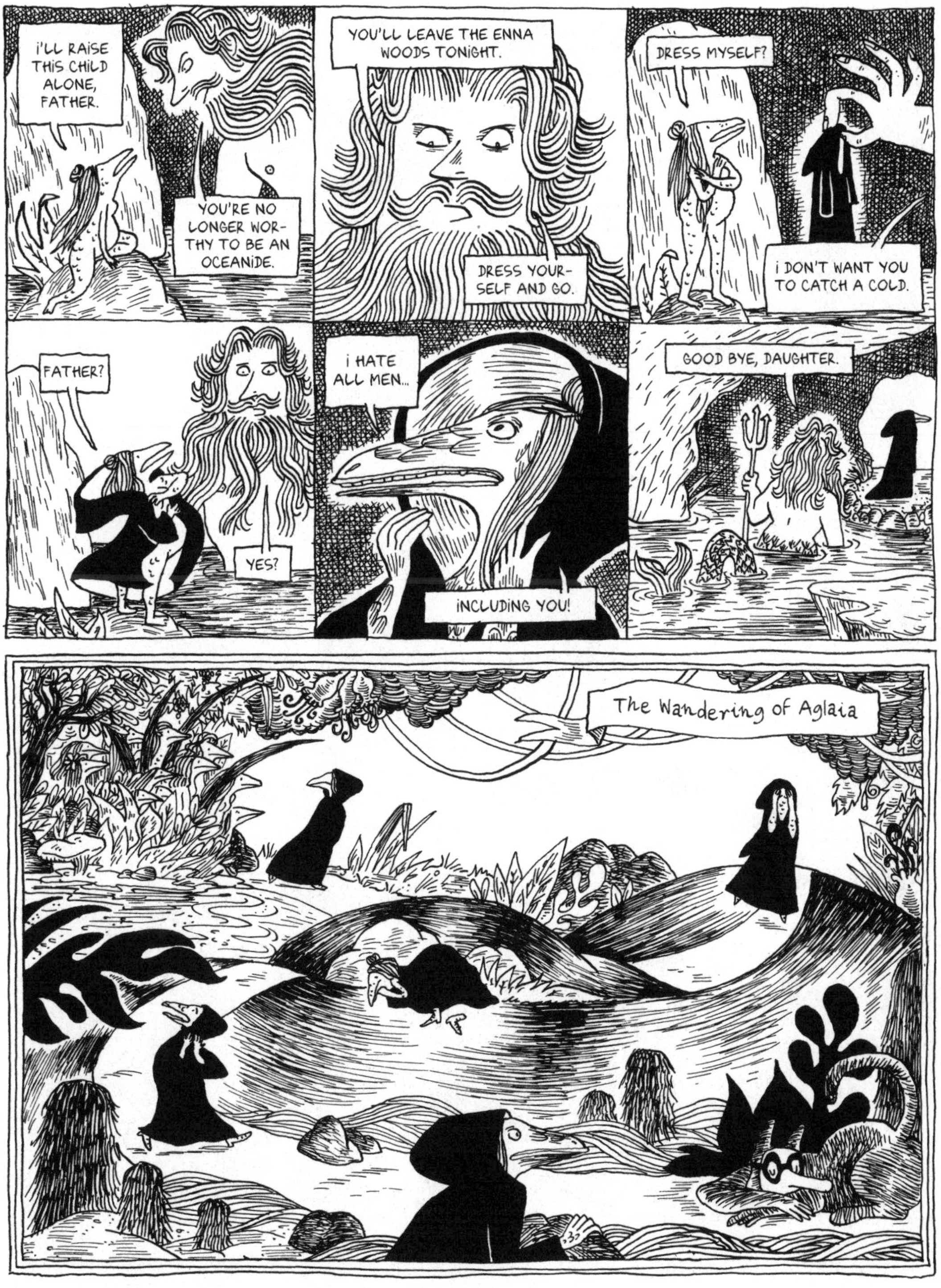
I'LL RAISE THIS CHILD ALONE, FATHER.
YOU'RE NO LONGER WOR-THY TO BE AN OCEANIDE.
YOU'LL LEAVE THE ENNA WOODS TONIGHT.
DRESS YOUR-SELF AND GO.
DRESS MYSELF?
I DON'T WANT YOU TO CATCH A COLD.
FATHER?
YES?
I HATE ALL MEN...
INCLUDING YOU!
GOOD BYE, DAUGHTER.
The Wandering of Aglaia

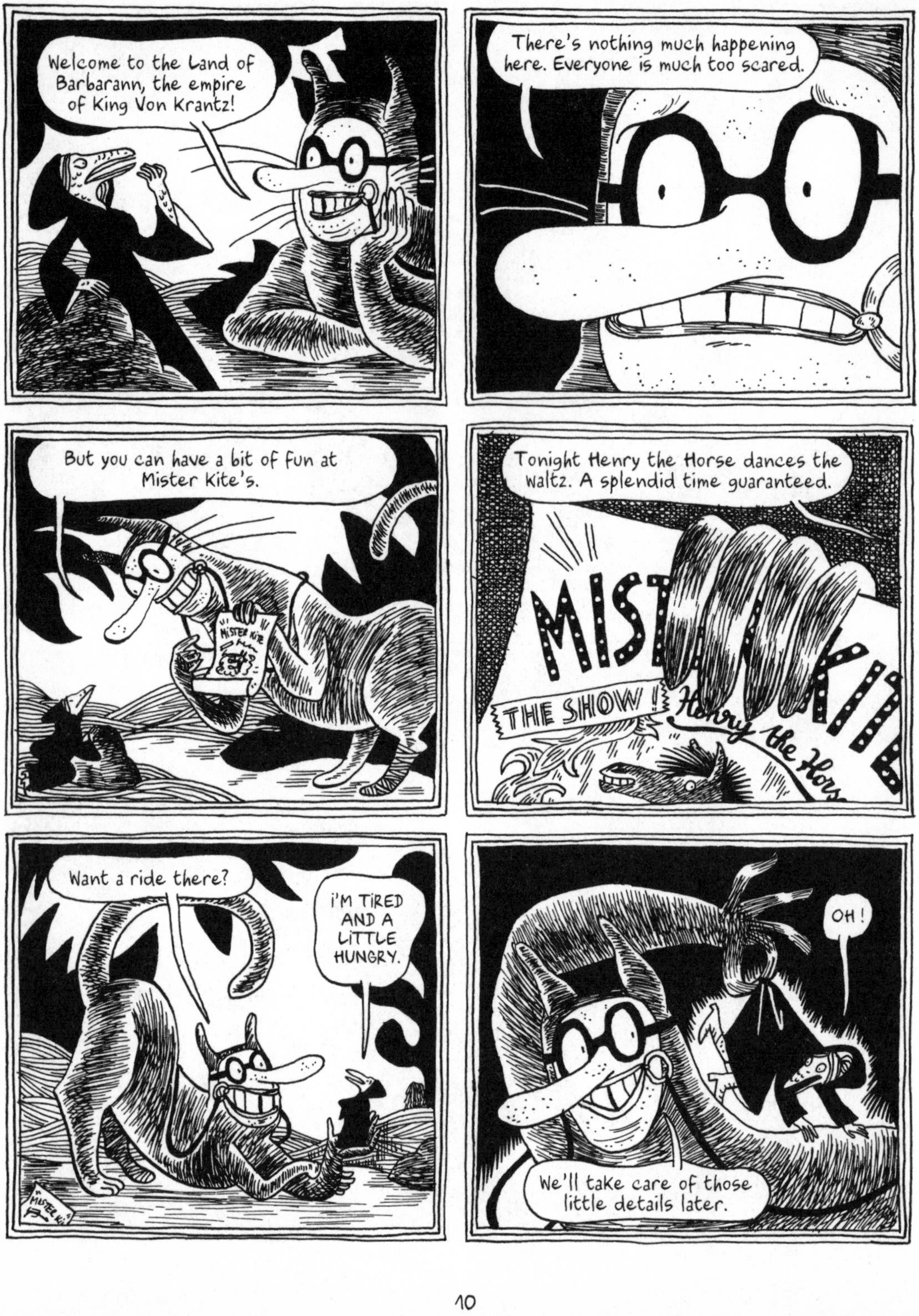
Welcome to the Land of Barbarann, the empire of King Von Krantz!
There's nothing much happening here. Everyone is much too scared.
But you can have a bit of fun at Mister Kite's.
MISTER KITE
Tonight Henry the Horse dances the waltz. A splendid time guaranteed.
MIST
KITE
THE SHOW!
Henry the Hors
Want a ride there?
I'M TIRED AND A LITTLE HUNGRY.
OH!
We'll take care of those little details later.

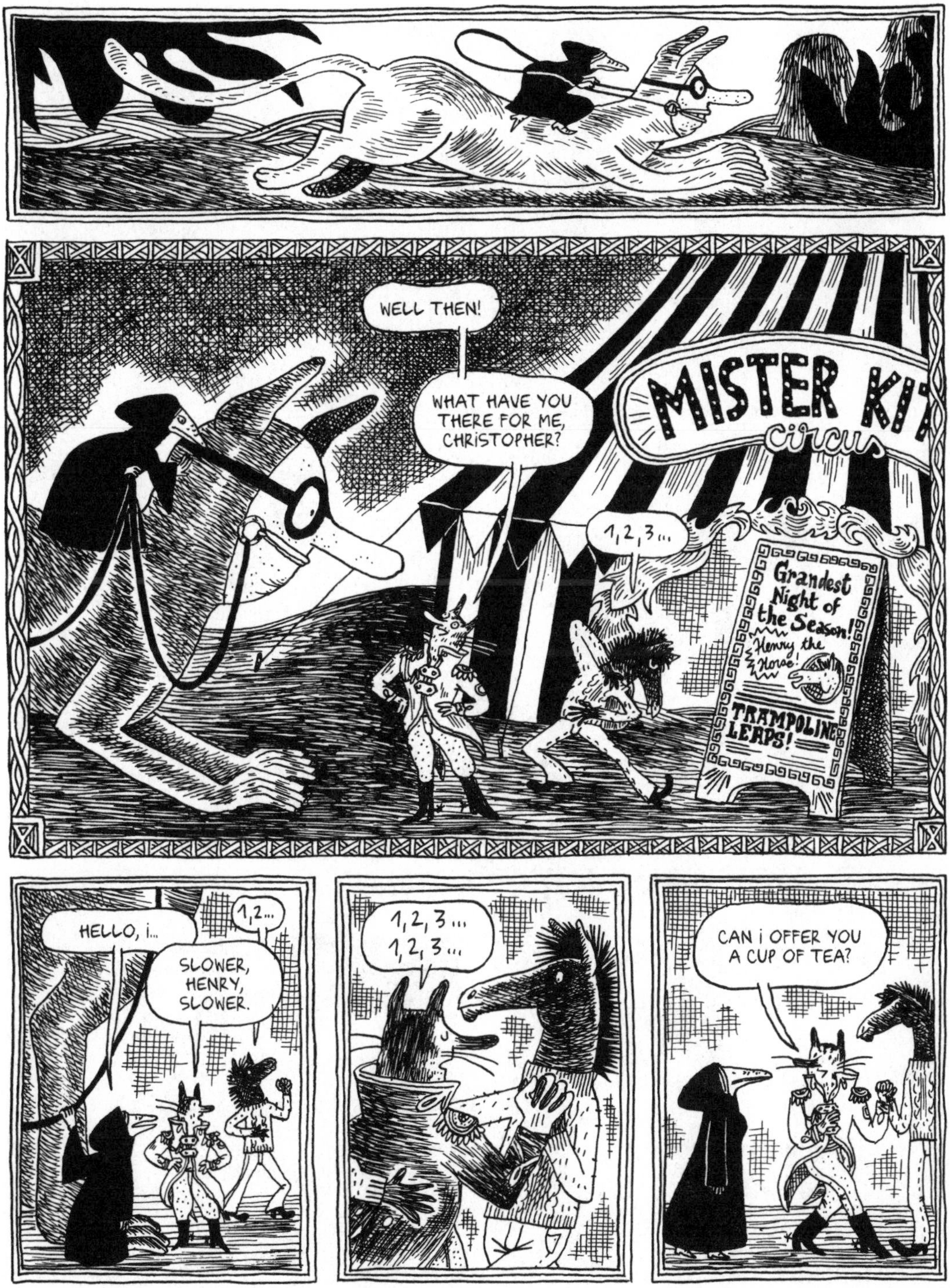
WELL THEN!
WHAT HAVE YOU THERE FOR ME, CHRISTOPHER?
MISTER KIT
circus
1,2,3...
Grandest Night of the Season!
Henry the Horse!
TRAMPOLINE LEAPS!
HELLO, i...
1,2...
SLOWER, HENRY, SLOWER.
1,2,3...
1,2,3...
CAN i OFFER YOU A CUP OF TEA?

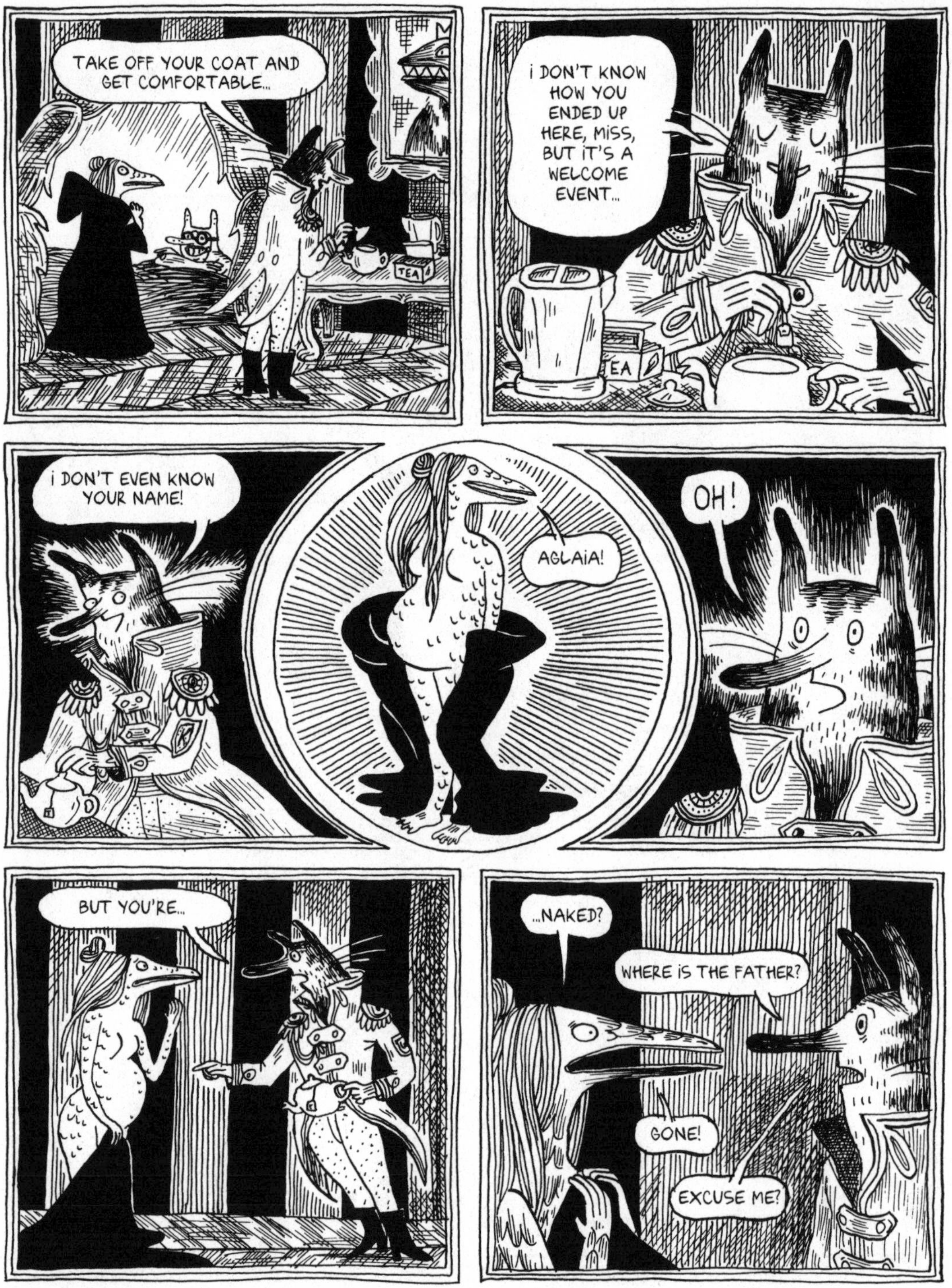

TAKE OFF YOUR COAT AND GET COMFORTABLE...
TEA
I DON'T KNOW HOW YOU ENDED UP HERE, MISS, BUT IT'S A WELCOME EVENT...
TEA
I DON'T EVEN KNOW YOUR NAME!
AGLAIA!
OH!
BUT YOU'RE...
...NAKED?
WHERE IS THE FATHER?
GONE!
EXCUSE ME?

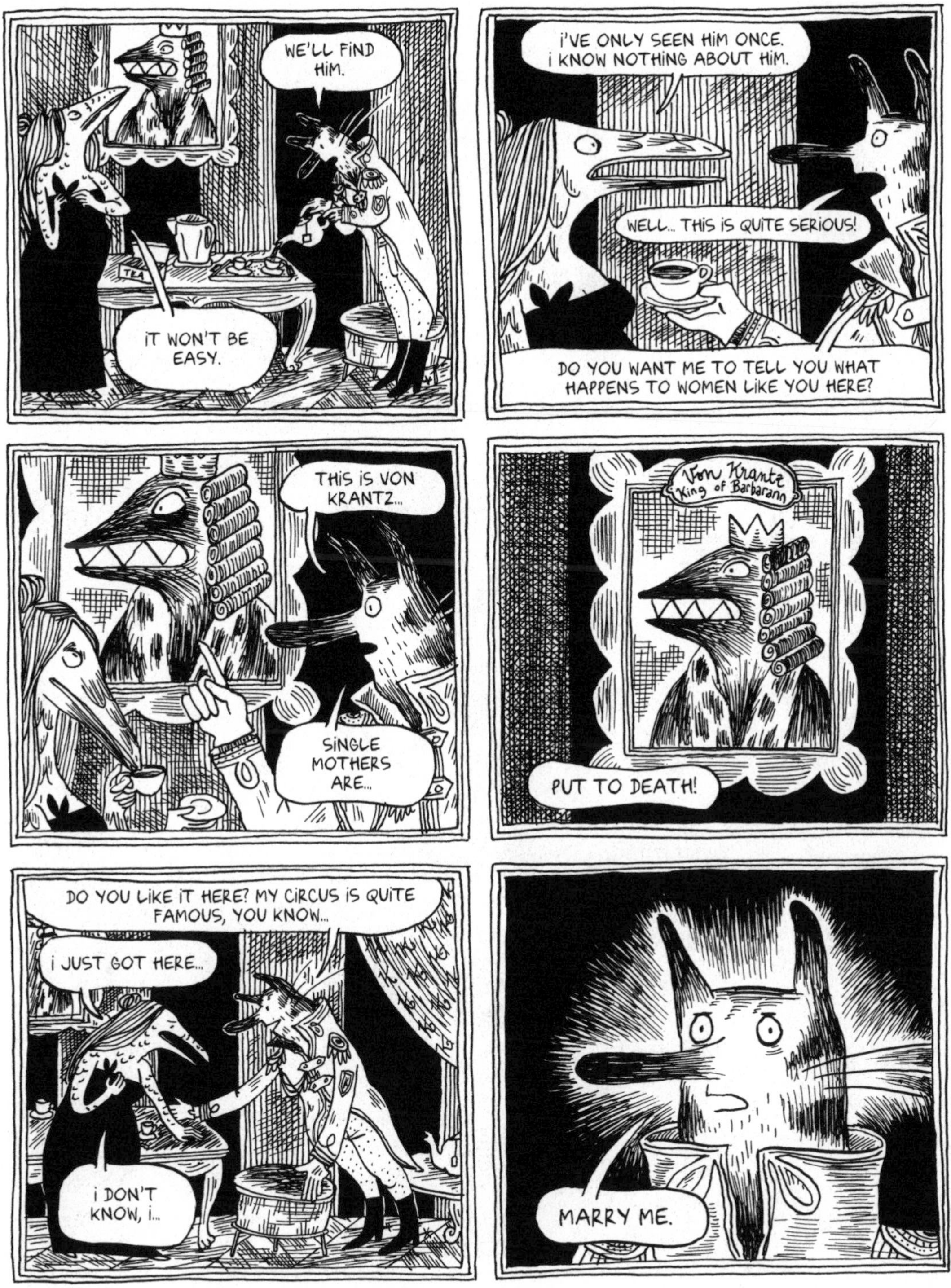
WE'LL FIND HIM.
IT WON'T BE EASY.
TEA
I'VE ONLY SEEN HIM ONCE. I KNOW NOTHING ABOUT HIM.
WELL... THIS IS QUITE SERIOUS!
DO YOU WANT ME TO TELL YOU WHAT HAPPENS TO WOMEN LIKE YOU HERE?
THIS IS VON KRANTZ...
SINGLE MOTHERS ARE...
Von Krantz King of Barbarann
PUT TO DEATH!
DO YOU LIKE IT HERE? MY CIRCUS IS QUITE FAMOUS, YOU KNOW...
I JUST GOT HERE...
I DON'T KNOW, I...
MARRY ME.

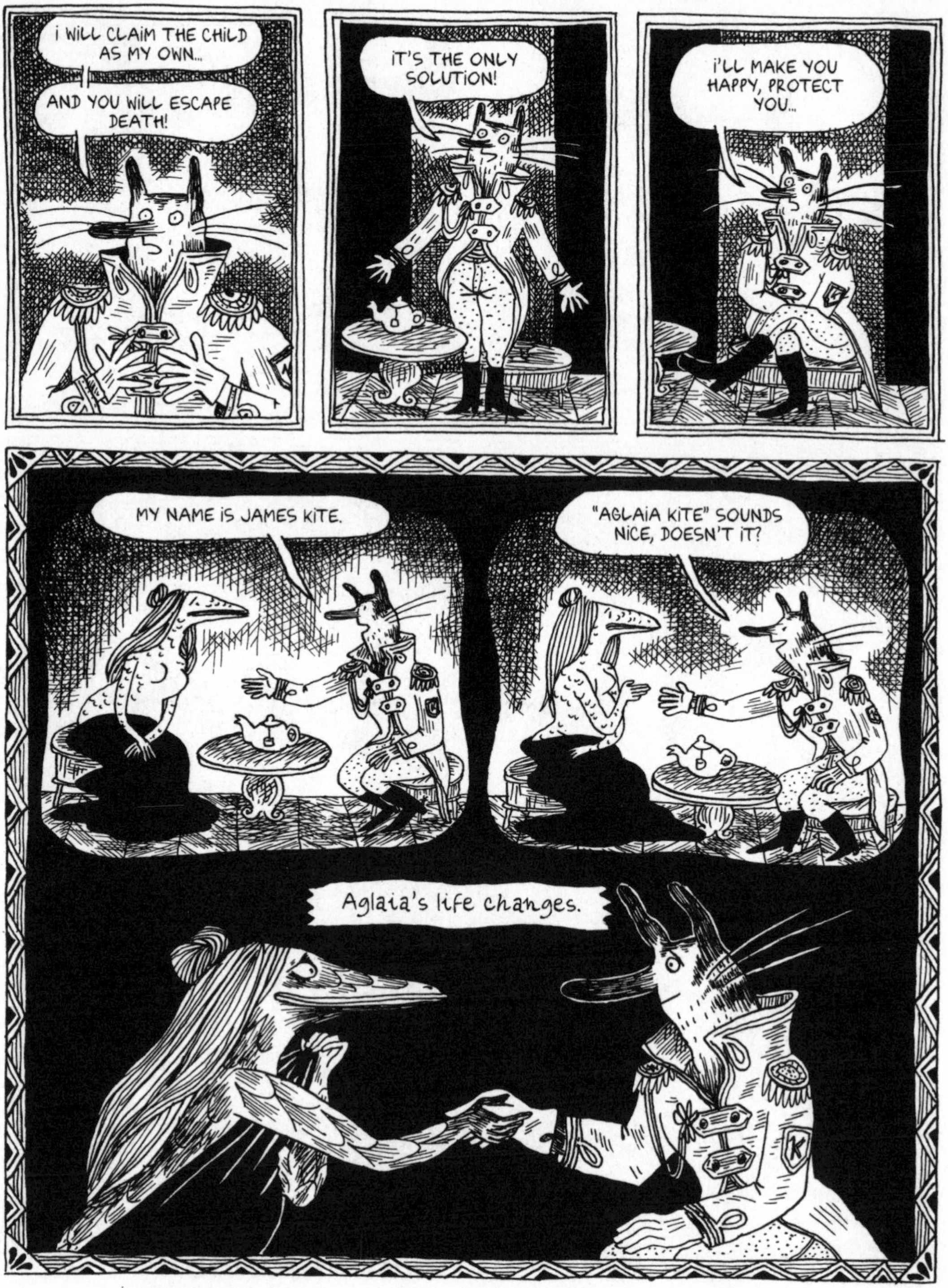
I WILL CLAIM THE CHILD AS MY OWN...
AND YOU WILL ESCAPE DEATH!
IT'S THE ONLY SOLUTION!
I'LL MAKE YOU HAPPY, PROTECT YOU...
MY NAME IS JAMES KITE.
"AGLAIA KITE" SOUNDS NICE, DOESN'T IT?
Aglaia's life changes.

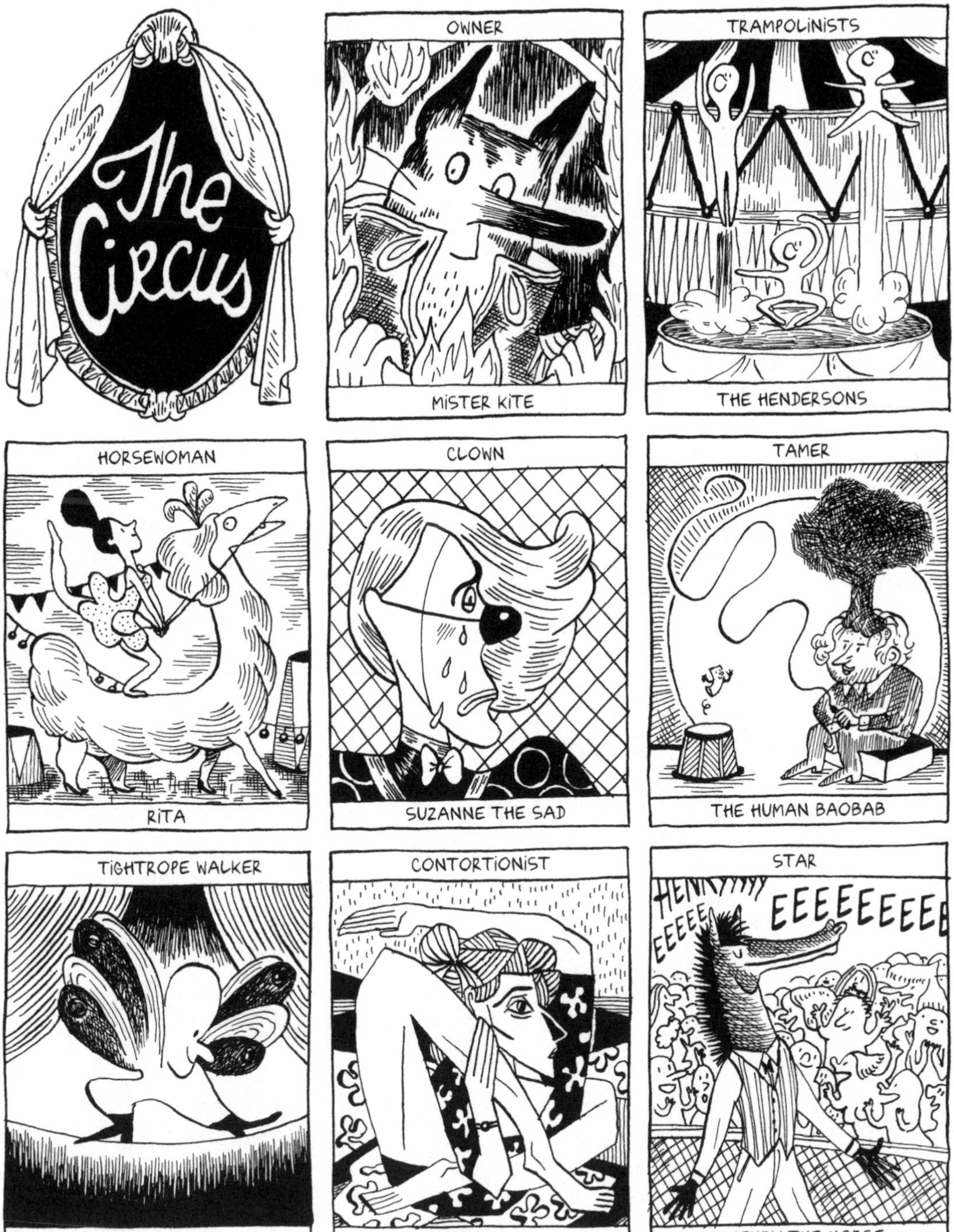
The Circus
OWNER
MISTER KITE
TRAMPOLINISTS
THE HENDERSONS
HORSEWOMAN
RITA
CLOWN
SUZANNE THE SAD
TAMER
THE HUMAN BAOBAB
TIGHTROPE WALKER
BOBBY WINGS
CONTORTIONIST
MADAME Z
STAR
HENRYYYYY
EEEEE
EEEEEEEEE
HENRY THE HORSE

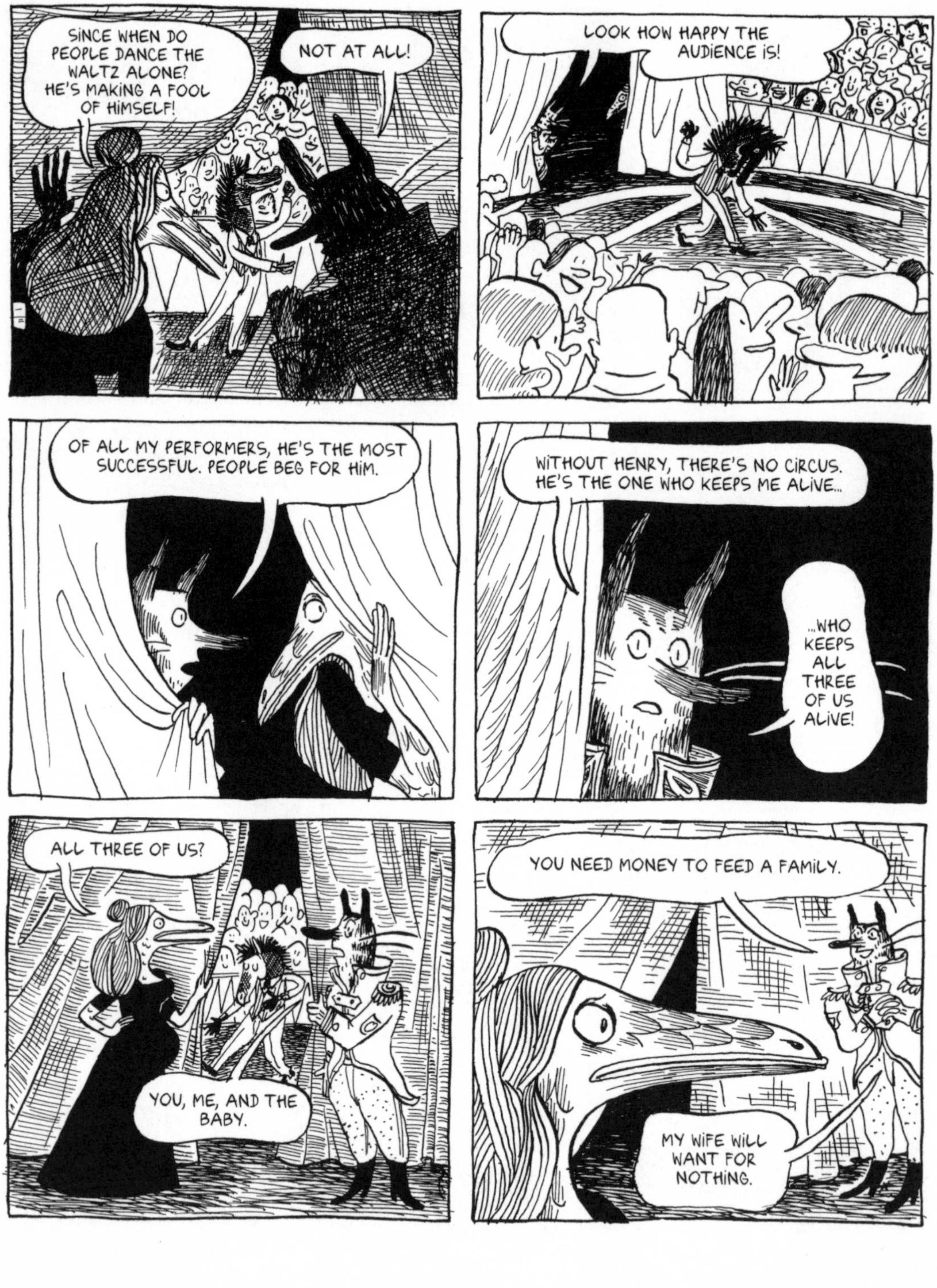

SINCE WHEN DO PEOPLE DANCE THE WALTZ ALONE? HE'S MAKING A FOOL OF HIMSELF!
NOT AT ALL!
LOOK HOW HAPPY THE AUDIENCE IS!
OF ALL MY PERFORMERS, HE'S THE MOST SUCCESSFUL. PEOPLE BEG FOR HIM.
WITHOUT HENRY, THERE'S NO CIRCUS. HE'S THE ONE WHO KEEPS ME ALIVE...
...WHO KEEPS ALL THREE OF US ALIVE!
ALL THREE OF US?
YOU, ME, AND THE BABY.
YOU NEED MONEY TO FEED A FAMILY.
MY WIFE WILL WANT FOR NOTHING.

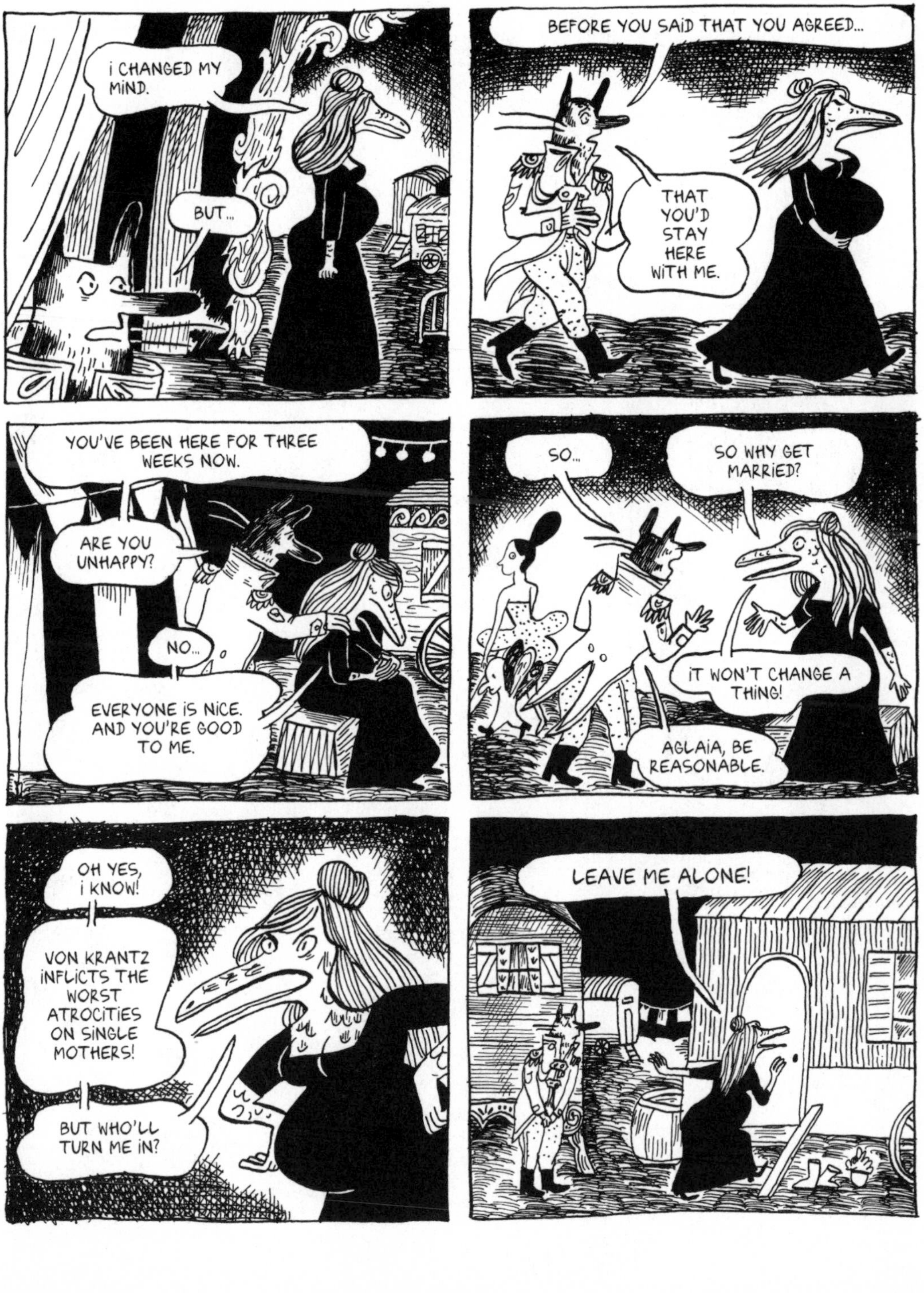
I CHANGED MY MIND.
BUT...
BEFORE YOU SAID THAT YOU AGREED...
THAT YOU'D STAY HERE WITH ME.
YOU'VE BEEN HERE FOR THREE WEEKS NOW.
ARE YOU UNHAPPY?
NO...
EVERYONE IS NICE. AND YOU'RE GOOD TO ME.
SO...
SO WHY GET MARRIED?
IT WON'T CHANGE A THING!
AGLAIA, BE REASONABLE.
OH YES, I KNOW!
VON KRANTZ INFLICTS THE WORST ATROCITIES ON SINGLE MOTHERS!
BUT WHO'LL TURN ME IN?
LEAVE ME ALONE!

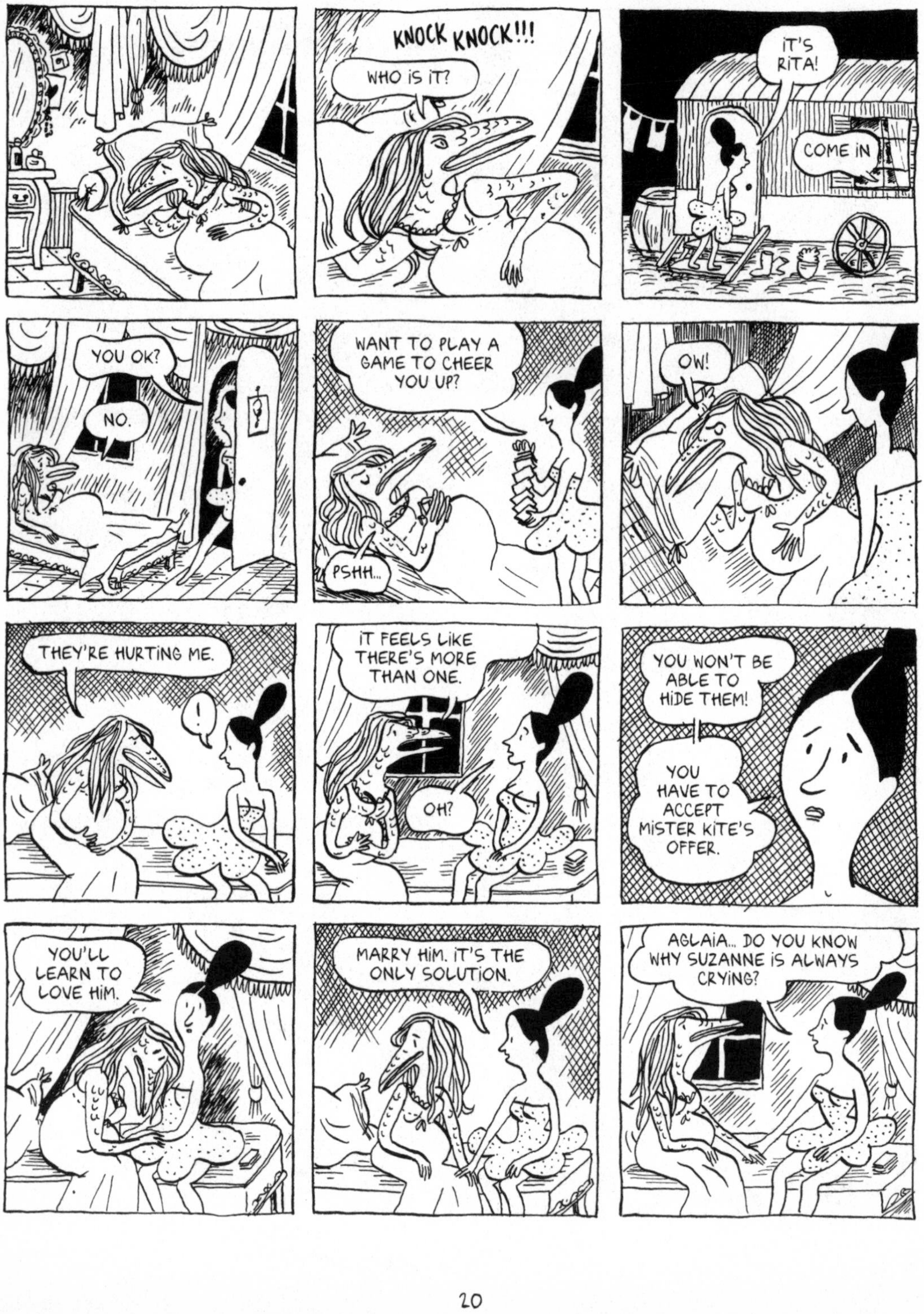
KNOCK KNOCK!!!
WHO IS IT?
IT'S RITA!
COME IN
YOU OK?
NO.
WANT TO PLAY A GAME TO CHEER YOU UP?
PSHH...
OW!
THEY'RE HURTING ME.
!
IT FEELS LIKE THERE'S MORE THAN ONE.
OH?
YOU WON'T BE ABLE TO HIDE THEM!
YOU HAVE TO ACCEPT MISTER KITE'S OFFER.
YOU'LL LEARN TO LOVE HIM.
MARRY HIM. IT'S THE ONLY SOLUTION.
AGLAIA... DO YOU KNOW WHY SUZANNE IS ALWAYS CRYING?

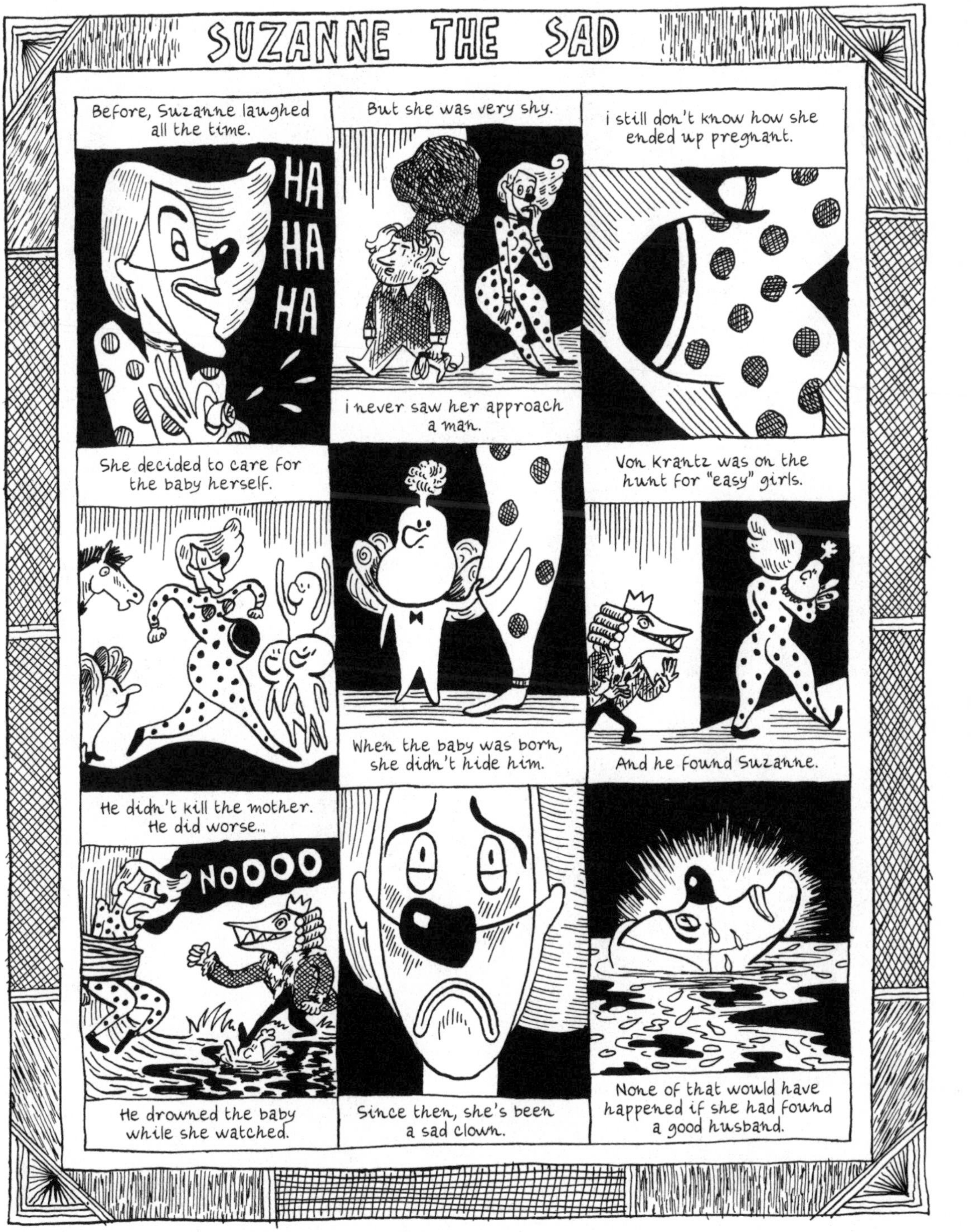
SUZANNE THE SAD
Before, Suzanne laughed all the time.
HA HA HA
But she was very shy.
i never saw her approach a man.
i still don't know how she ended up pregnant.
She decided to care for the baby herself.
When the baby was born, she didn't hide him.
Von Krantz was on the hunt for "easy" girls.
And he found Suzanne.
He didn't kill the mother. He did worse...
NOOOO
He drowned the baby while she watched.
Since then, she's been a sad clown.
None of that would have happened if she had found a good husband.

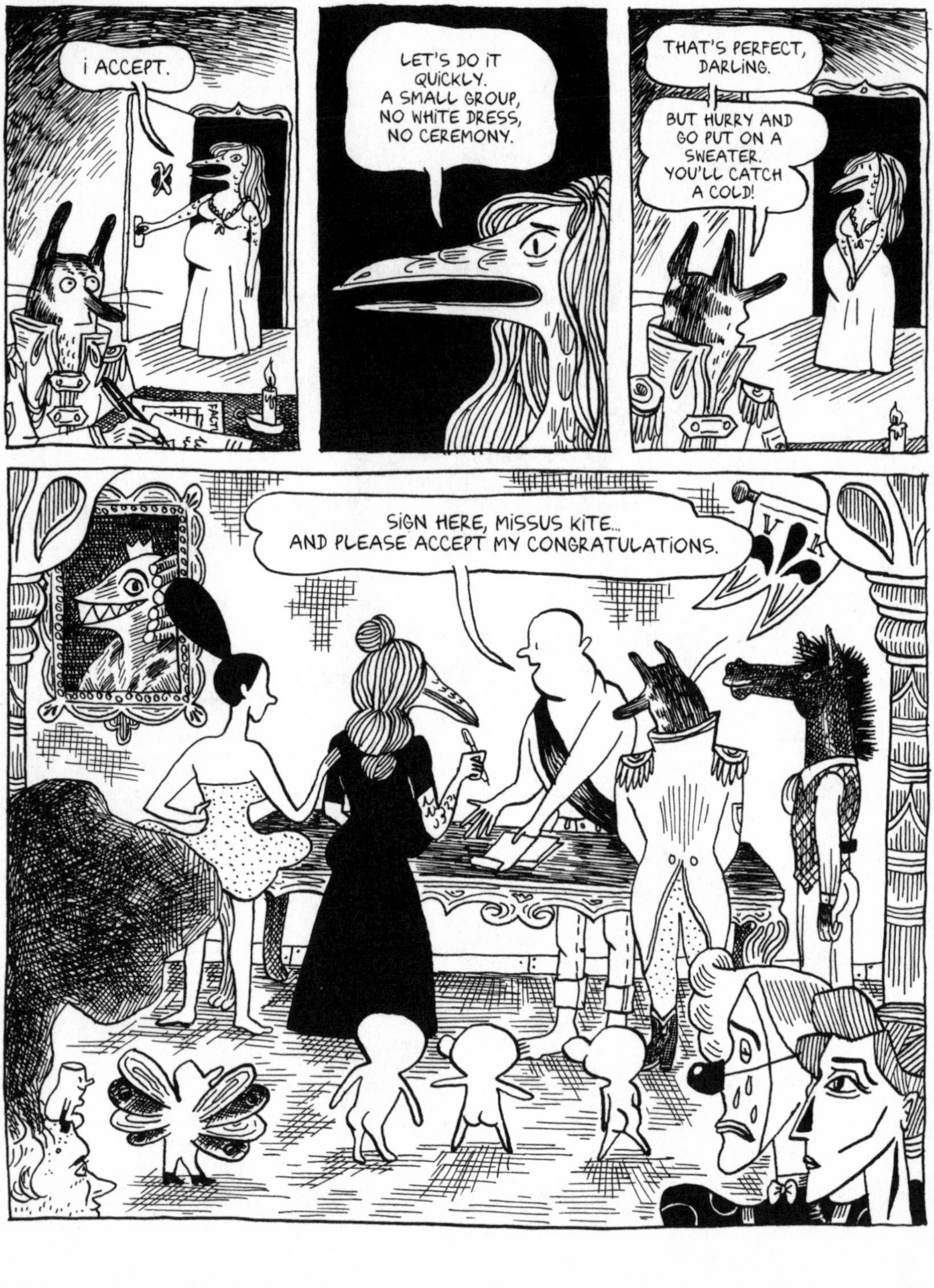
I ACCEPT.
LET'S DO IT QUICKLY. A SMALL GROUP, NO WHITE DRESS, NO CEREMONY.
THAT'S PERFECT, DARLING.
BUT HURRY AND GO PUT ON A SWEATER. YOU'LL CATCH A COLD!
SIGN HERE, MISSUS KITE... AND PLEASE ACCEPT MY CONGRATULATIONS.

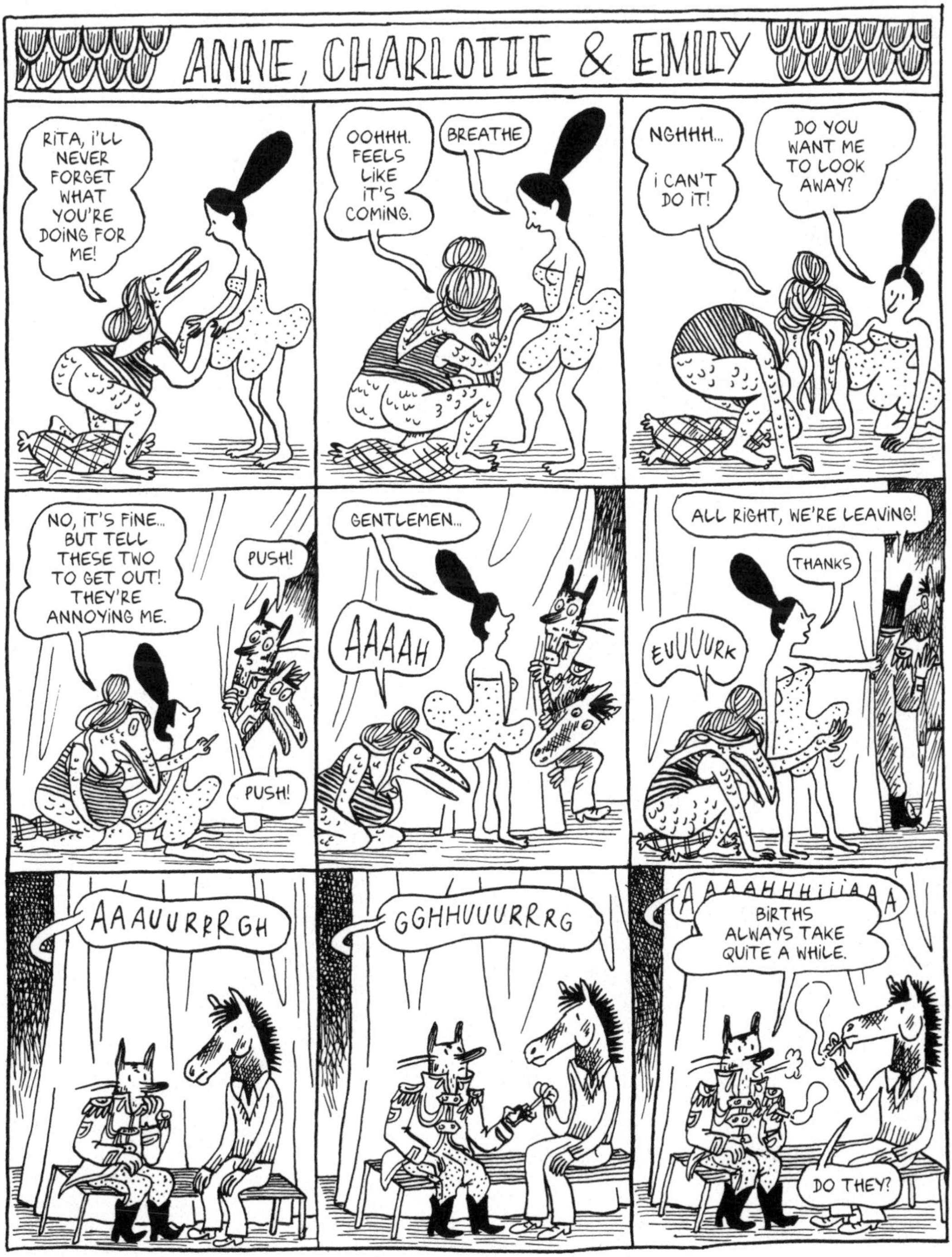
ANNE, CHARLOTTE & EMILY
RITA, I'LL NEVER FORGET WHAT YOU'RE DOING FOR ME!
OOHHH. FEELS LIKE IT'S COMING.
BREATHE
NGHHH... I CAN'T DO IT!
DO YOU WANT ME TO LOOK AWAY?
NO, IT'S FINE... BUT TELL THESE TWO TO GET OUT! THEY'RE ANNOYING ME.
PUSH!
PUSH!
GENTLEMEN...
AAAAH
ALL RIGHT, WE'RE LEAVING!
THANKS
EVUUURK
AAAUURRRGH
GGHHUUURRRG
AAAAHHHiiiiAAAA
BIRTHS ALWAYS TAKE QUITE A WHILE.
DO THEY?

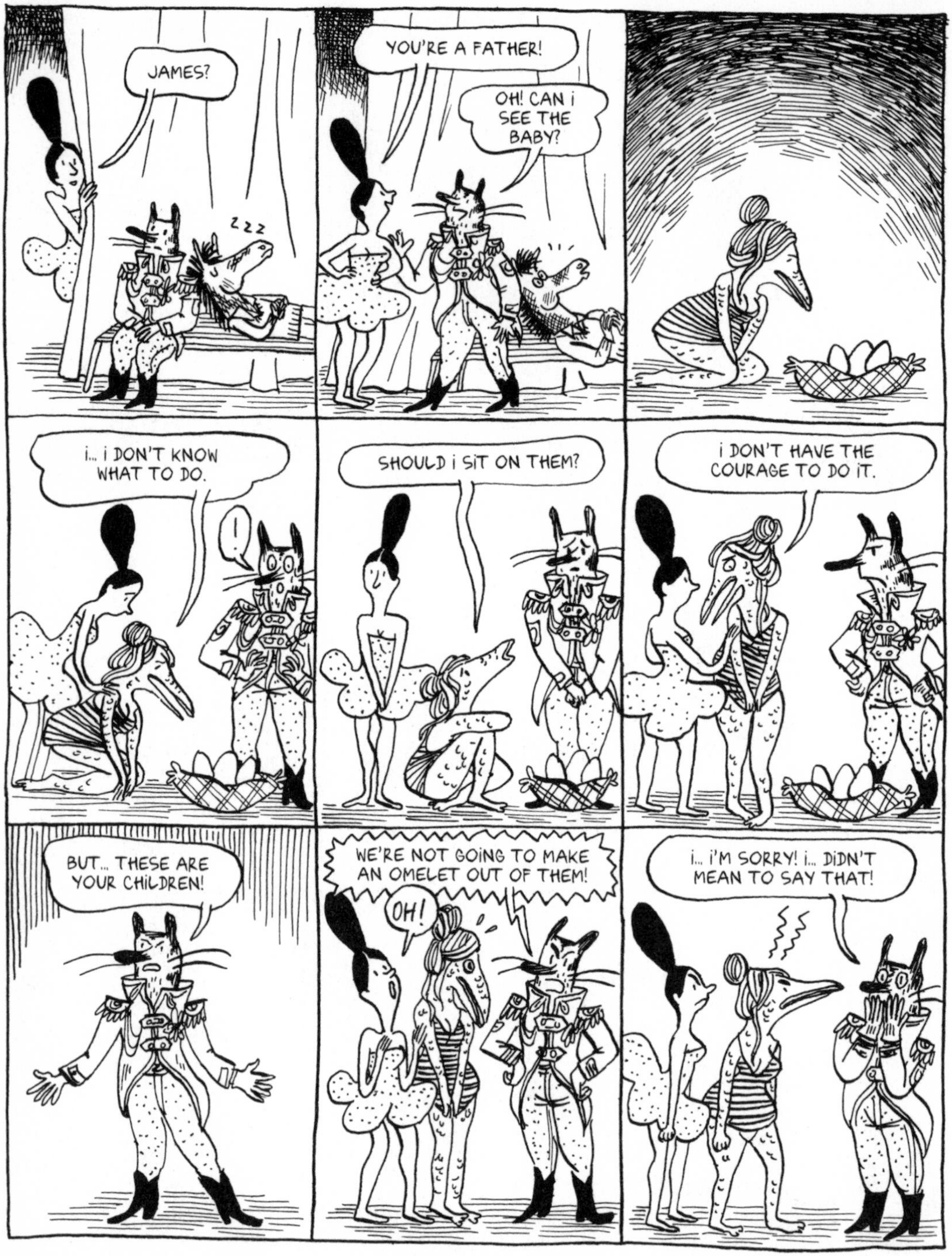

JAMES?
YOU'RE A FATHER!
OH! CAN i SEE THE BABY?
i... i DON'T KNOW WHAT TO DO.
SHOULD i SIT ON THEM?
i DON'T HAVE THE COURAGE TO DO iT.
BUT... THESE ARE YOUR CHILDREN!
WE'RE NOT GOING TO MAKE AN OMELET OUT OF THEM!
OH!
i... i'M SORRY! i... DIDN'T MEAN TO SAY THAT!

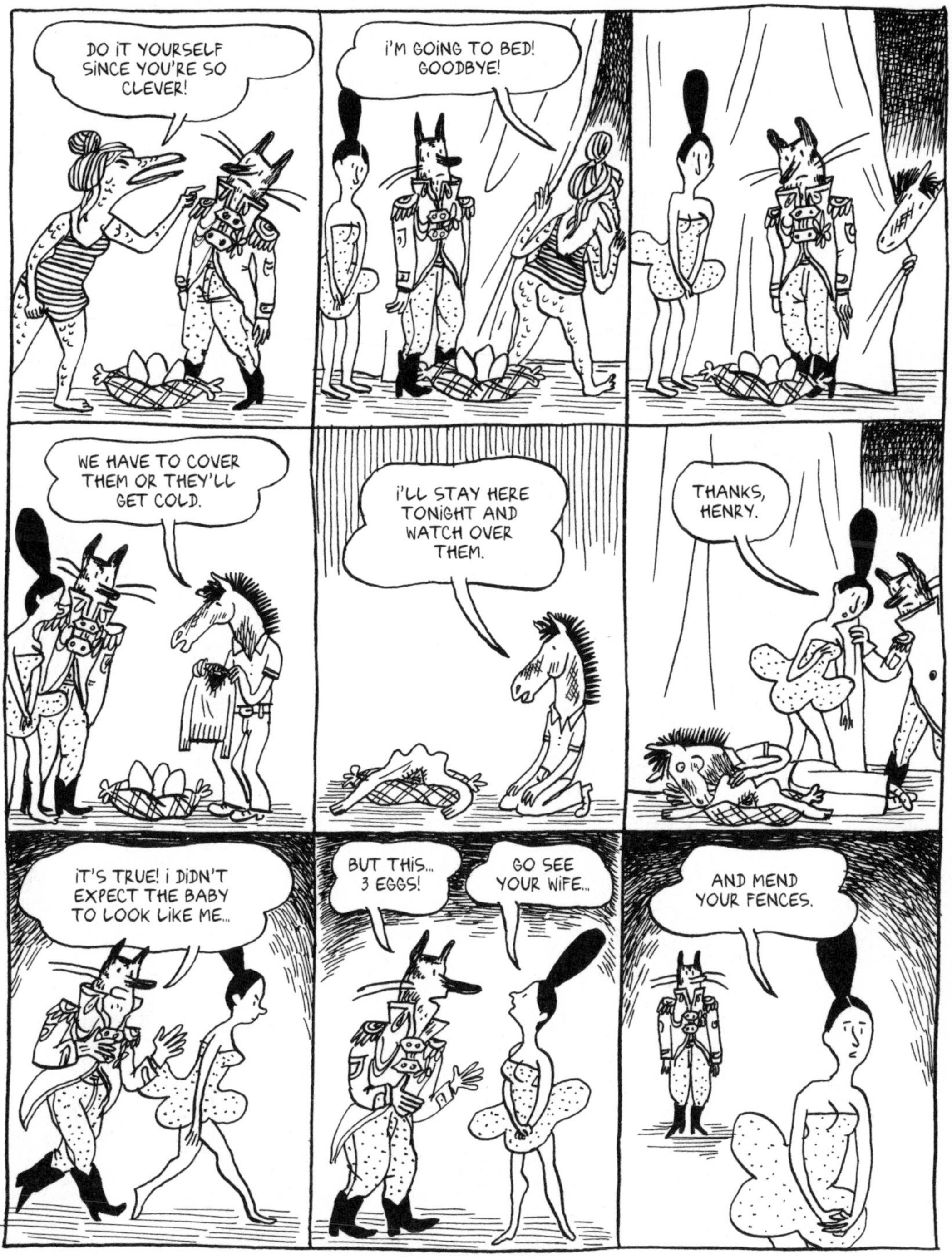
DO IT YOURSELF SINCE YOU'RE SO CLEVER!
I'M GOING TO BED! GOODBYE!
WE HAVE TO COVER THEM OR THEY'LL GET COLD.
I'LL STAY HERE TONIGHT AND WATCH OVER THEM.
THANKS, HENRY.
IT'S TRUE! I DIDN'T EXPECT THE BABY TO LOOK LIKE ME...
BUT THIS... 3 EGGS!
GO SEE YOUR WIFE...
AND MEND YOUR FENCES.

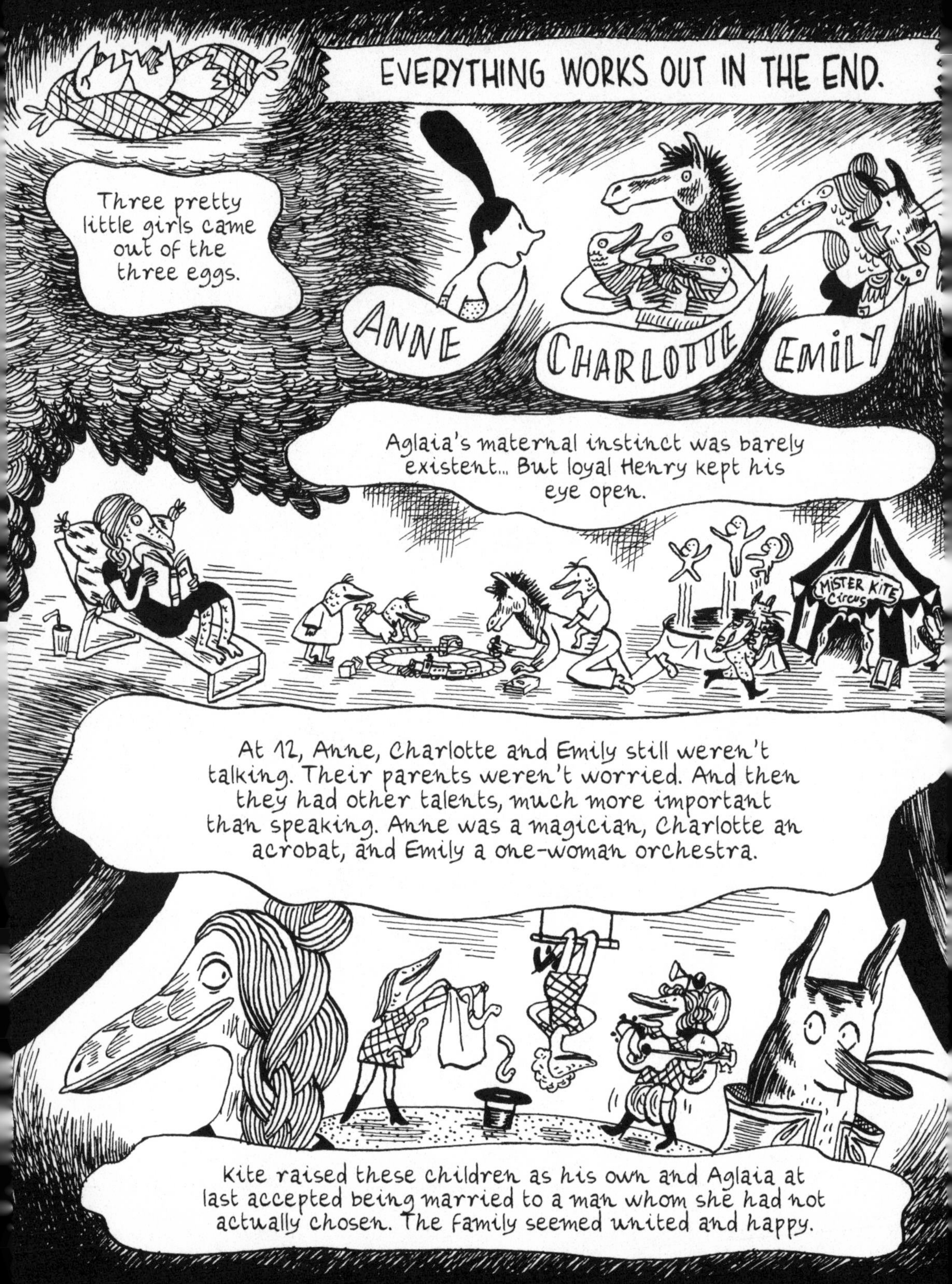

EVERYTHING WORKS OUT IN THE END.
Three pretty little girls came out of the three eggs.
ANNE
CHARLOTTE
EMILY
Aglaia's maternal instinct was barely existent... But loyal Henry kept his eye open.
MISTER KITE Circus
At 12, Anne, Charlotte and Emily still weren't talking. Their parents weren't worried. And then they had other talents, much more important than speaking. Anne was a magician, Charlotte an acrobat, and Emily a one-woman orchestra.
Kite raised these children as his own and Aglaia at last accepted being married to a man whom she had not actually chosen. The family seemed united and happy.

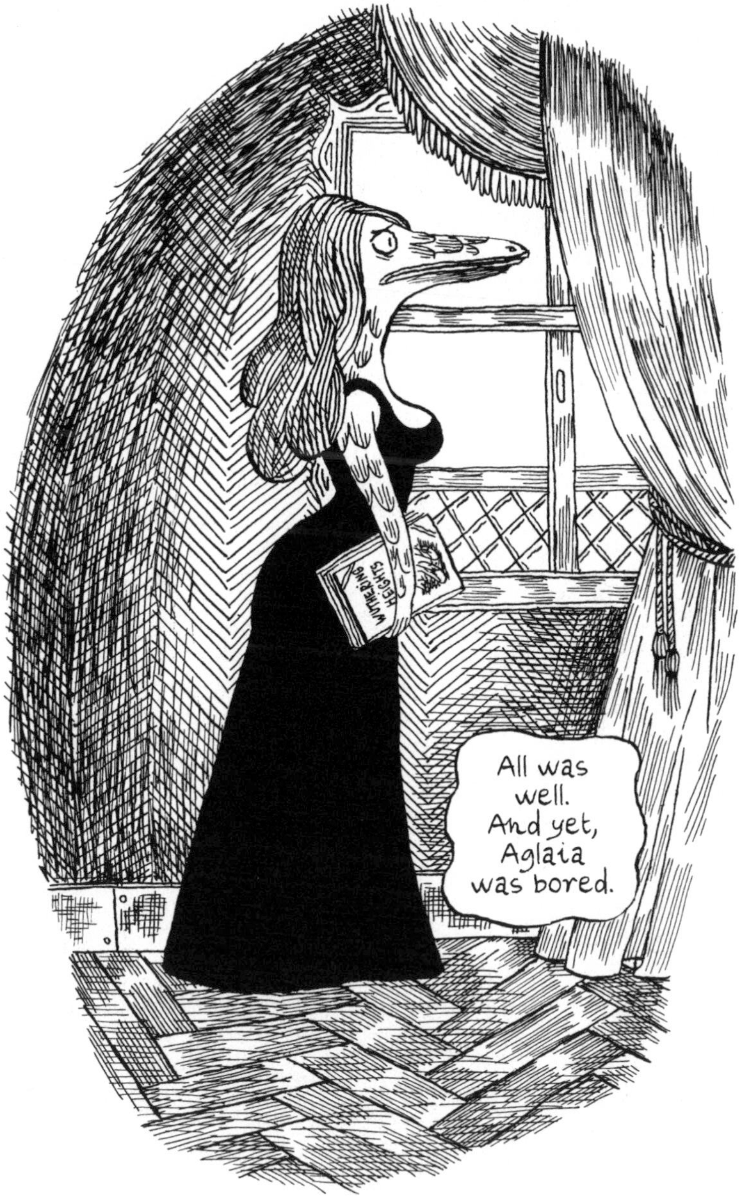
WUTHERING HEIGHTS
All was well. And yet, Aglaia was bored.

INTERLUDE FOR SIMONE, THE KING'S SECRETARY

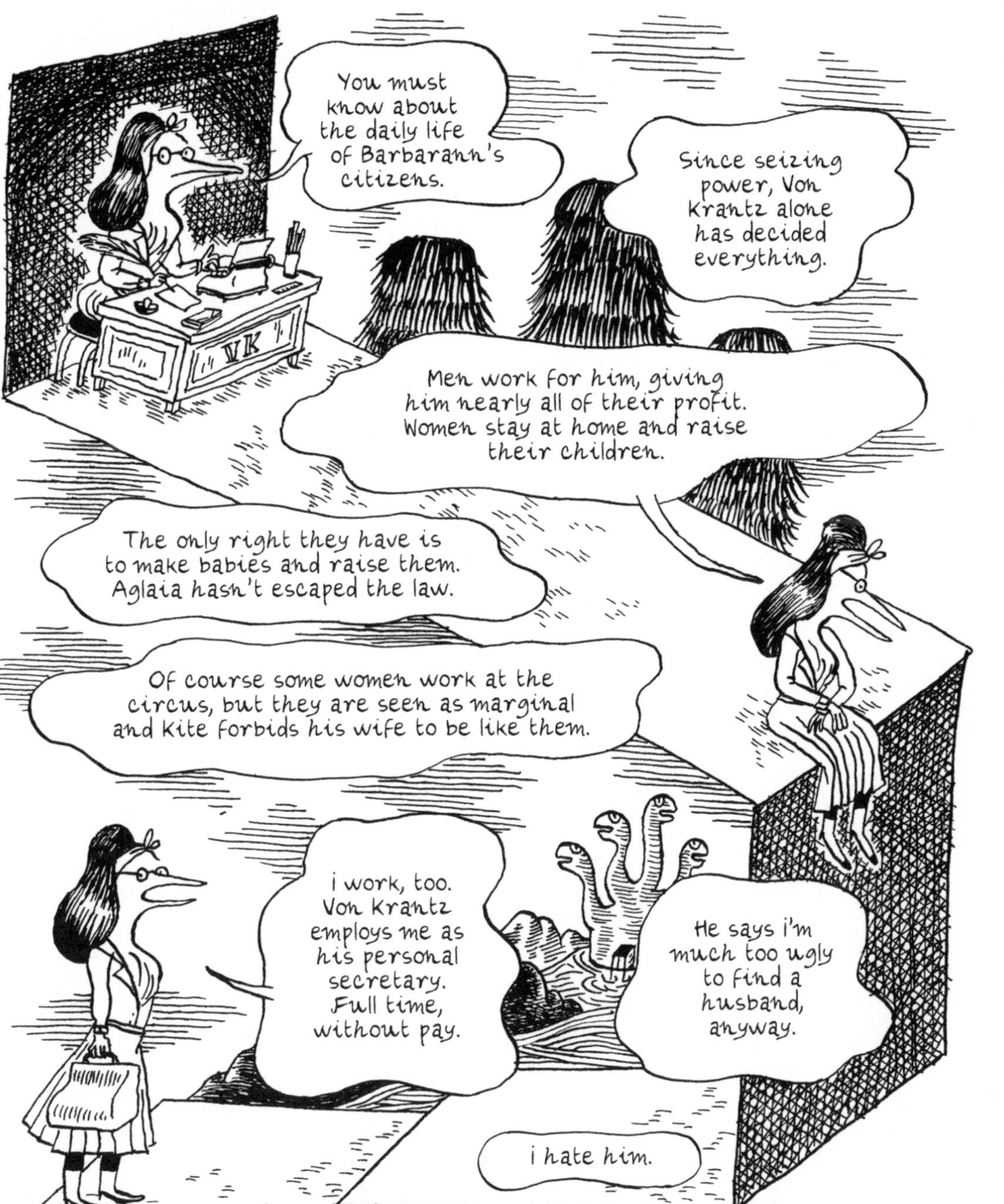

You must know about the daily life of Barbarann's citizens.
Since seizing power, Von Krantz alone has decided everything.
VK
Men work for him, giving him nearly all of their profit. Women stay at home and raise their children.
The only right they have is to make babies and raise them. Aglaia hasn't escaped the law.
Of course some women work at the circus, but they are seen as marginal and Kite forbids his wife to be like them.
I work, too. Von Krantz employs me as his personal secretary. Full time, without pay.
He says I'm much too ugly to find a husband, anyway.
I hate him.
Everyone hates him.

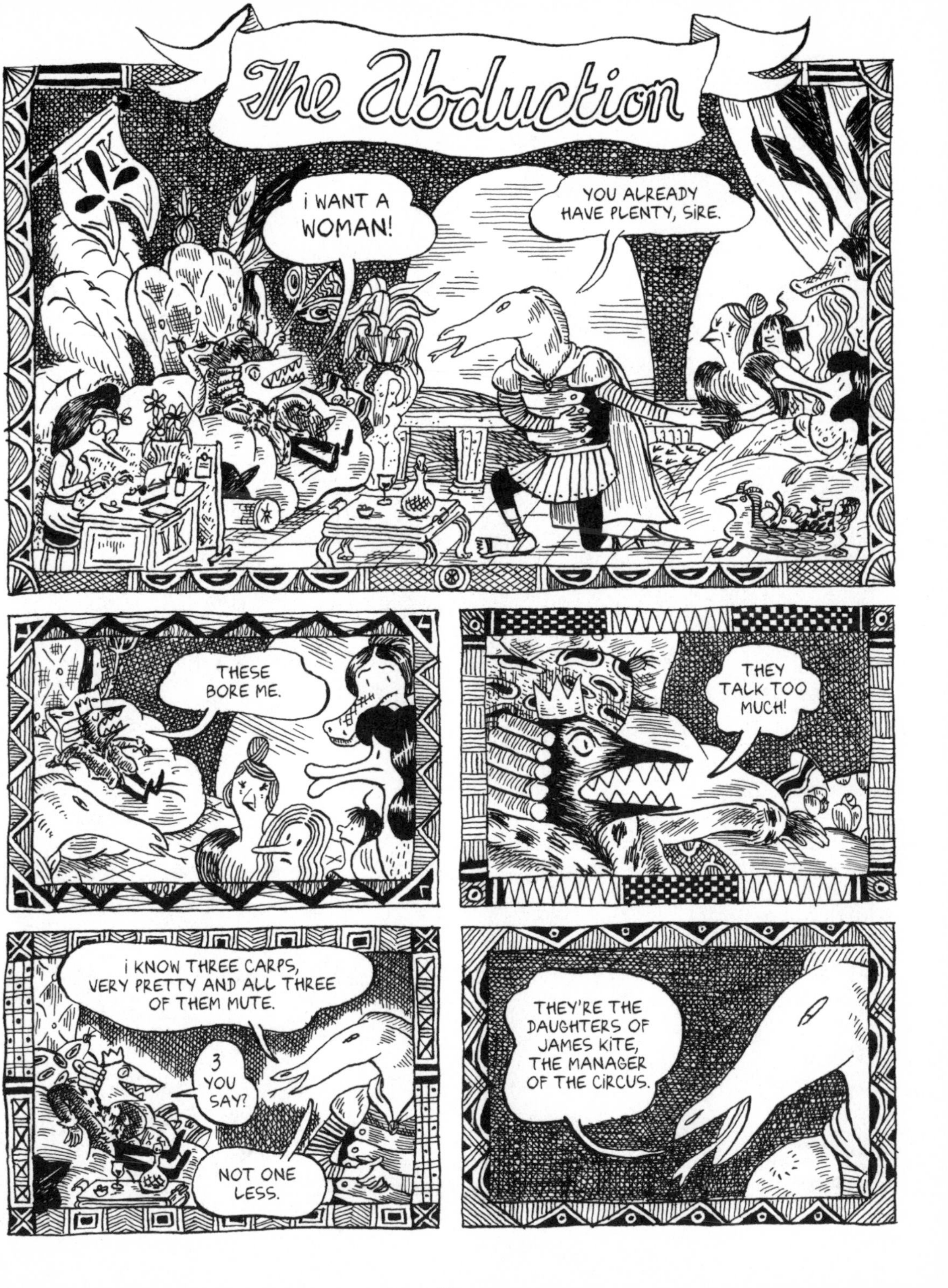
The Abduction
i WANT A WOMAN!
YOU ALREADY HAVE PLENTY, SiRE.
THESE BORE ME.
THEY TALK TOO MUCH!
i KNOW THREE CARPS, VERY PRETTY AND ALL THREE OF THEM MUTE.
3 YOU SAY?
NOT ONE LESS.
THEY'RE THE DAUGHTERS OF JAMES KiTE, THE MANAGER OF THE CiRCUS.

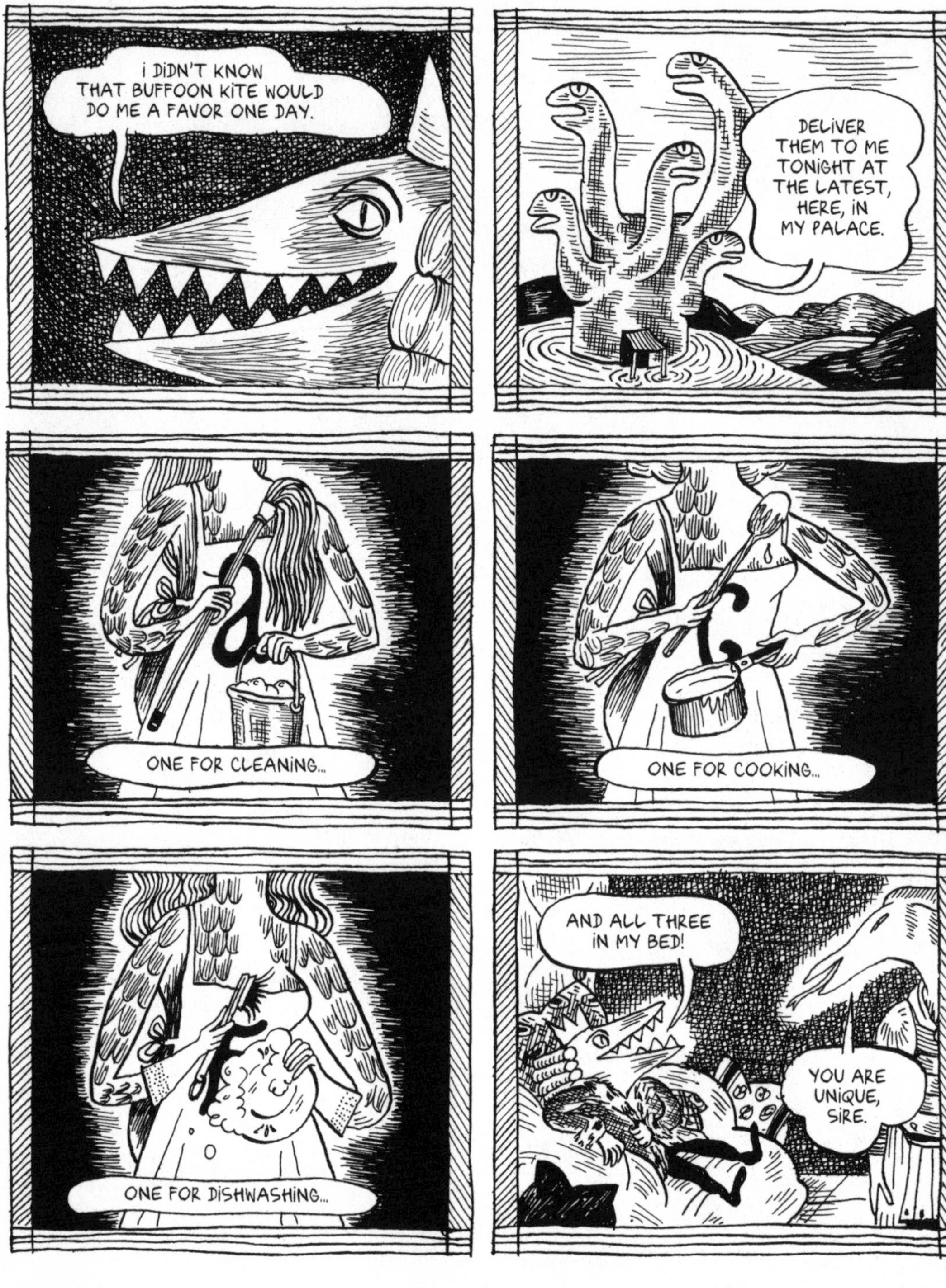
I DIDN'T KNOW THAT BUFFOON KITE WOULD DO ME A FAVOR ONE DAY.
DELIVER THEM TO ME TONIGHT AT THE LATEST, HERE, IN MY PALACE.
ONE FOR CLEANING...
ONE FOR COOKING...
ONE FOR DISHWASHING...
AND ALL THREE IN MY BED!
YOU ARE UNIQUE, SIRE.

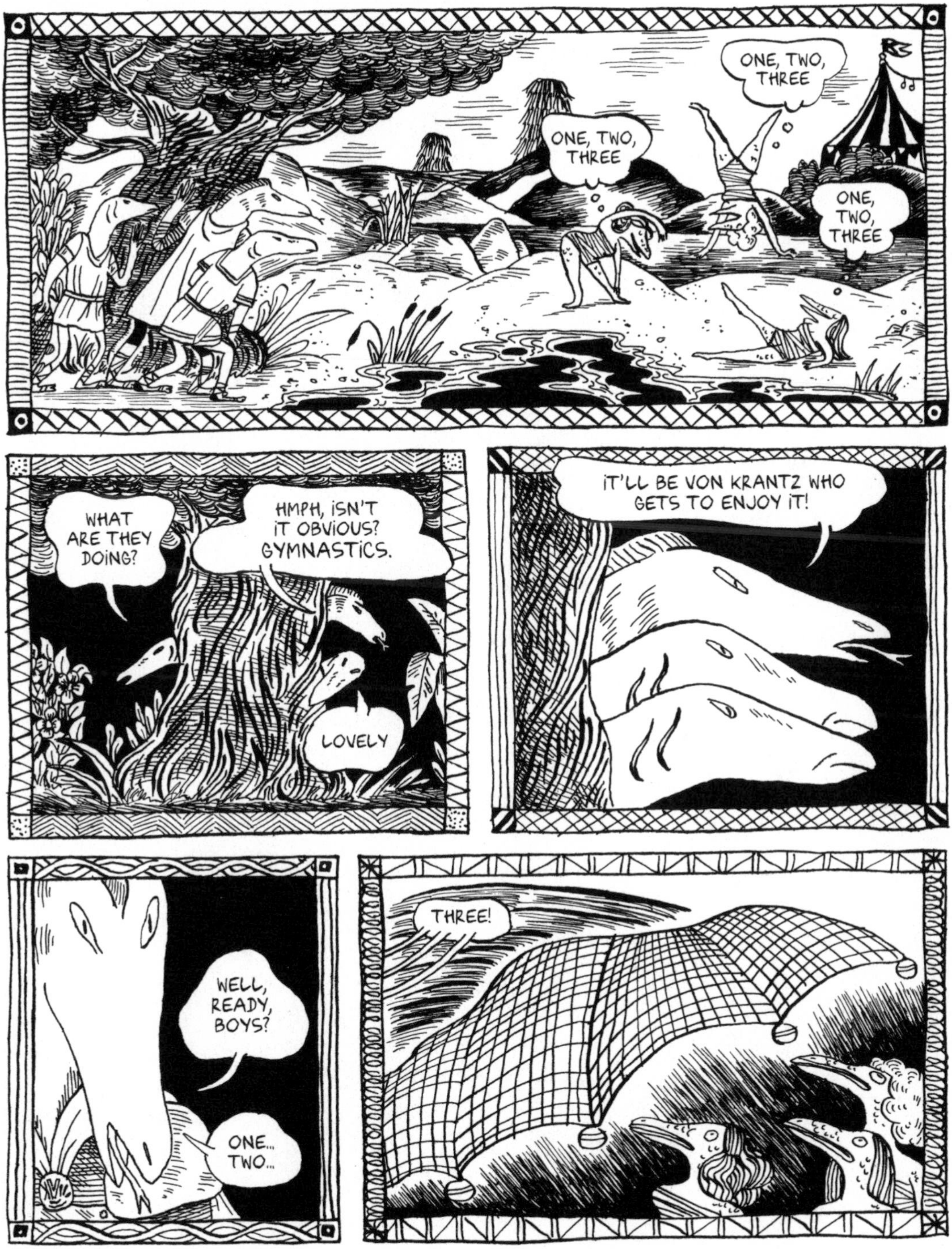

ONE, TWO, THREE
ONE, TWO, THREE
ONE, TWO, THREE
WHAT ARE THEY DOING?
HMPH, ISN'T IT OBVIOUS? GYMNASTICS.
LOVELY
IT'LL BE VON KRANTZ WHO GETS TO ENJOY IT!
WELL, READY, BOYS?
ONE... TWO...
THREE!

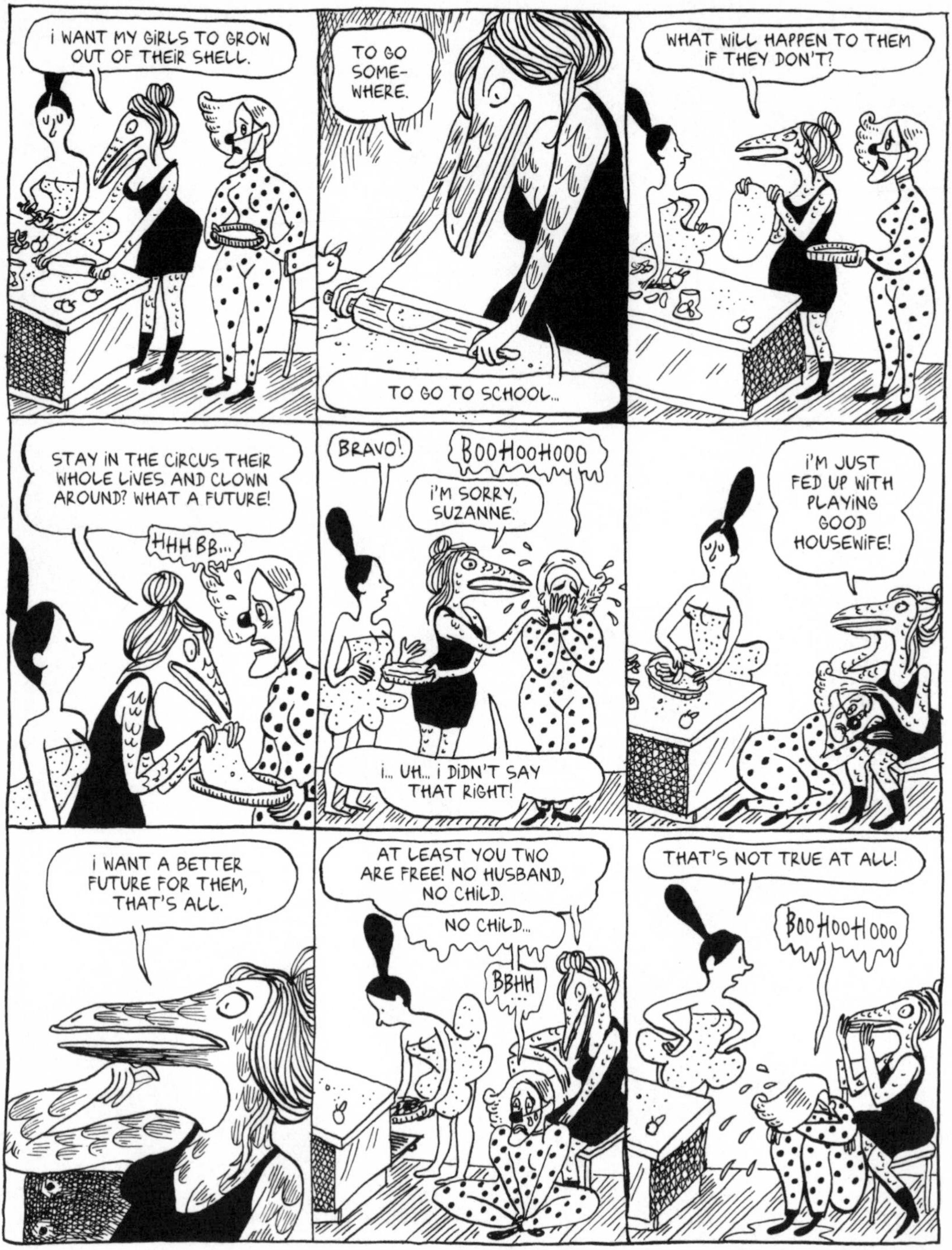
I WANT MY GIRLS TO GROW OUT OF THEIR SHELL.
TO GO SOME-WHERE.
TO GO TO SCHOOL...
WHAT WILL HAPPEN TO THEM IF THEY DON'T?
STAY IN THE CIRCUS THEIR WHOLE LIVES AND CLOWN AROUND? WHAT A FUTURE!
HHHBB...
BRAVO!
BOOHOOHOOO
I'M SORRY, SUZANNE.
I... UH... I DIDN'T SAY THAT RIGHT!
I'M JUST FED UP WITH PLAYING GOOD HOUSEWIFE!
I WANT A BETTER FUTURE FOR THEM, THAT'S ALL.
AT LEAST YOU TWO ARE FREE! NO HUSBAND, NO CHILD.
NO CHILD...
BBHH
THAT'S NOT TRUE AT ALL!
BOOHOOHOOO

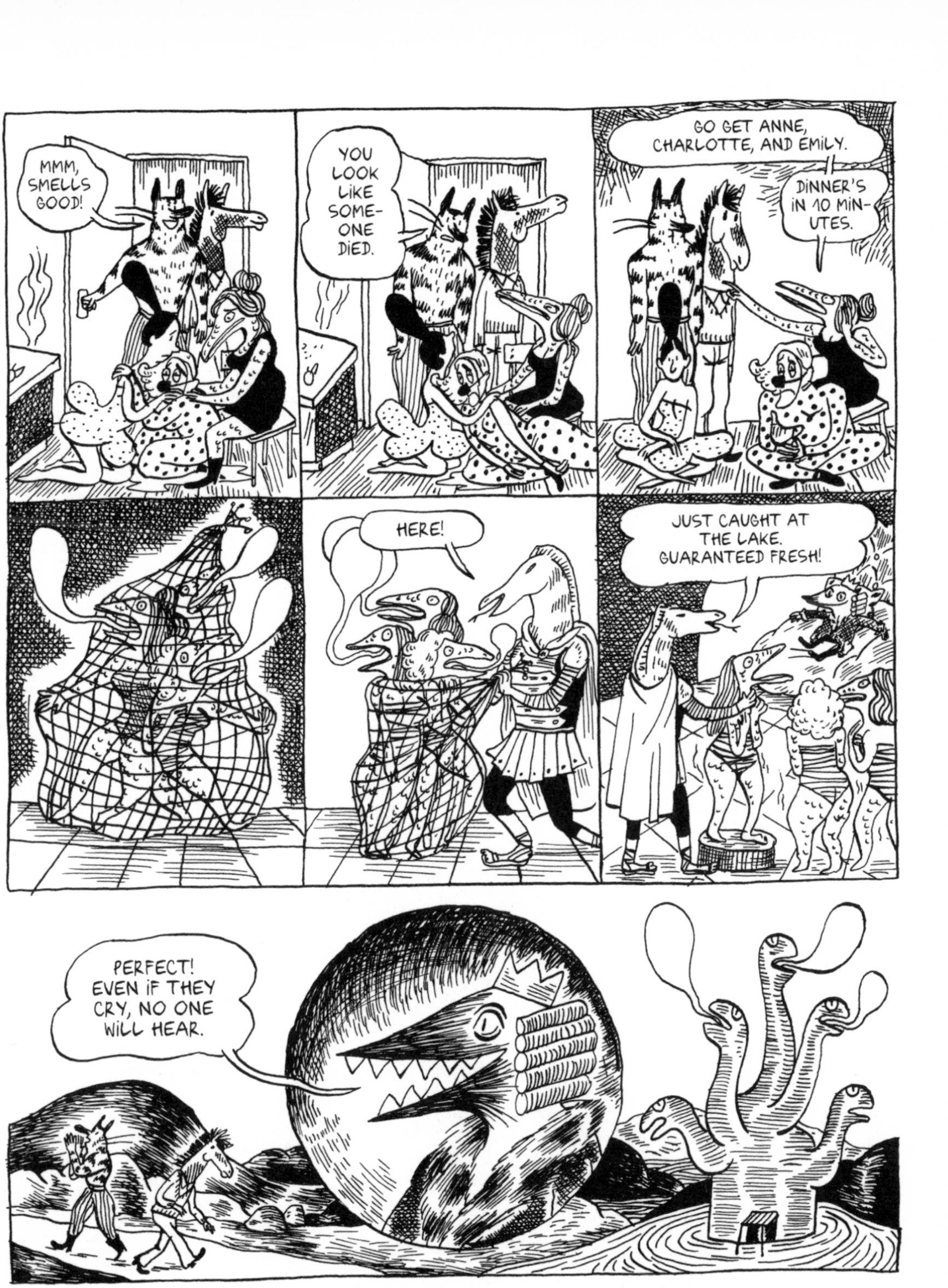
MMM, SMELLS GOOD!
YOU LOOK LIKE SOME-ONE DIED.
GO GET ANNE, CHARLOTTE, AND EMILY.
DINNER'S IN 10 MIN-UTES.
HERE!
JUST CAUGHT AT THE LAKE. GUARANTEED FRESH!
PERFECT! EVEN IF THEY CRY, NO ONE WILL HEAR.

INTERLUDE FOR SIMONE, THE KING'S FORMER SECRETARY

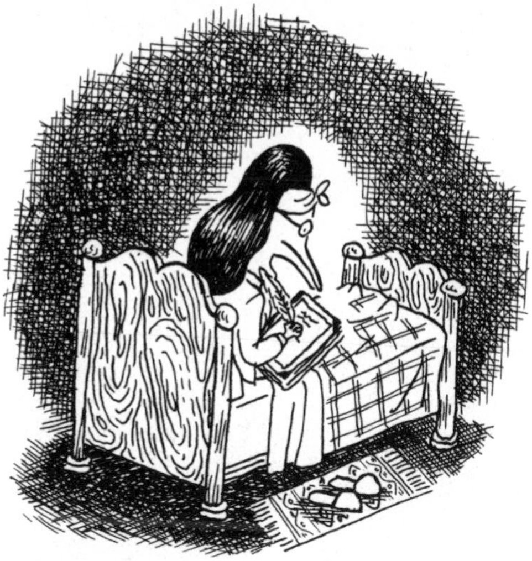

Aglaia,

i beg you to burn this letter after reading it.

i know where your daughters are.

Von Krantz is holding them prisoner in the three highest towers of the Palace.

Each door is dangerously guarded. it is not easy to get in.

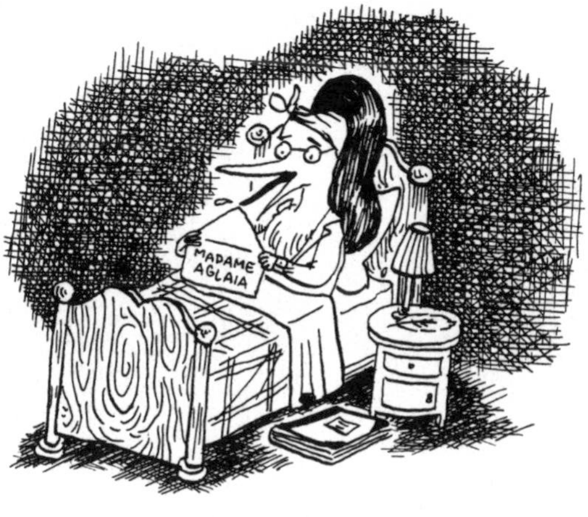
MADAME AGLAIA

But it is possible to get close to your children. Use your head.

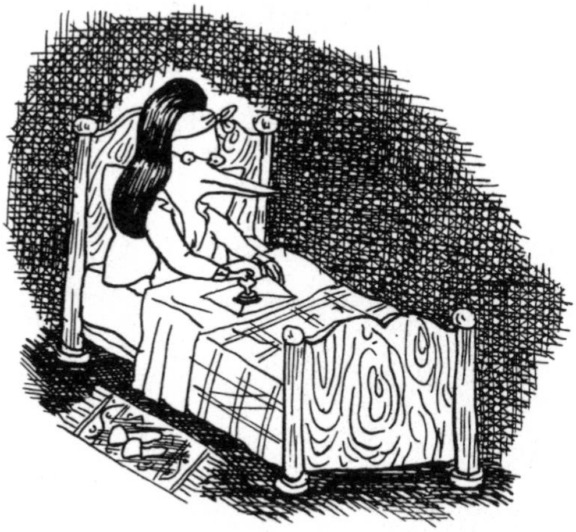

i know Von Krantz well. He's not a very clever man. it will be easy to set a trap.

A position for a secretary has just opened. isn't that a good start?

Warmly,

AGLAIA'S VICTORY

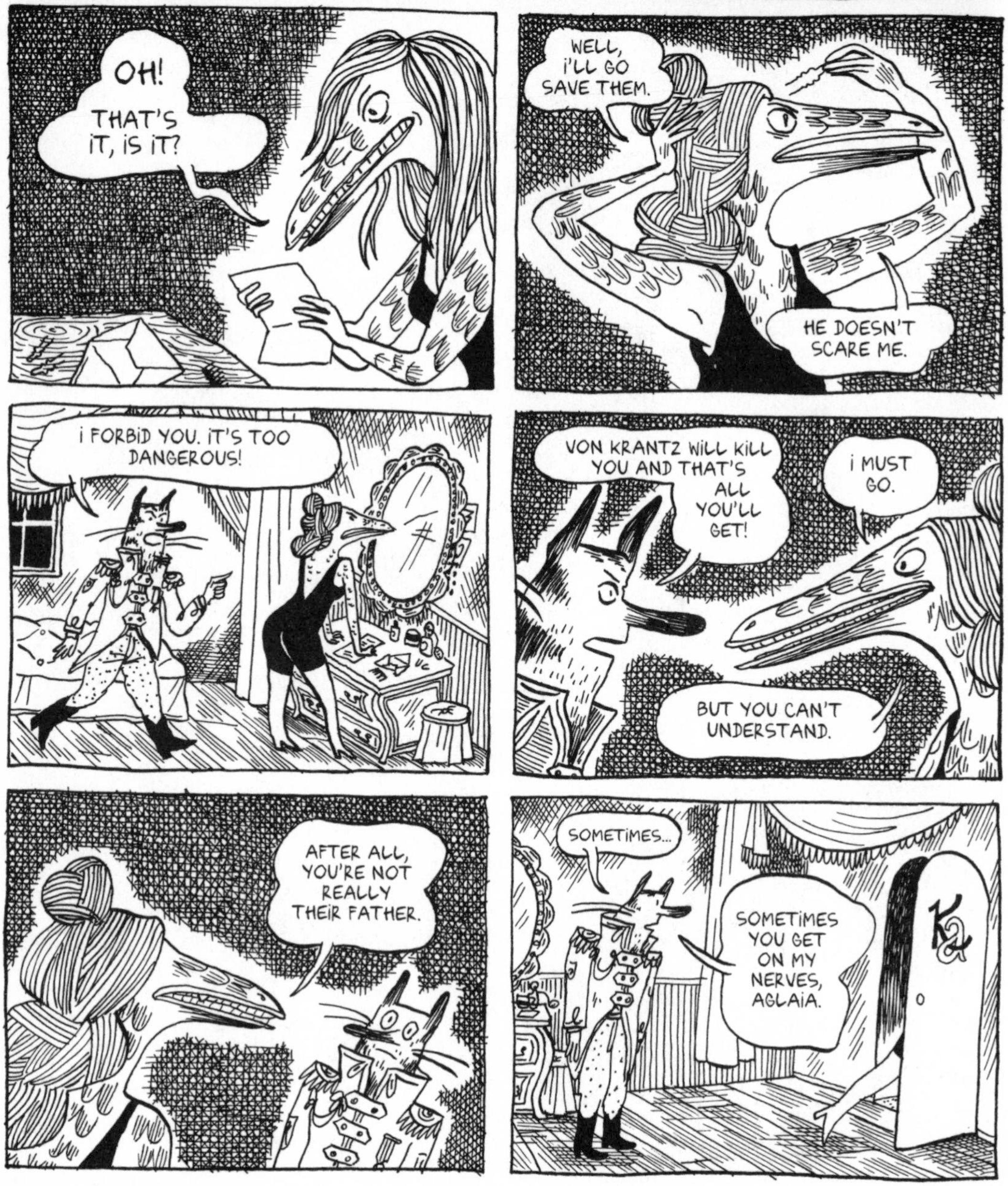
OH!
THAT'S IT, IS IT?
WELL, I'LL GO SAVE THEM.
HE DOESN'T SCARE ME.
I FORBID YOU. IT'S TOO DANGEROUS!
VON KRANTZ WILL KILL YOU AND THAT'S ALL YOU'LL GET!
I MUST GO.
BUT YOU CAN'T UNDERSTAND.
AFTER ALL, YOU'RE NOT REALLY THEIR FATHER.
SOMETIMES...
SOMETIMES YOU GET ON MY NERVES, AGLAIA.

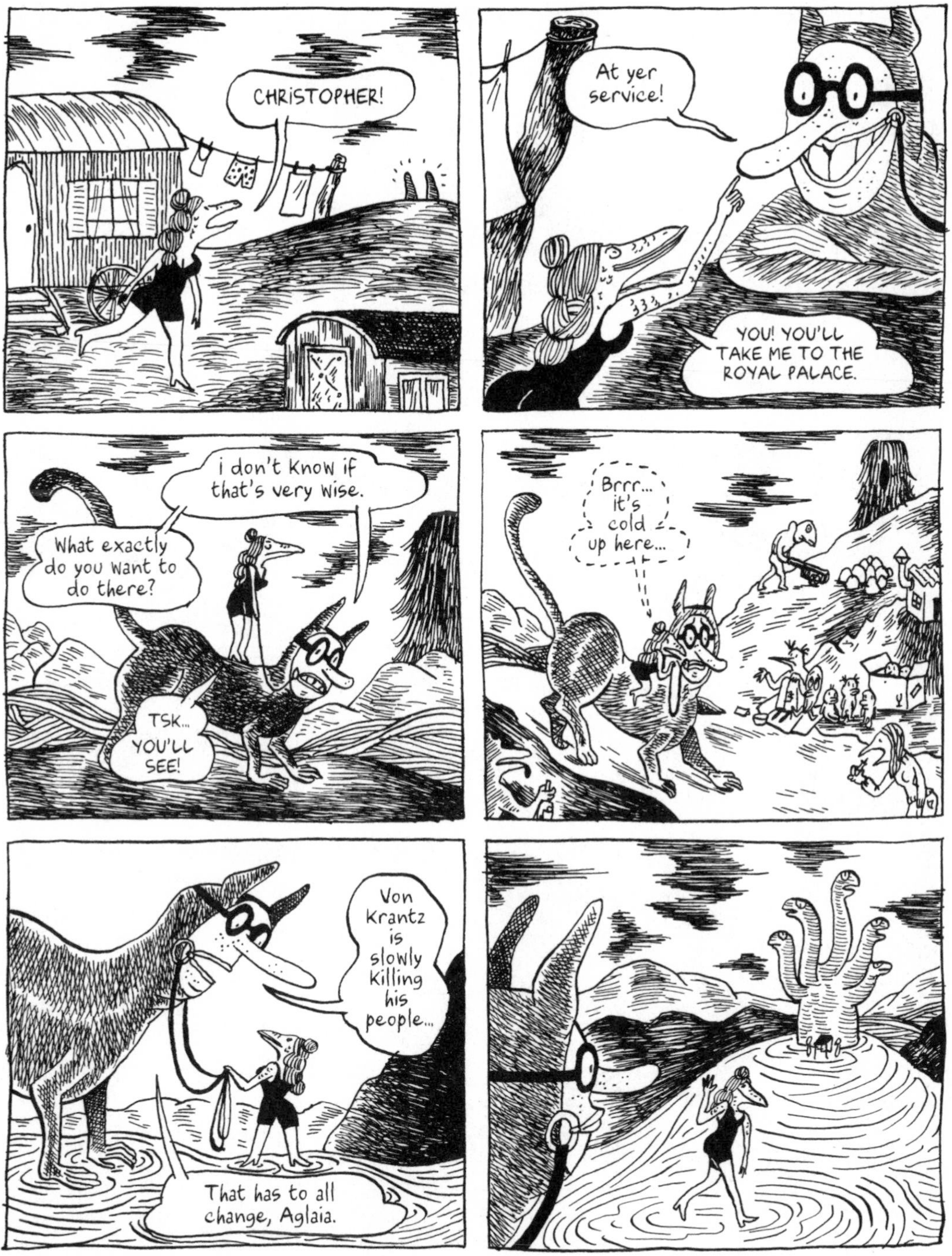

CHRISTOPHER!
At yer service!
YOU! YOU'LL TAKE ME TO THE ROYAL PALACE.
What exactly do you want to do there?
i don't Know if that's very wise.
TSK... YOU'LL SEE!
Brrr... it's cold up here...
Von Krantz is slowly killing his people...
That has to all change, Aglaia.

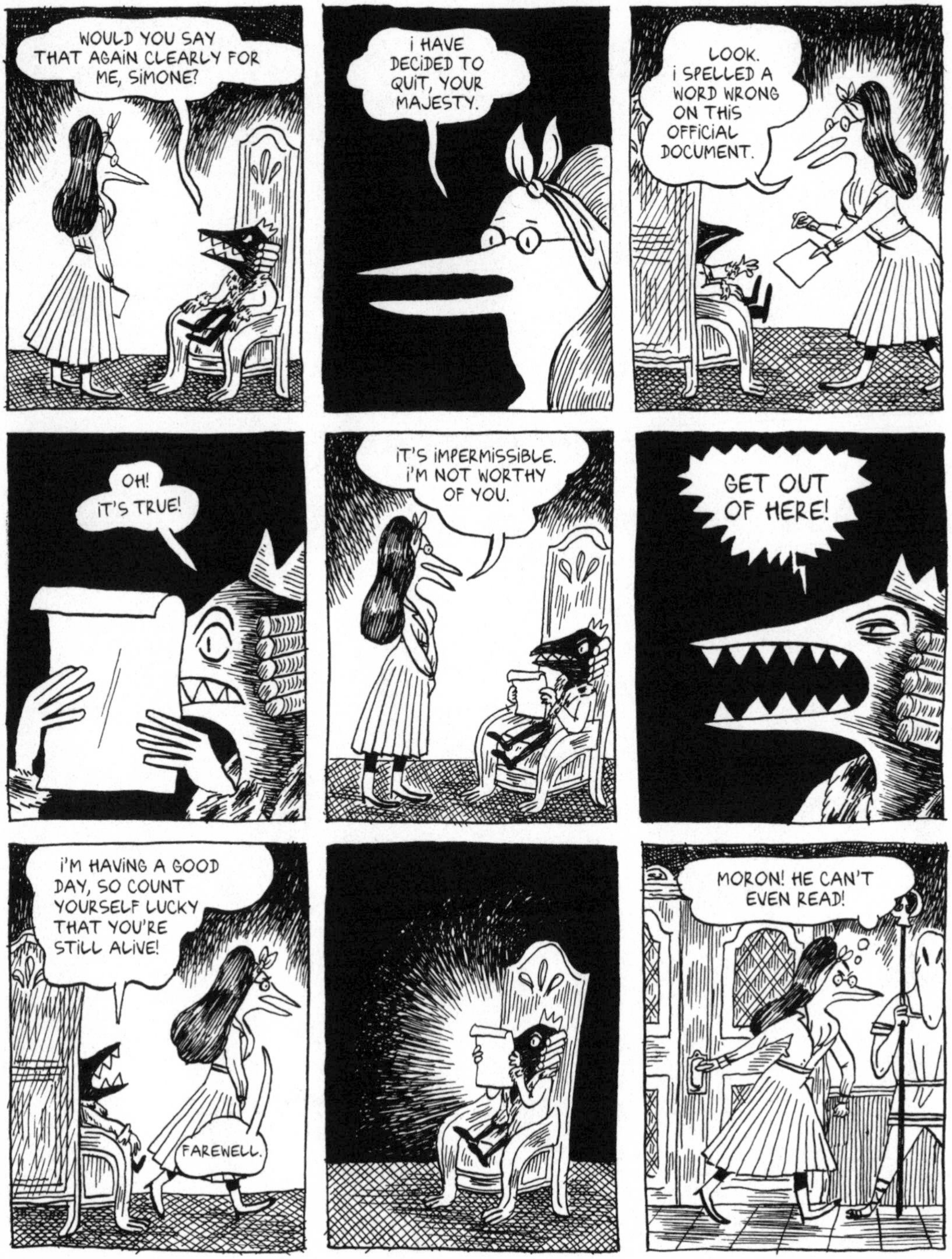
WOULD YOU SAY THAT AGAIN CLEARLY FOR ME, SIMONE?
I HAVE DECIDED TO QUIT, YOUR MAJESTY.
LOOK. I SPELLED A WORD WRONG ON THIS OFFICIAL DOCUMENT.
OH! IT'S TRUE!
IT'S IMPERMISSIBLE. I'M NOT WORTHY OF YOU.
GET OUT OF HERE!
I'M HAVING A GOOD DAY, SO COUNT YOURSELF LUCKY THAT YOU'RE STILL ALIVE!
FAREWELL.
MORON! HE CAN'T EVEN READ!

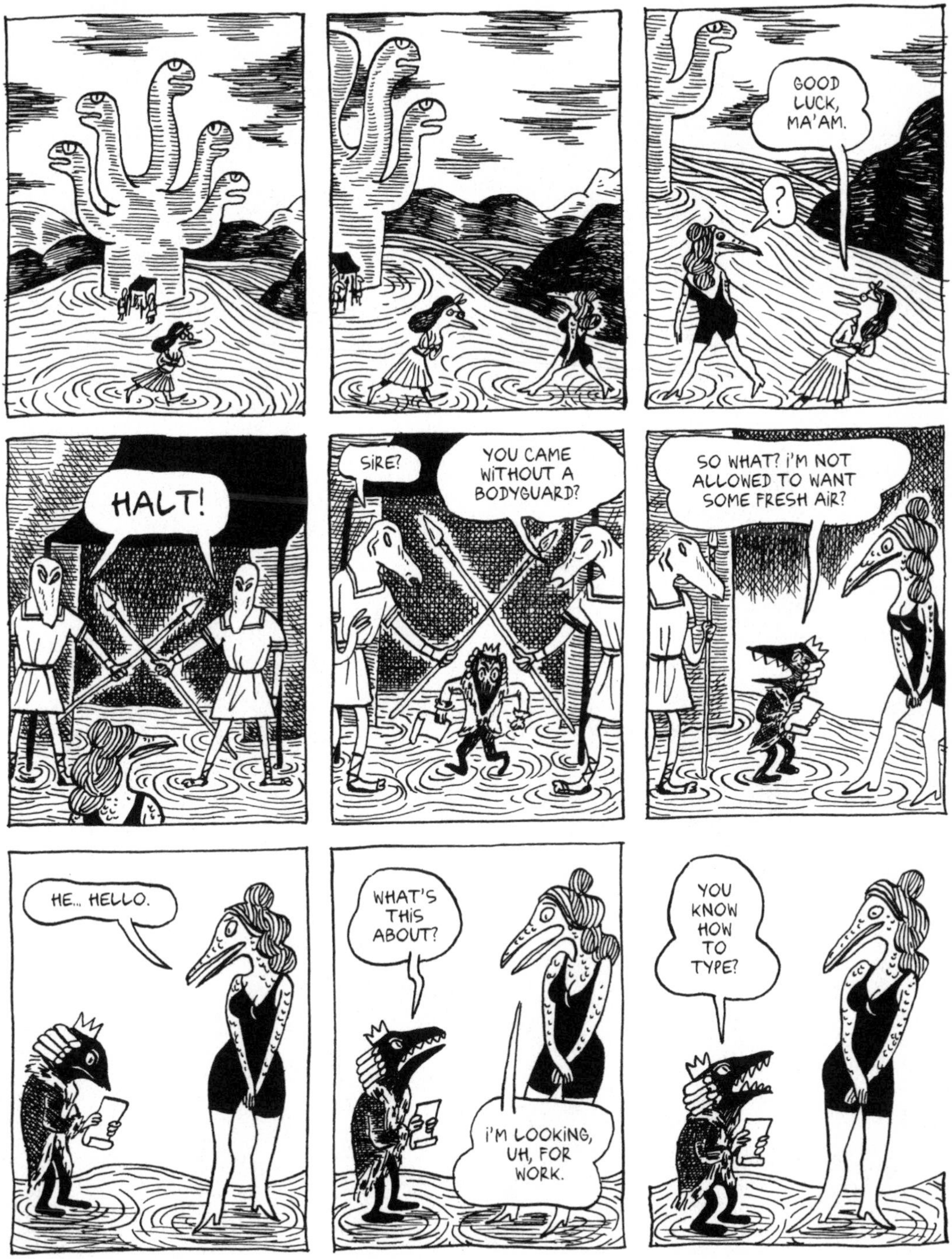
GOOD LUCK, MA'AM.
?
HALT!
SIRE?
YOU CAME WITHOUT A BODYGUARD?
SO WHAT? I'M NOT ALLOWED TO WANT SOME FRESH AIR?
HE... HELLO.
WHAT'S THIS ABOUT?
I'M LOOKING, UH, FOR WORK.
YOU KNOW HOW TO TYPE?

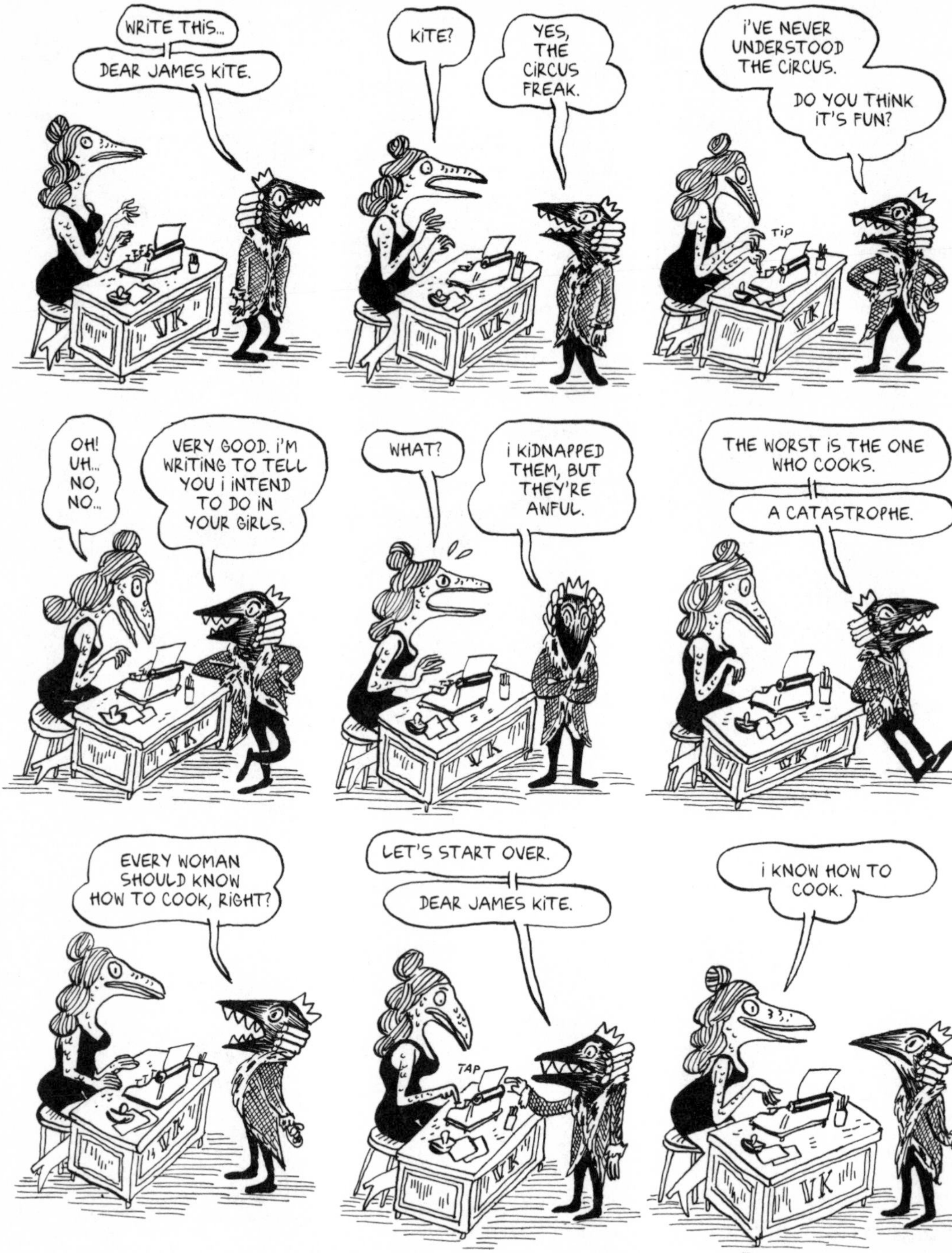
WRITE THIS...
DEAR JAMES KITE.
KITE?
YES, THE CIRCUS FREAK.
I'VE NEVER UNDERSTOOD THE CIRCUS.
DO YOU THINK IT'S FUN?
TIP
OH! UH... NO, NO...
VERY GOOD. I'M WRITING TO TELL YOU I INTEND TO DO IN YOUR GIRLS.
WHAT?
I KIDNAPPED THEM, BUT THEY'RE AWFUL.
THE WORST IS THE ONE WHO COOKS.
A CATASTROPHE.
EVERY WOMAN SHOULD KNOW HOW TO COOK, RIGHT?
LET'S START OVER.
DEAR JAMES KITE.
TAP
I KNOW HOW TO COOK.

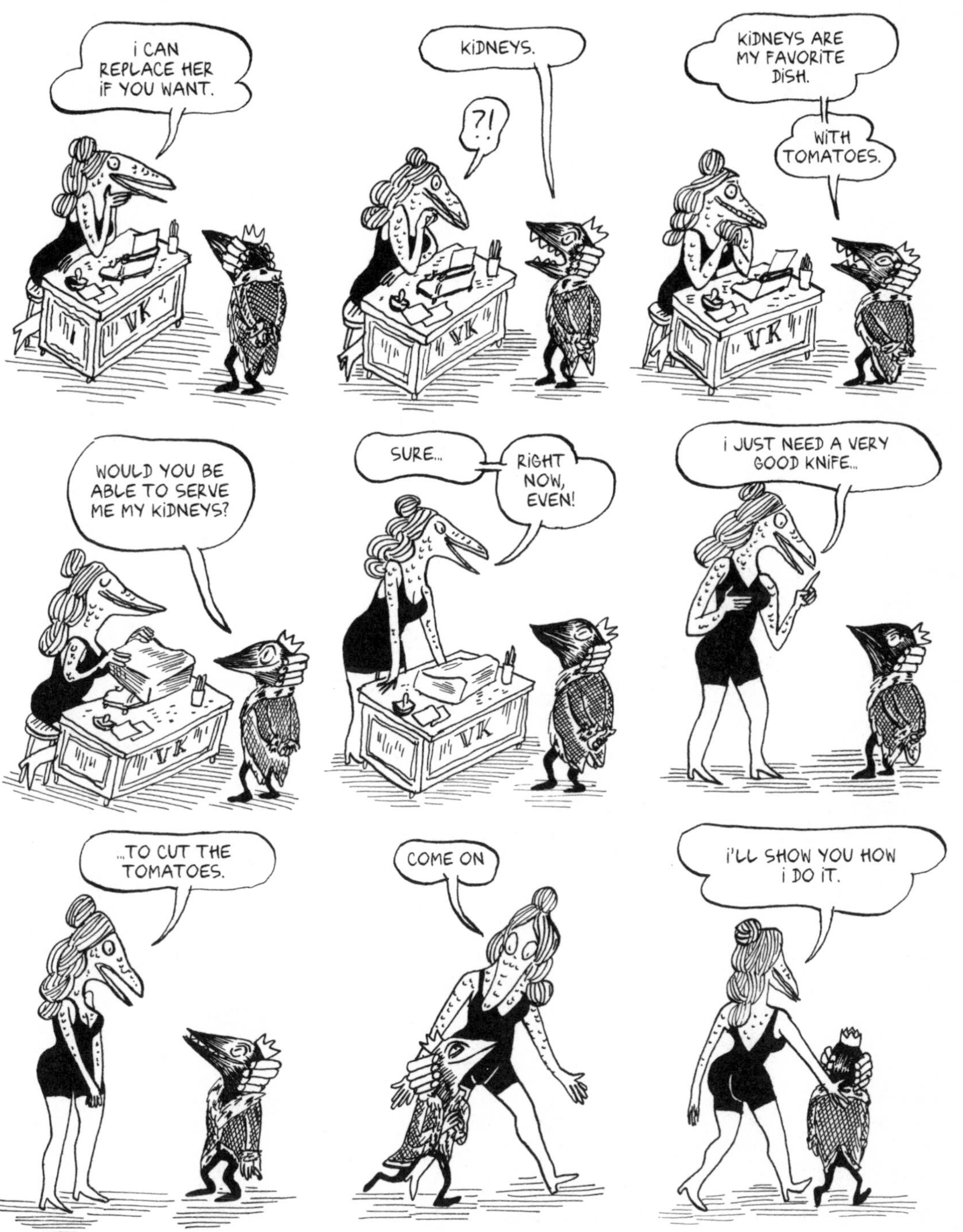
i CAN REPLACE HER iF YOU WANT.
KiDNEYS.
?!
KiDNEYS ARE MY FAVORiTE DiSH.
WiTH TOMATOES.
WOULD YOU BE ABLE TO SERVE ME MY KiDNEYS?
SURE...
RiGHT NOW, EVEN!
i JUST NEED A VERY GOOD KNiFE...
...TO CUT THE TOMATOES.
COME ON
i'LL SHOW YOU HOW i DO iT.

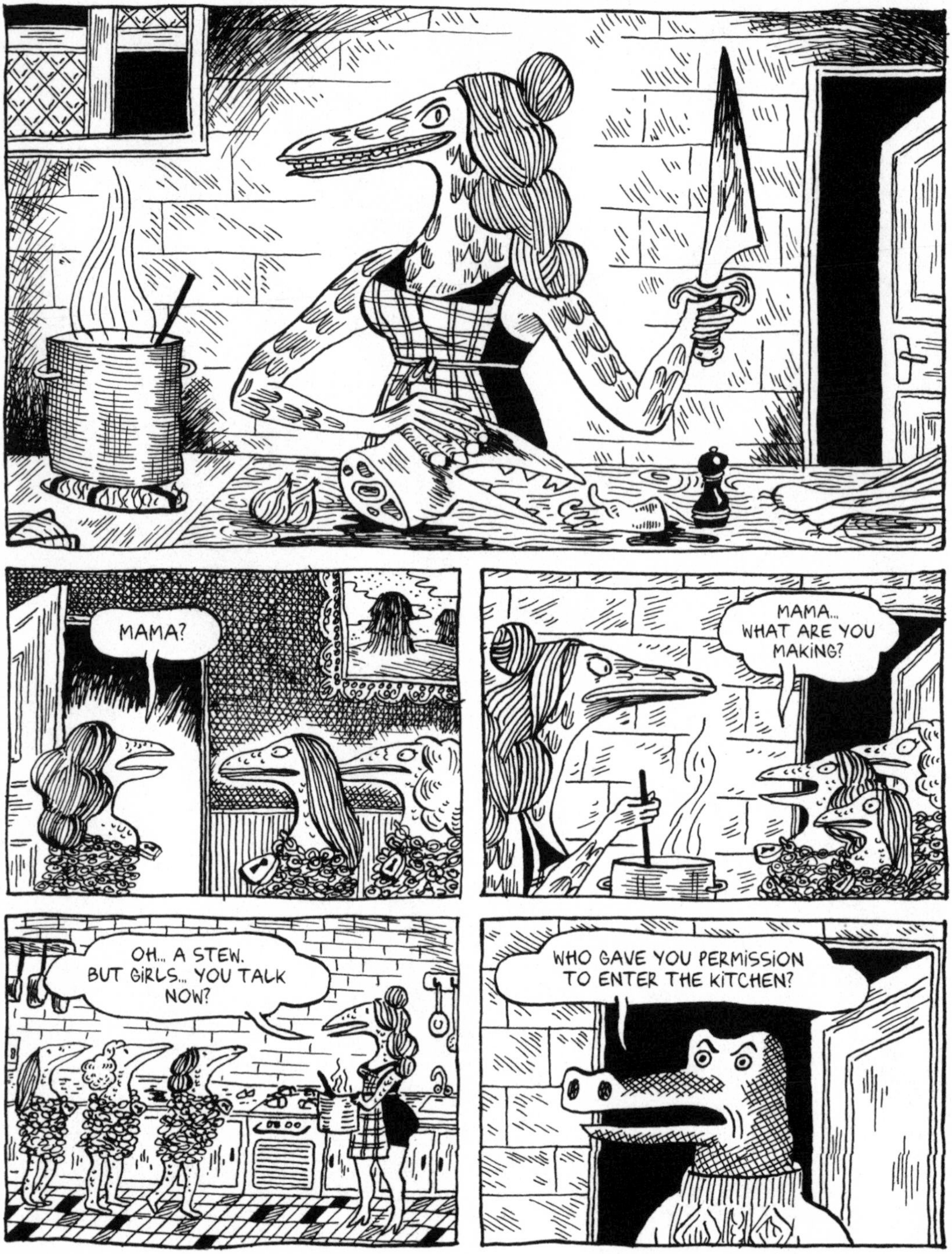
MAMA?
MAMA... WHAT ARE YOU MAKING?
OH... A STEW. BUT GIRLS... YOU TALK NOW?
WHO GAVE YOU PERMISSION TO ENTER THE KITCHEN?

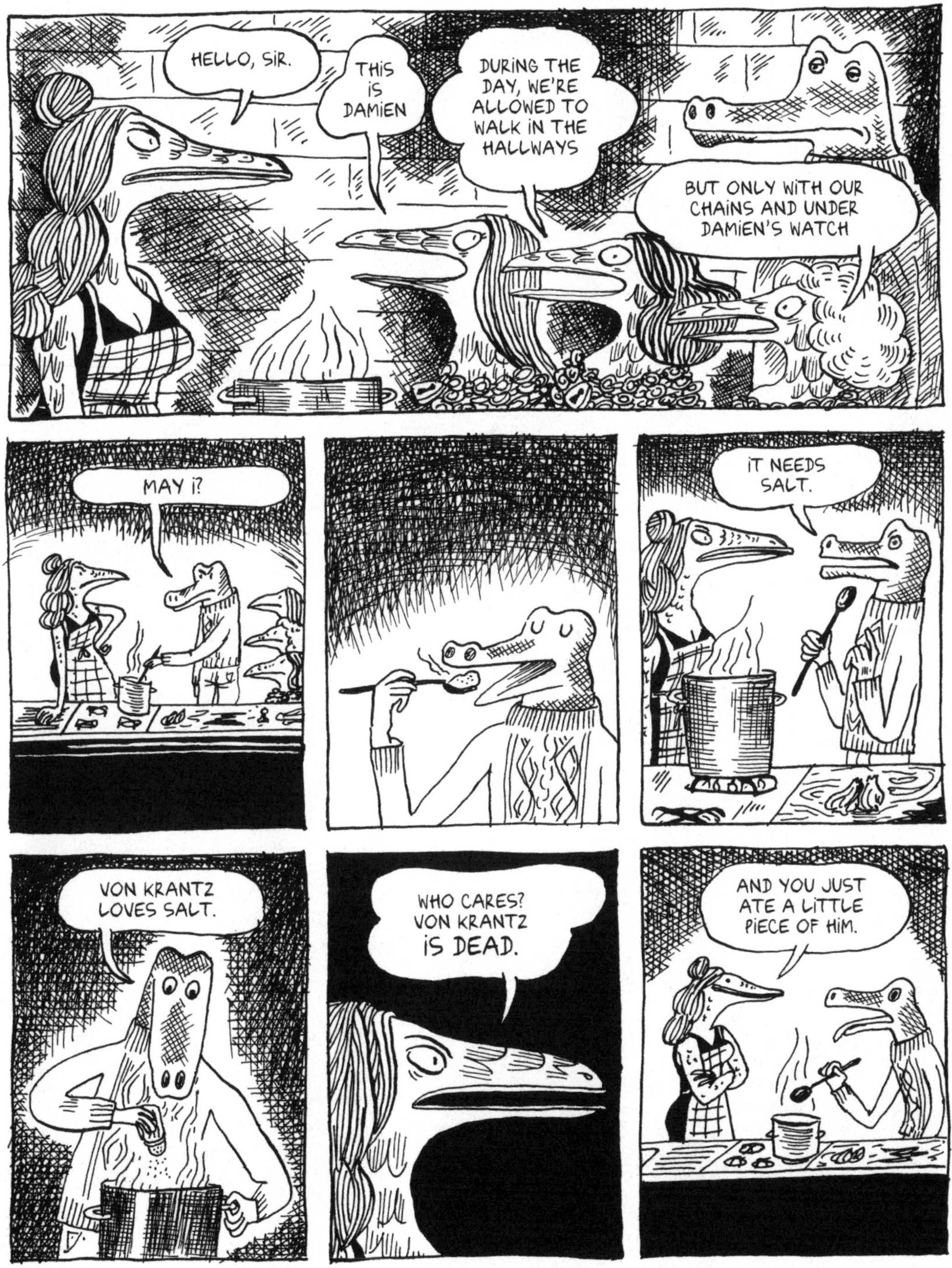
HELLO, SIR.
THIS IS DAMIEN
DURING THE DAY, WE'RE ALLOWED TO WALK IN THE HALLWAYS
BUT ONLY WITH OUR CHAINS AND UNDER DAMIEN'S WATCH
MAY I?
IT NEEDS SALT.
VON KRANTZ LOVES SALT.
WHO CARES? VON KRANTZ IS DEAD.
AND YOU JUST ATE A LITTLE PIECE OF HIM.

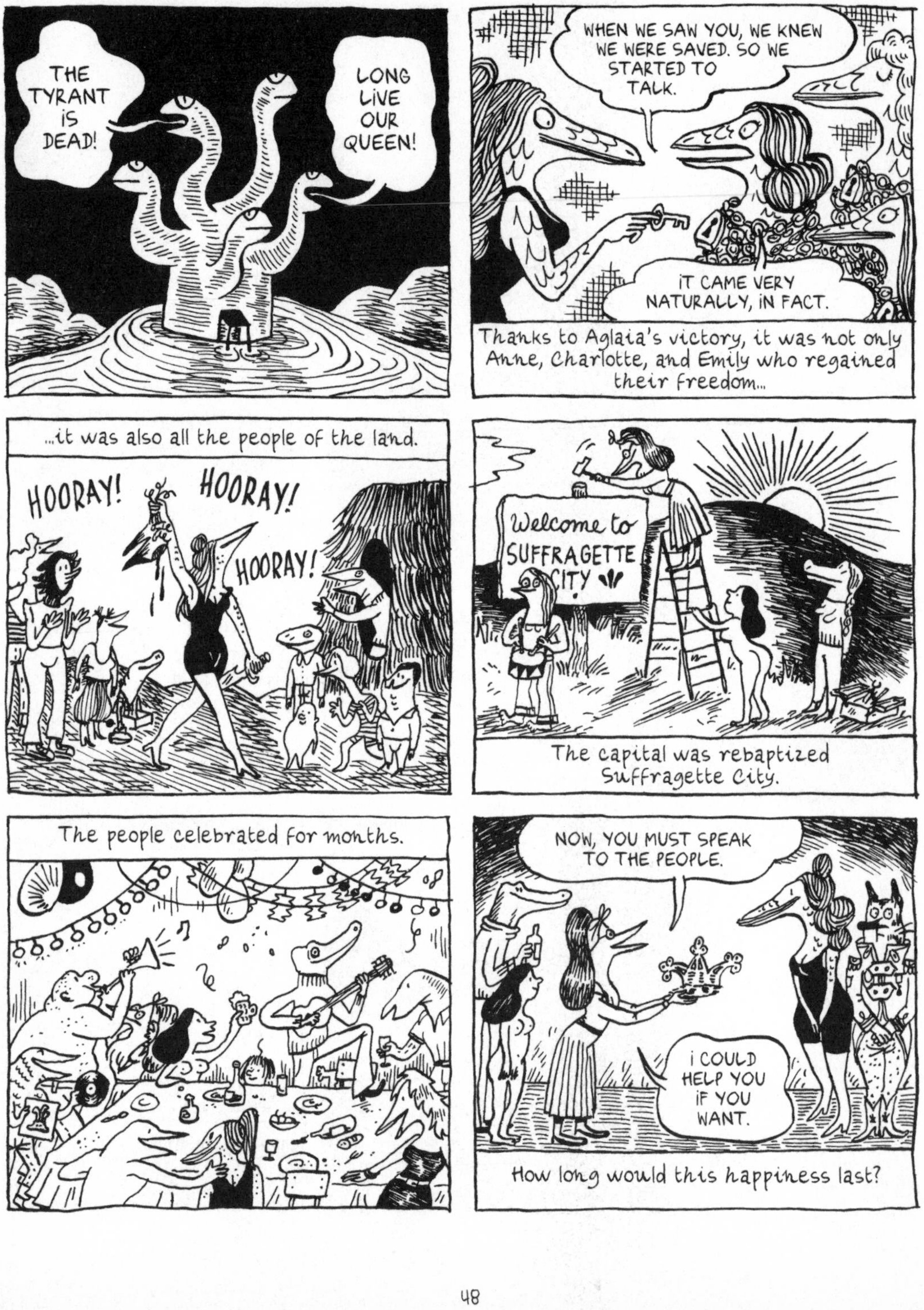
THE TYRANT IS DEAD!
LONG LIVE OUR QUEEN!
WHEN WE SAW YOU, WE KNEW WE WERE SAVED. SO WE STARTED TO TALK.
IT CAME VERY NATURALLY, IN FACT.
Thanks to Aglaia's victory, it was not only Anne, Charlotte, and Emily who regained their freedom...
...it was also all the people of the land.
HOORAY!
HOORAY!
HOORAY!
Welcome to SUFFRAGETTE CITY
The capital was rebaptized Suffragette City.
The people celebrated for months.
NOW, YOU MUST SPEAK TO THE PEOPLE.
I COULD HELP YOU IF YOU WANT.
How long would this happiness last?

INTERLUDE FOR SIMONE, THE QUEEN'S POLITICAL ADVISOR

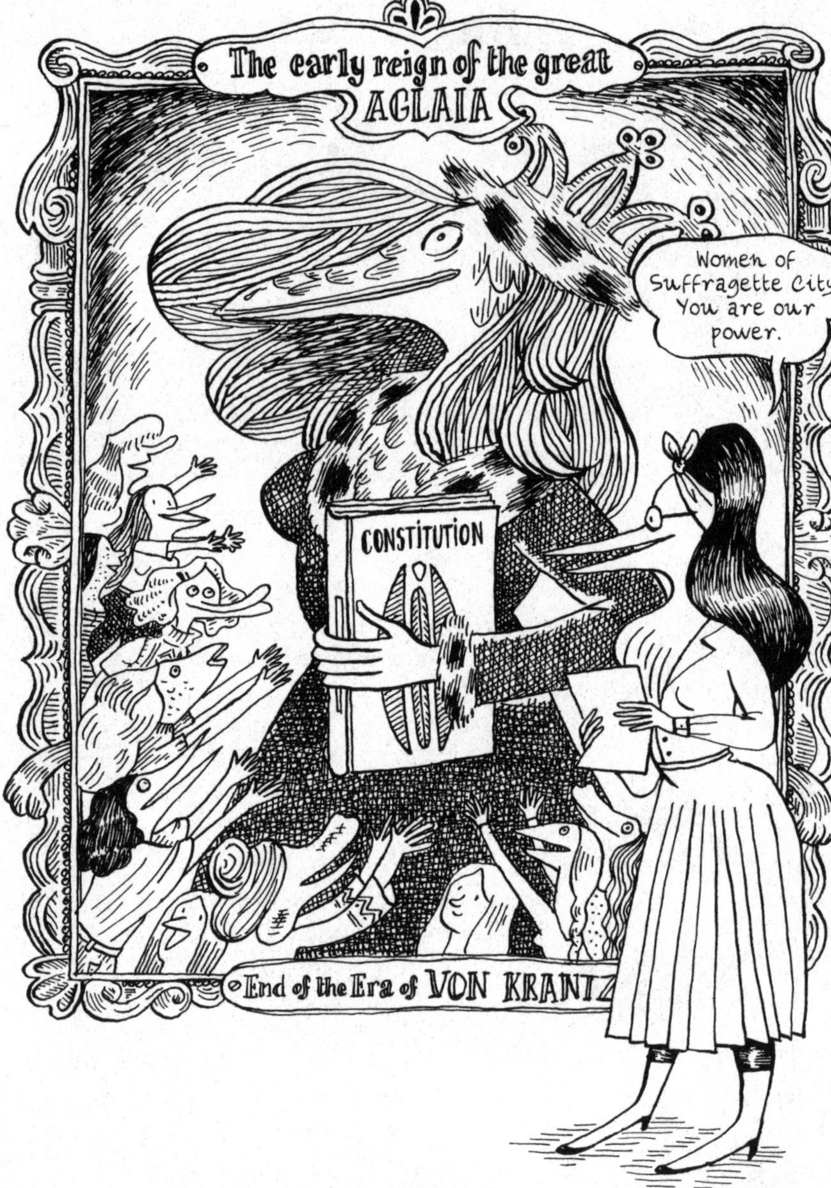
The early reign of the great AGLAIA
Women of Suffragette City, You are our power.
CONSTITUTION
End of the Era of VON KRANTZ

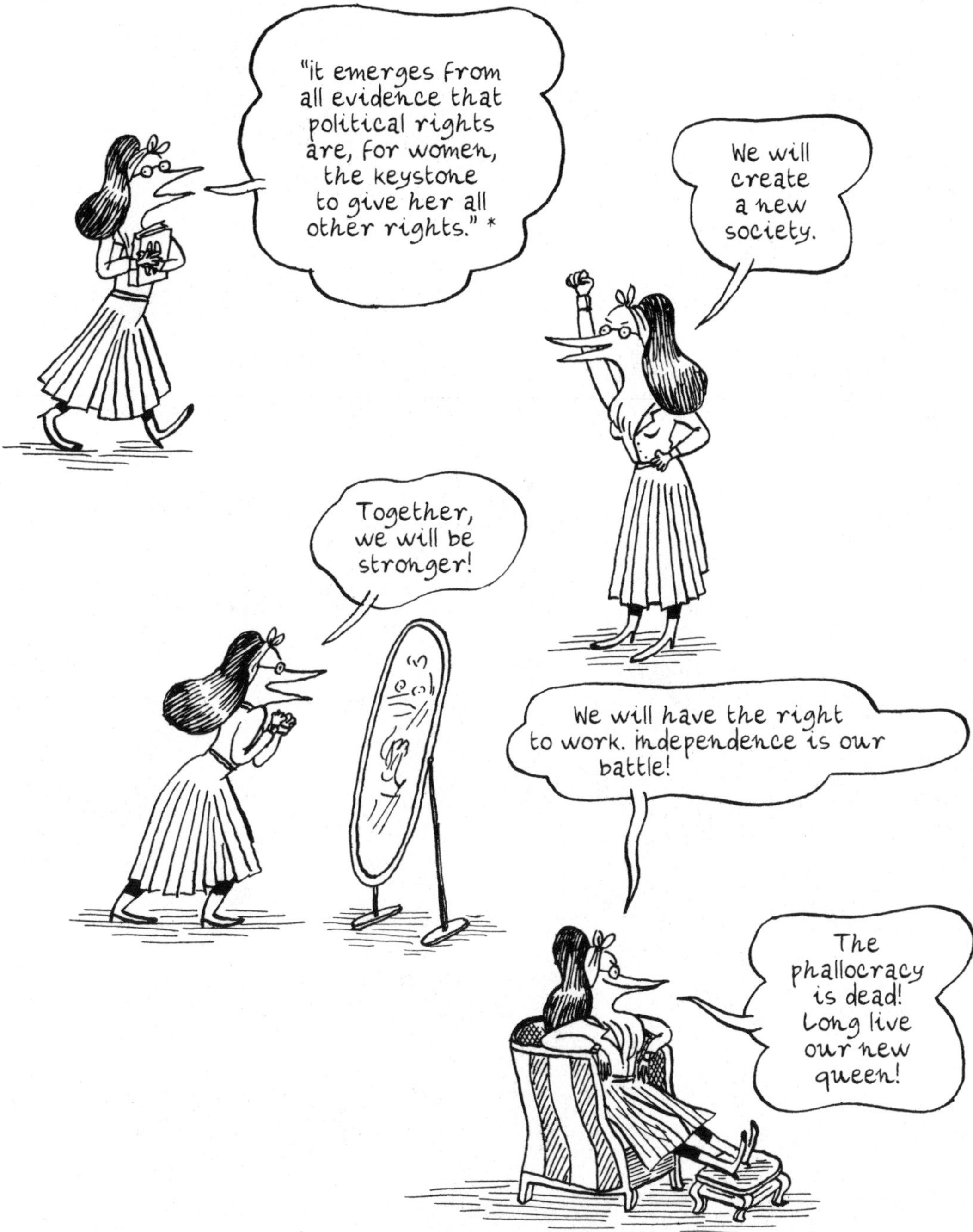
"it emerges from all evidence that political rights are, for women, the keystone to give her all other rights." *
We will create a new society.
Together, we will be stronger!
We will have the right to work. independence is our battle!
The phallocracy is dead! Long live our new queen!

* HUBERTINE AUCLERT, "THE CITIZENESS," FEBRUARY 13, 1881

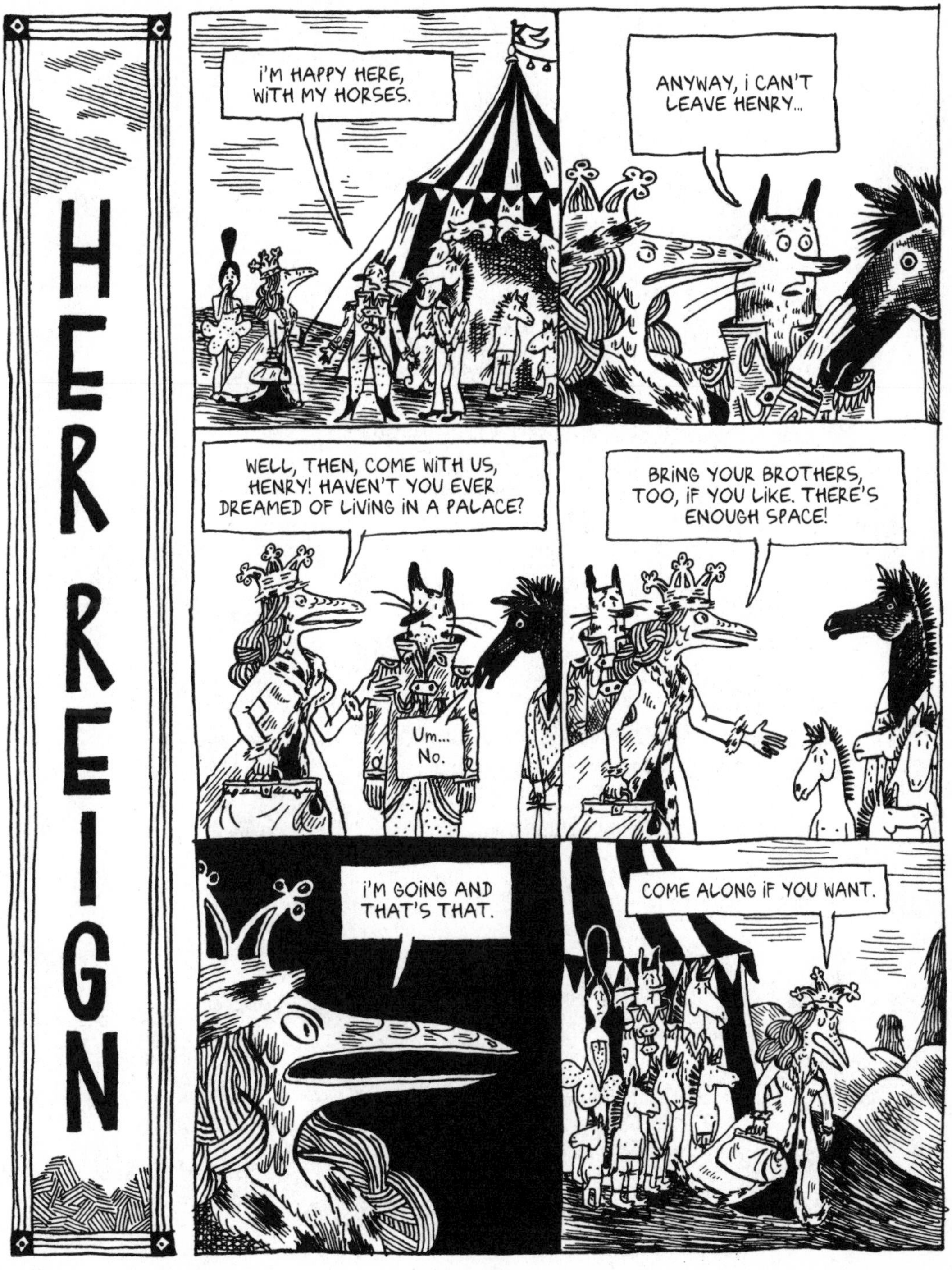
HER REIGN
I'M HAPPY HERE, WITH MY HORSES.
ANYWAY, I CAN'T LEAVE HENRY...
WELL, THEN, COME WITH US, HENRY! HAVEN'T YOU EVER DREAMED OF LIVING IN A PALACE?
Um... No.
BRING YOUR BROTHERS, TOO, IF YOU LIKE. THERE'S ENOUGH SPACE!
I'M GOING AND THAT'S THAT.
COME ALONG IF YOU WANT.

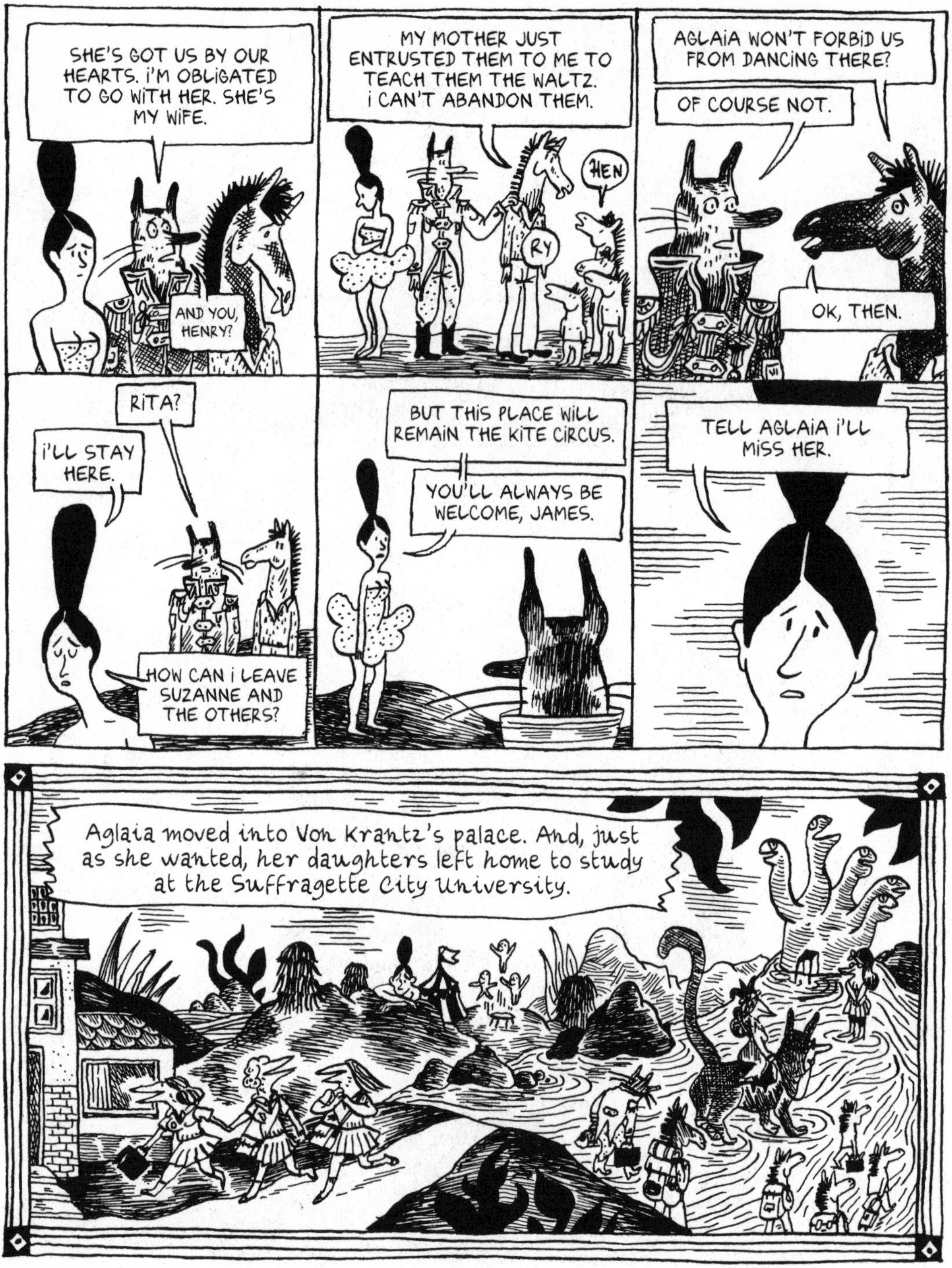
SHE'S GOT US BY OUR HEARTS. i'M OBLIGATED TO GO WITH HER. SHE'S MY WIFE.
AND YOU, HENRY?
MY MOTHER JUST ENTRUSTED THEM TO ME TO TEACH THEM THE WALTZ. i CAN'T ABANDON THEM.
HEN
RY
AGLAiA WON'T FORBiD US FROM DANCiNG THERE?
OF COURSE NOT.
OK, THEN.
RiTA?
i'LL STAY HERE.
HOW CAN i LEAVE SUZANNE AND THE OTHERS?
BUT THiS PLACE WiLL REMAiN THE KiTE CiRCUS.
YOU'LL ALWAYS BE WELCOME, JAMES.
TELL AGLAiA i'LL MiSS HER.
Aglaia moved into Von Krantz's palace. And, just as she wanted, her daughters left home to study at the Suffragette City University.

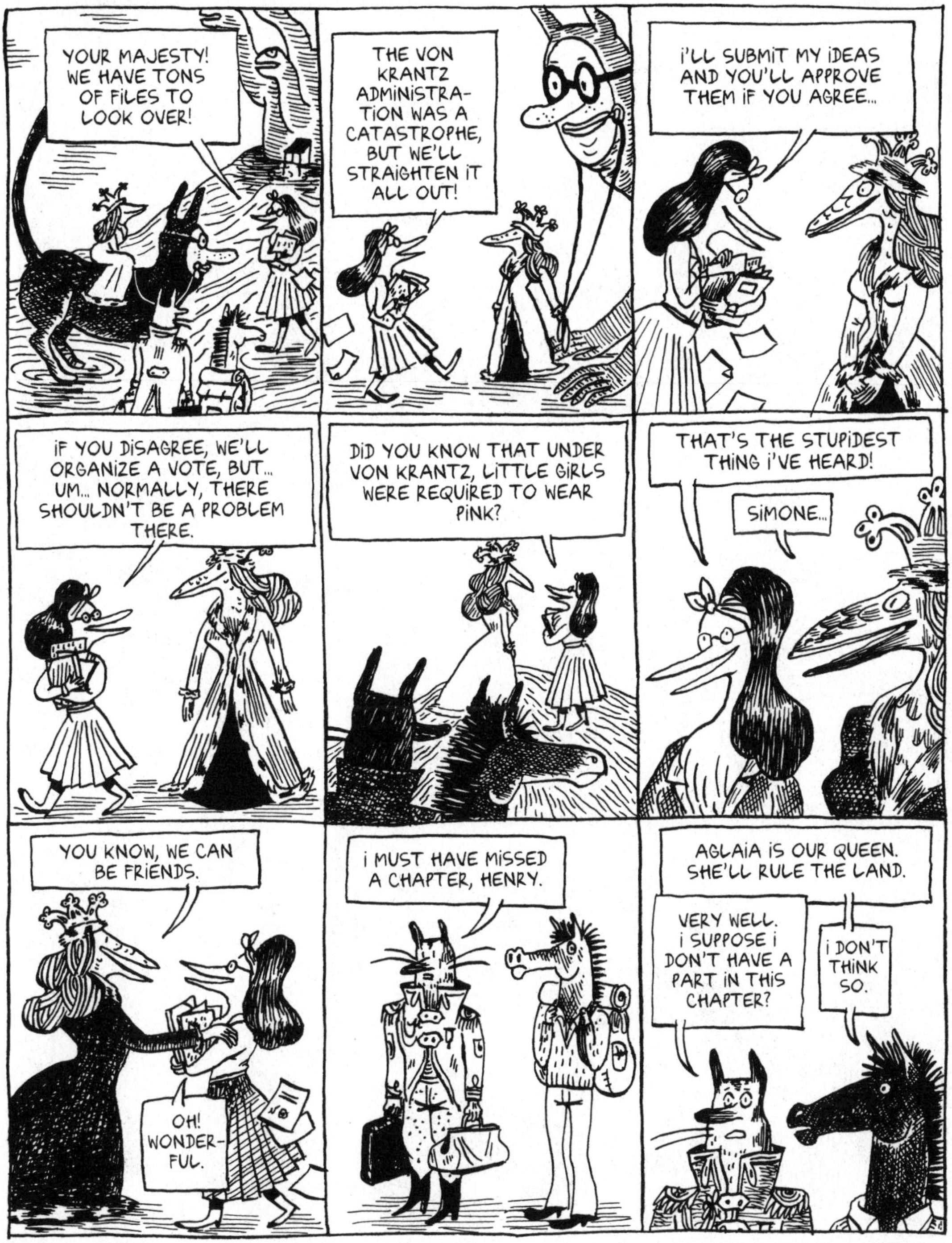
YOUR MAJESTY! WE HAVE TONS OF FILES TO LOOK OVER!
THE VON KRANTZ ADMINISTRATION WAS A CATASTROPHE, BUT WE'LL STRAIGHTEN IT ALL OUT!
I'LL SUBMIT MY IDEAS AND YOU'LL APPROVE THEM IF YOU AGREE...
IF YOU DISAGREE, WE'LL ORGANIZE A VOTE, BUT... UM... NORMALLY, THERE SHOULDN'T BE A PROBLEM THERE.
DID YOU KNOW THAT UNDER VON KRANTZ, LITTLE GIRLS WERE REQUIRED TO WEAR PINK?
THAT'S THE STUPIDEST THING I'VE HEARD!
SIMONE...
YOU KNOW, WE CAN BE FRIENDS.
OH! WONDERFUL.
I MUST HAVE MISSED A CHAPTER, HENRY.
AGLAIA IS OUR QUEEN. SHE'LL RULE THE LAND.
VERY WELL. I SUPPOSE I DON'T HAVE A PART IN THIS CHAPTER?
I DON'T THINK SO.

Sometime later...

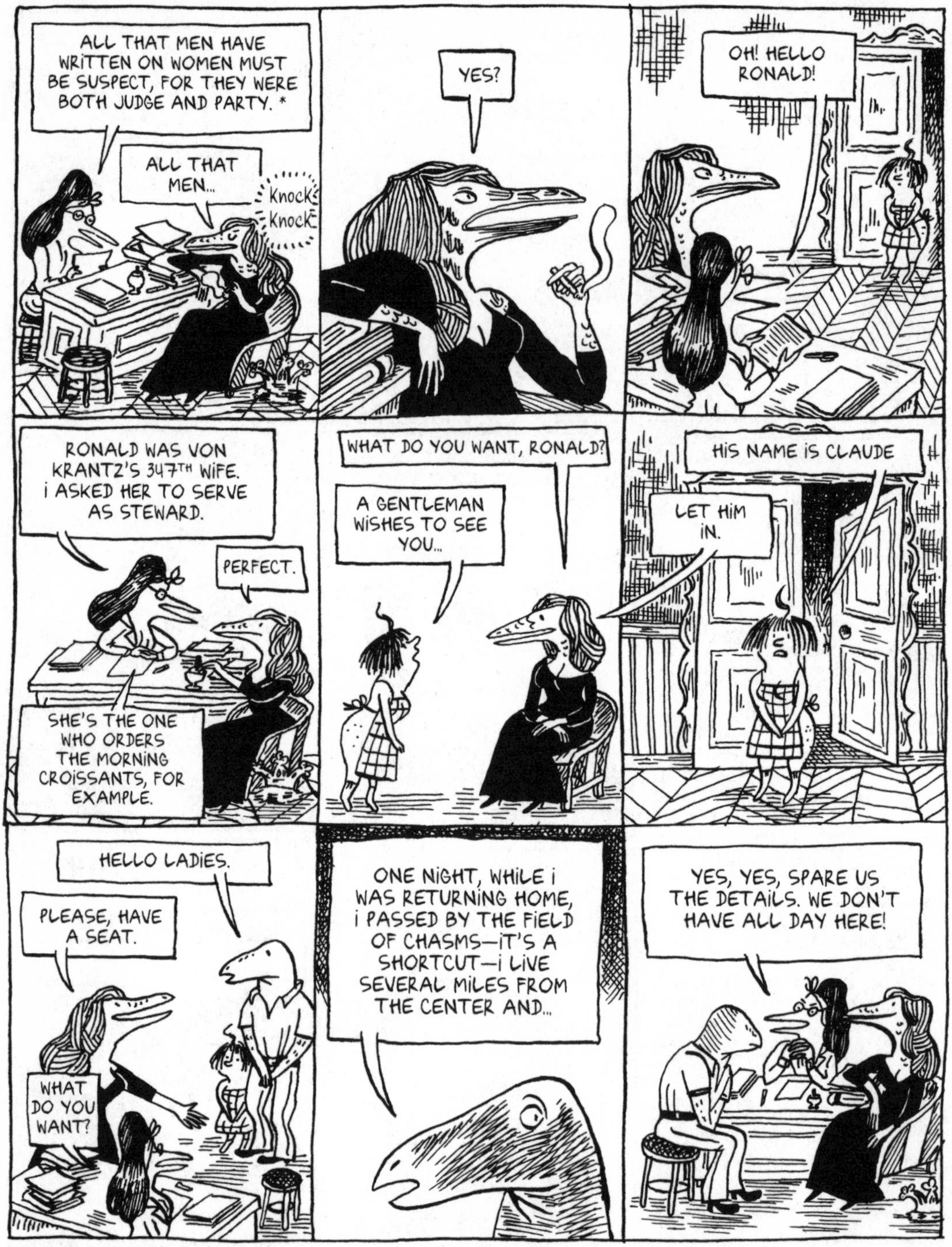
ALL THAT MEN HAVE WRITTEN ON WOMEN MUST BE SUSPECT, FOR THEY WERE BOTH JUDGE AND PARTY. *
ALL THAT MEN...
Knock Knock
YES?
OH! HELLO RONALD!
RONALD WAS VON KRANTZ'S 347TH WIFE. I ASKED HER TO SERVE AS STEWARD.
PERFECT.
SHE'S THE ONE WHO ORDERS THE MORNING CROISSANTS, FOR EXAMPLE.
WHAT DO YOU WANT, RONALD?
A GENTLEMAN WISHES TO SEE YOU...
HIS NAME IS CLAUDE
LET HIM IN.
HELLO LADIES.
PLEASE, HAVE A SEAT.
WHAT DO YOU WANT?
ONE NIGHT, WHILE I WAS RETURNING HOME, I PASSED BY THE FIELD OF CHASMS—IT'S A SHORTCUT—I LIVE SEVERAL MILES FROM THE CENTER AND...
YES, YES, SPARE US THE DETAILS. WE DON'T HAVE ALL DAY HERE!

* François Poullain de la Barre

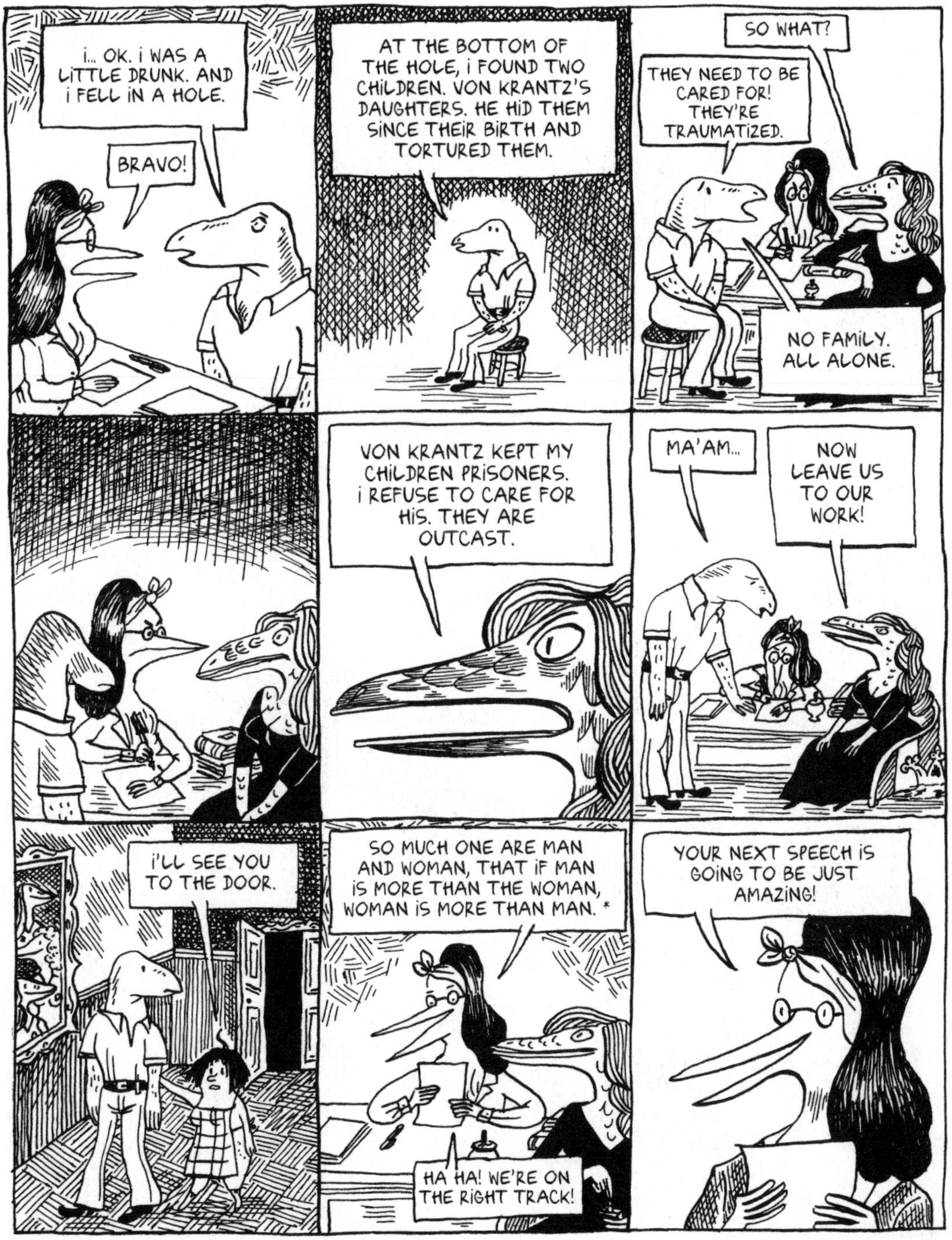
I... OK. I WAS A LITTLE DRUNK. AND I FELL IN A HOLE.
BRAVO!
AT THE BOTTOM OF THE HOLE, I FOUND TWO CHILDREN. VON KRANTZ'S DAUGHTERS. HE HID THEM SINCE THEIR BIRTH AND TORTURED THEM.
SO WHAT?
THEY NEED TO BE CARED FOR! THEY'RE TRAUMATIZED.
NO FAMILY. ALL ALONE.
VON KRANTZ KEPT MY CHILDREN PRISONERS. I REFUSE TO CARE FOR HIS. THEY ARE OUTCAST.
MA'AM...
NOW LEAVE US TO OUR WORK!
I'LL SEE YOU TO THE DOOR.
SO MUCH ONE ARE MAN AND WOMAN, THAT IF MAN IS MORE THAN THE WOMAN, WOMAN IS MORE THAN MAN. *
HA HA! WE'RE ON THE RIGHT TRACK!
YOUR NEXT SPEECH IS GOING TO BE JUST AMAZING!

* Marie le Jars de Gournay

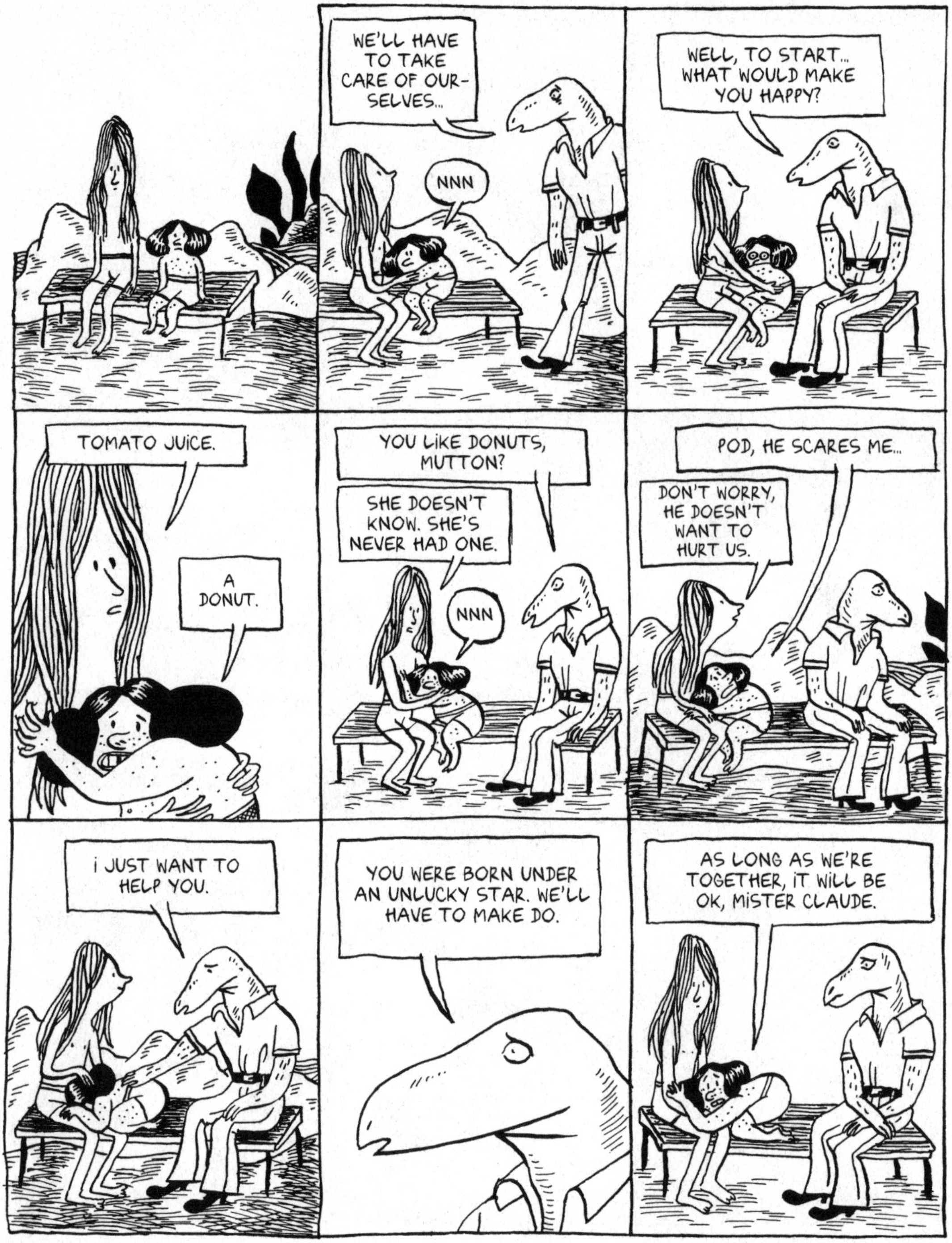
WE'LL HAVE TO TAKE CARE OF OUR-SELVES...
NNN
WELL, TO START... WHAT WOULD MAKE YOU HAPPY?
TOMATO JUICE.
A DONUT.
YOU LIKE DONUTS, MUTTON?
SHE DOESN'T KNOW. SHE'S NEVER HAD ONE.
NNN
POD, HE SCARES ME...
DON'T WORRY, HE DOESN'T WANT TO HURT US.
I JUST WANT TO HELP YOU.
YOU WERE BORN UNDER AN UNLUCKY STAR. WE'LL HAVE TO MAKE DO.
AS LONG AS WE'RE TOGETHER, IT WILL BE OK, MISTER CLAUDE.

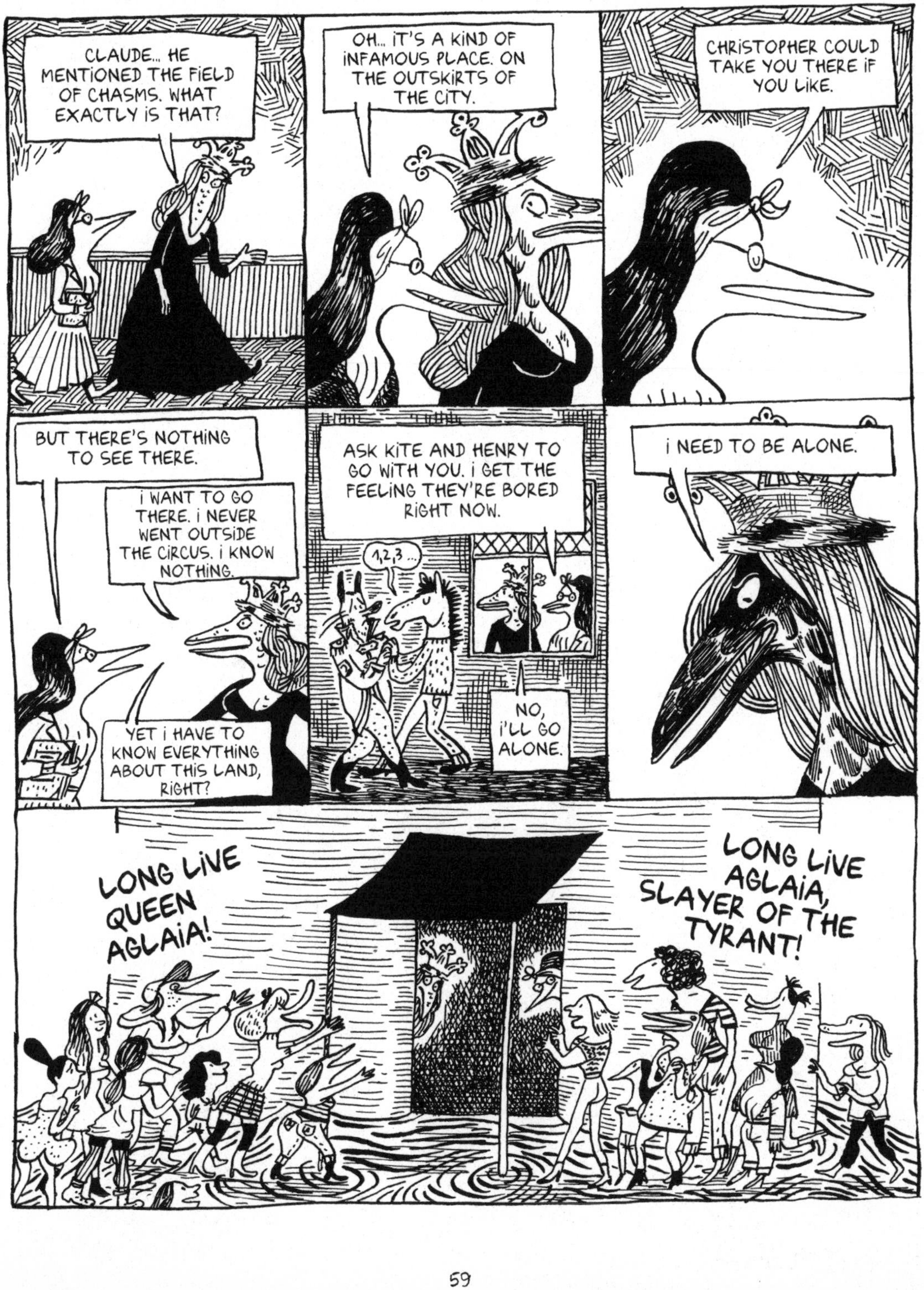
CLAUDE... HE MENTIONED THE FIELD OF CHASMS. WHAT EXACTLY IS THAT?
OH... IT'S A KIND OF INFAMOUS PLACE. ON THE OUTSKIRTS OF THE CITY.
CHRISTOPHER COULD TAKE YOU THERE IF YOU LIKE.
BUT THERE'S NOTHING TO SEE THERE.
I WANT TO GO THERE. I NEVER WENT OUTSIDE THE CIRCUS. I KNOW NOTHING.
YET I HAVE TO KNOW EVERYTHING ABOUT THIS LAND, RIGHT?
ASK KITE AND HENRY TO GO WITH YOU. I GET THE FEELING THEY'RE BORED RIGHT NOW.
1,2,3 ...
NO, I'LL GO ALONE.
I NEED TO BE ALONE.
LONG LIVE QUEEN AGLAIA!
LONG LIVE AGLAIA, SLAYER OF THE TYRANT!

iNTERLUDE FOR SiMONE, WOMAN iN THE SHADOWS

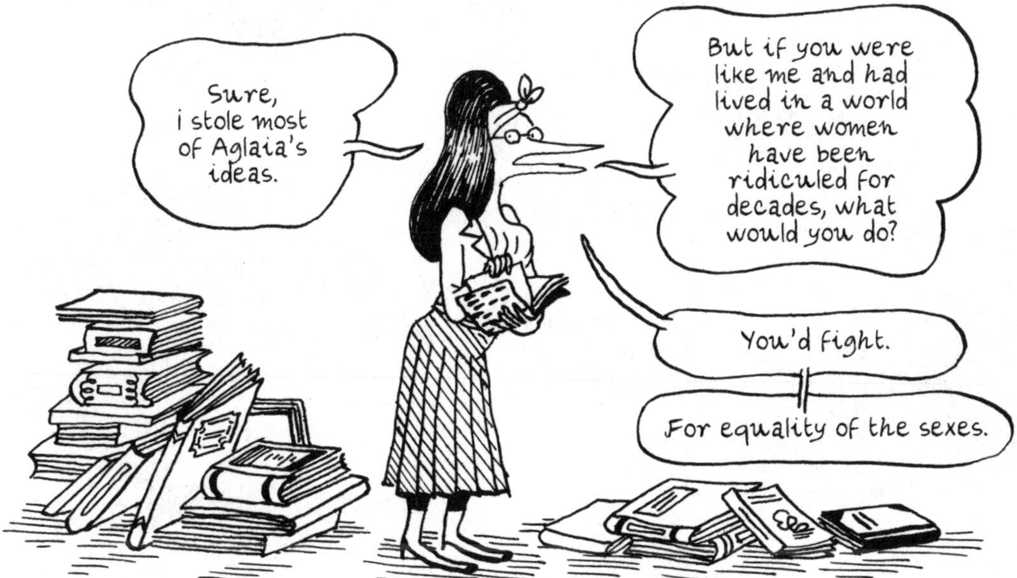
Sure, i stole most of Aglaia's ideas.
But if you were like me and had lived in a world where women have been ridiculed for decades, what would you do?
You'd fight.
For equality of the sexes.

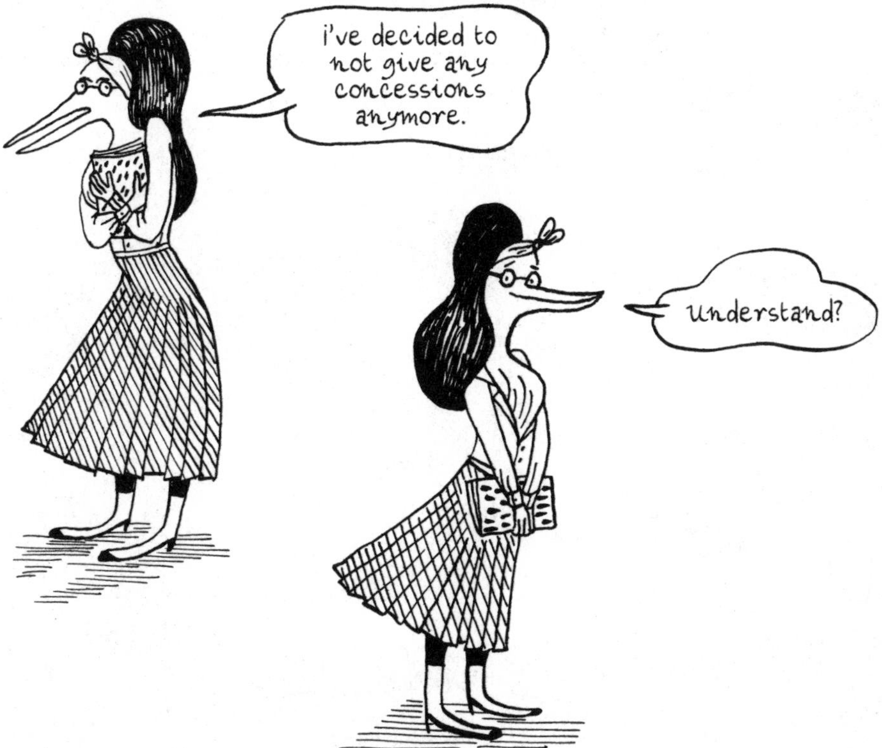
i've decided to not give any concessions anymore.
Understand?

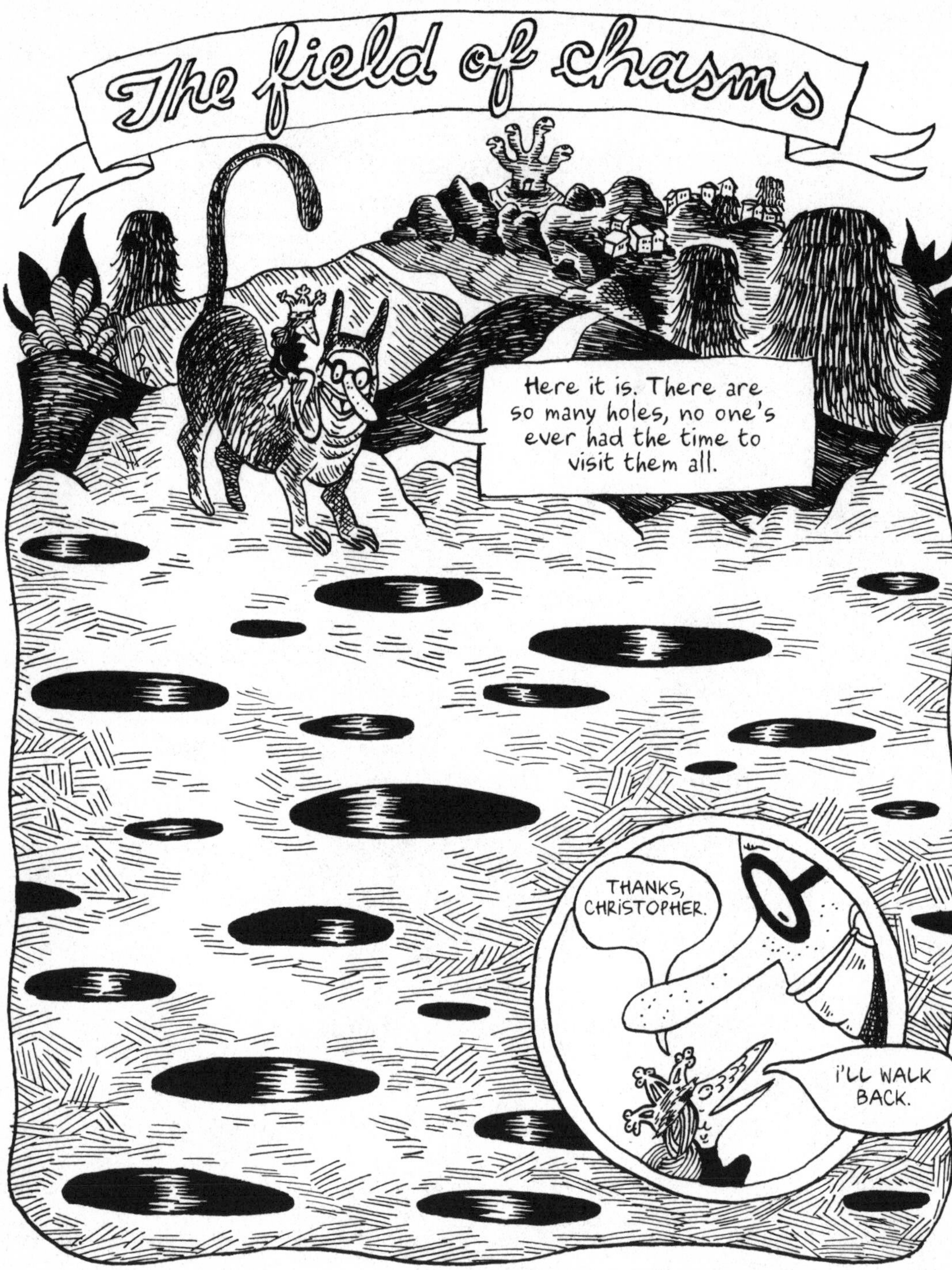
The field of chasms
Here it is. There are so many holes, no one's ever had the time to visit them all.
THANKS, CHRISTOPHER.
I'LL WALK BACK.

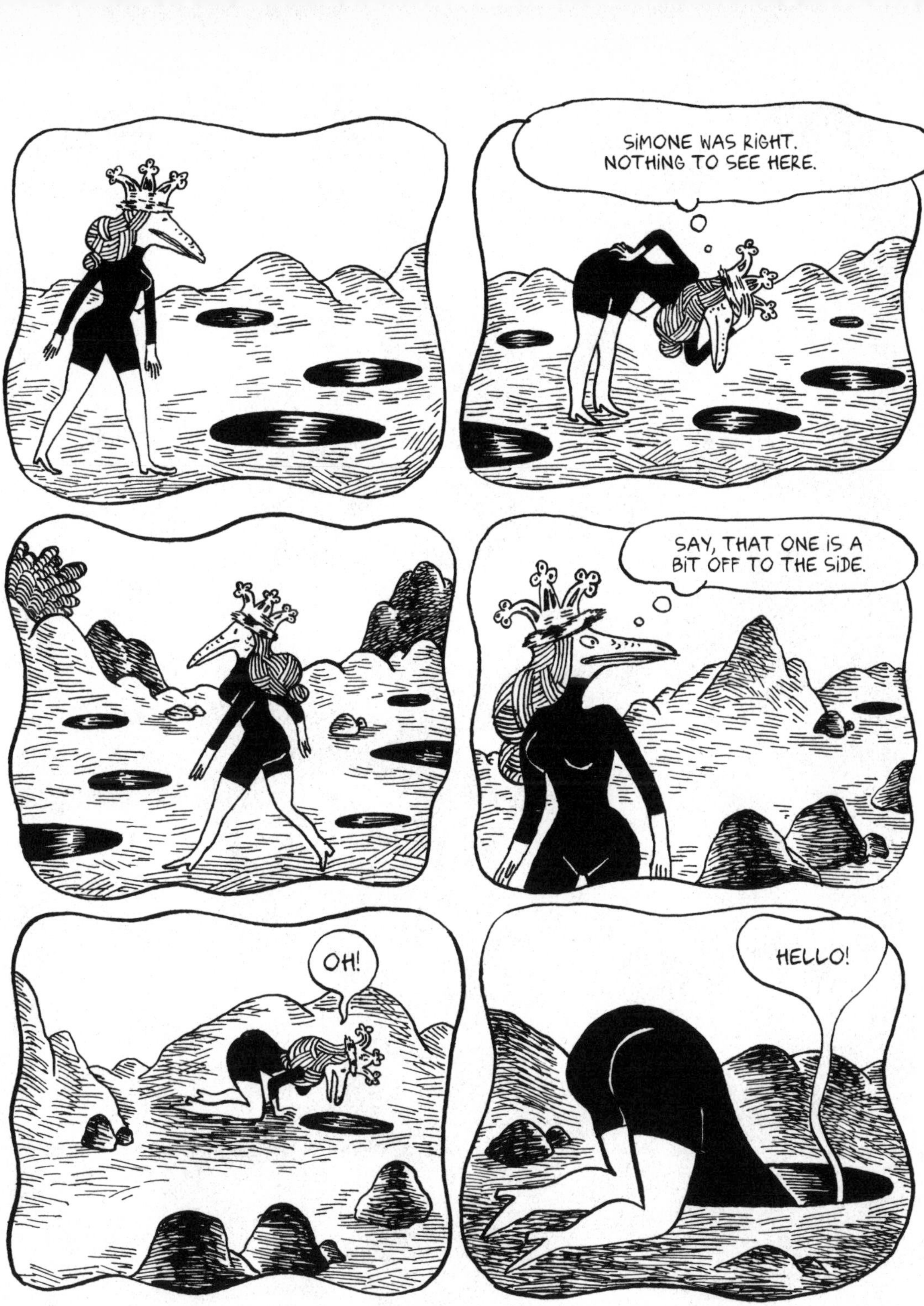
SIMONE WAS RIGHT. NOTHING TO SEE HERE.
SAY, THAT ONE IS A BIT OFF TO THE SIDE.
OH!
HELLO!

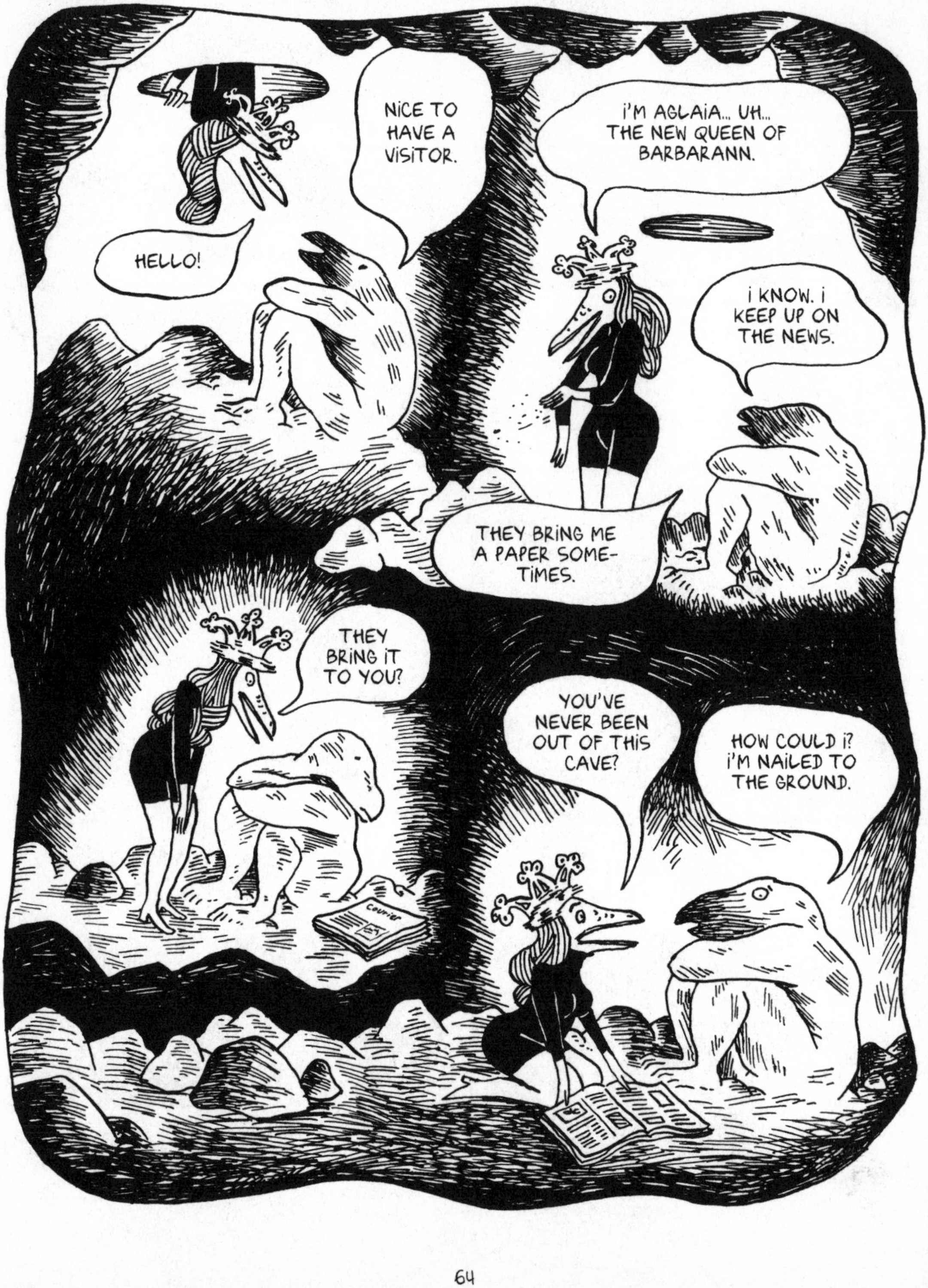
HELLO!
NICE TO HAVE A VISITOR.
I'M AGLAIA... UH... THE NEW QUEEN OF BARBARANN.
I KNOW. I KEEP UP ON THE NEWS.
THEY BRING ME A PAPER SOME-TIMES.
THEY BRING IT TO YOU?
YOU'VE NEVER BEEN OUT OF THIS CAVE?
HOW COULD I? I'M NAILED TO THE GROUND.
COURIER

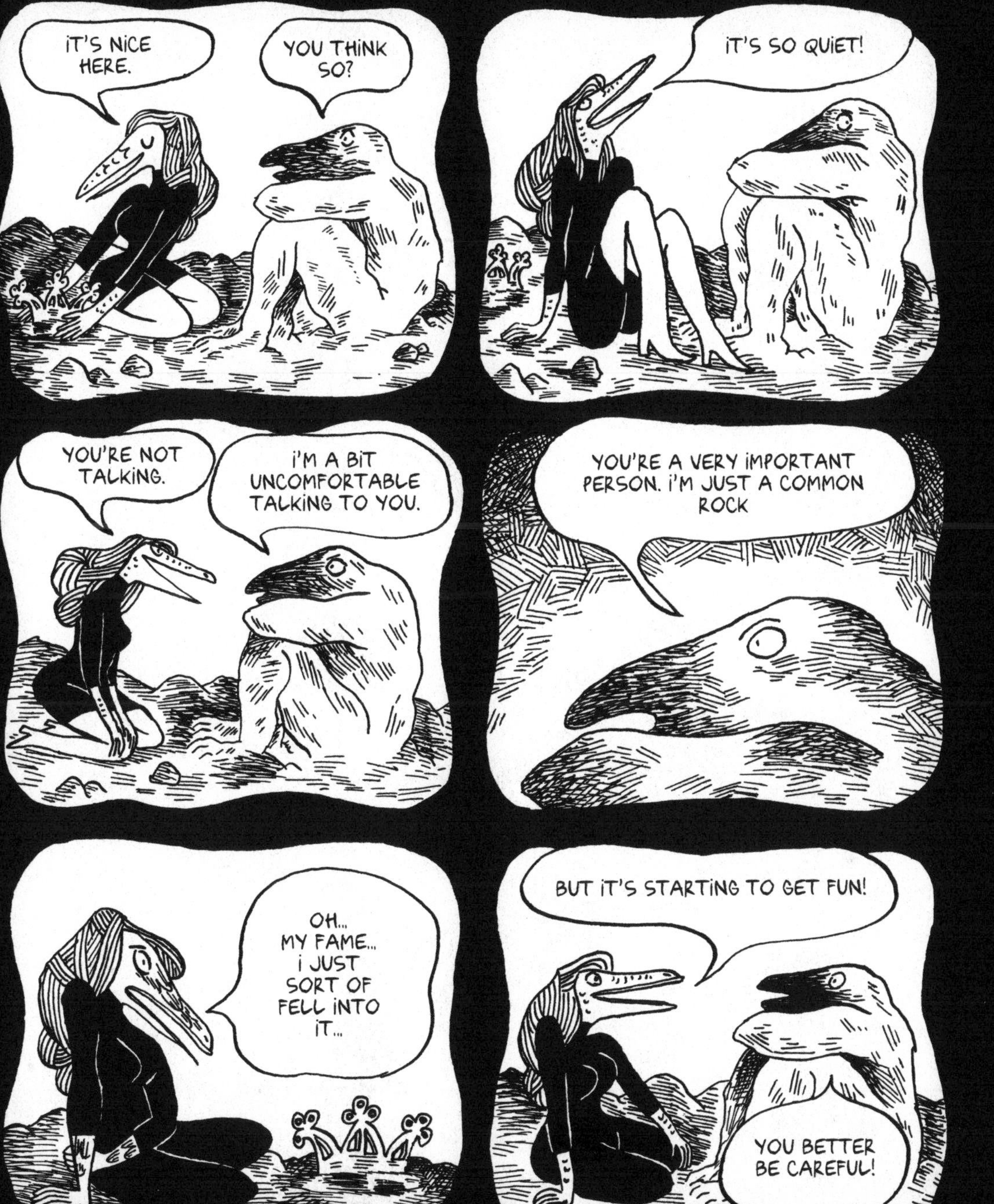
IT'S NICE HERE.
YOU THINK SO?
IT'S SO QUIET!
YOU'RE NOT TALKING.
I'M A BIT UNCOMFORTABLE TALKING TO YOU.
YOU'RE A VERY IMPORTANT PERSON. I'M JUST A COMMON ROCK
OH... MY FAME... I JUST SORT OF FELL INTO IT...
BUT IT'S STARTING TO GET FUN!
YOU BETTER BE CAREFUL!

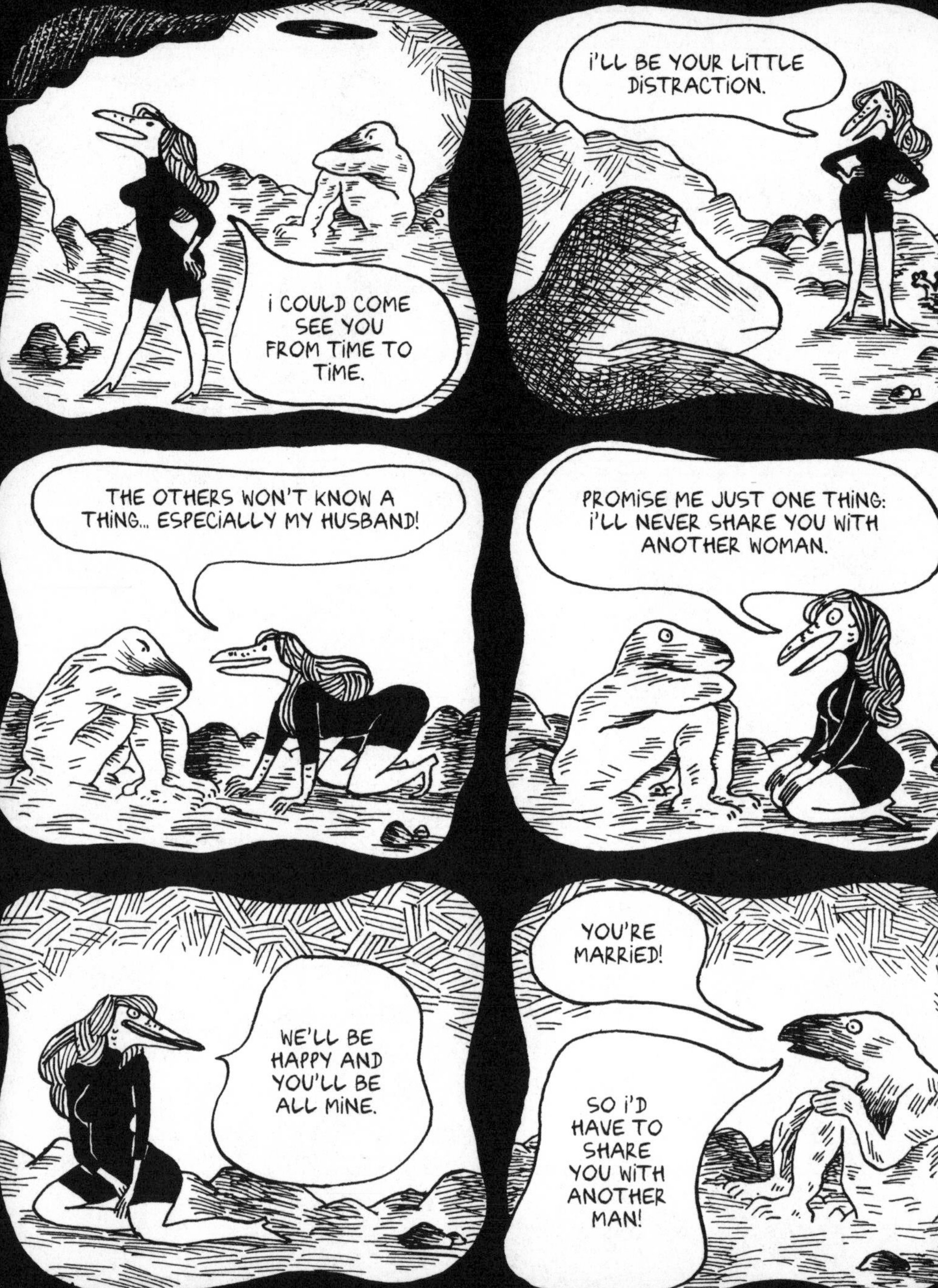
I COULD COME SEE YOU FROM TIME TO TIME.
I'LL BE YOUR LITTLE DISTRACTION.
THE OTHERS WON'T KNOW A THING... ESPECIALLY MY HUSBAND!
PROMISE ME JUST ONE THING: I'LL NEVER SHARE YOU WITH ANOTHER WOMAN.
WE'LL BE HAPPY AND YOU'LL BE ALL MINE.
YOU'RE MARRIED!
SO I'D HAVE TO SHARE YOU WITH ANOTHER MAN!

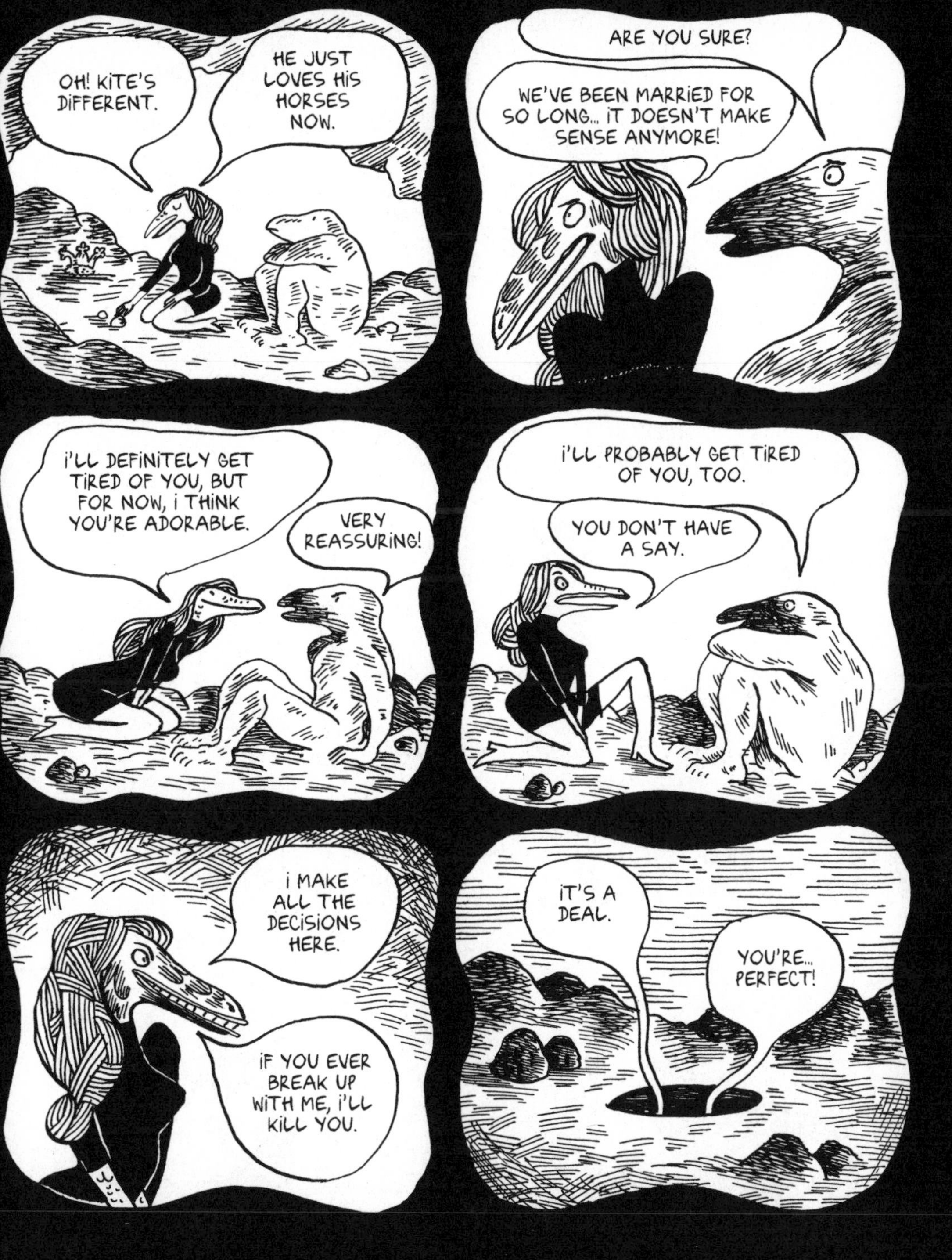
OH! KITE'S DIFFERENT.
HE JUST LOVES HIS HORSES NOW.
ARE YOU SURE?
WE'VE BEEN MARRIED FOR SO LONG... IT DOESN'T MAKE SENSE ANYMORE!
I'LL DEFINITELY GET TIRED OF YOU, BUT FOR NOW, I THINK YOU'RE ADORABLE.
VERY REASSURING!
I'LL PROBABLY GET TIRED OF YOU, TOO.
YOU DON'T HAVE A SAY.
I MAKE ALL THE DECISIONS HERE.
IF YOU EVER BREAK UP WITH ME, I'LL KILL YOU.
IT'S A DEAL.
YOU'RE... PERFECT!

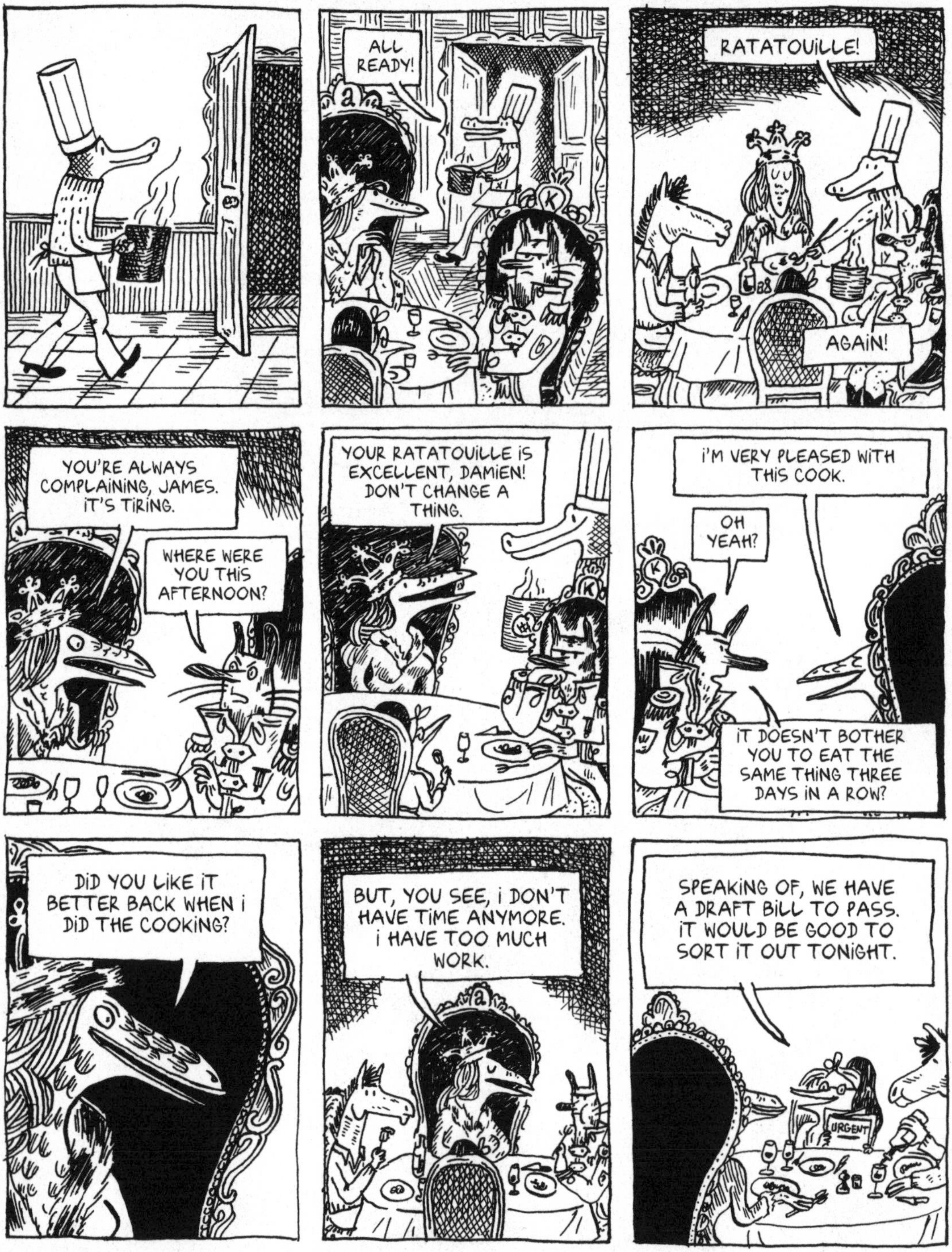
ALL READY!
RATATOUiLLE!
AGAiN!
YOU'RE ALWAYS COMPLAiNiNG, JAMES. iT'S TiRiNG.
WHERE WERE YOU THiS AFTERNOON?
YOUR RATATOUiLLE iS EXCELLENT, DAMiEN! DON'T CHANGE A THiNG.
i'M VERY PLEASED WiTH THiS COOK.
OH YEAH?
iT DOESN'T BOTHER YOU TO EAT THE SAME THiNG THREE DAYS iN A ROW?
DiD YOU LiKE iT BETTER BACK WHEN i DiD THE COOKiNG?
BUT, YOU SEE, i DON'T HAVE TiME ANYMORE. i HAVE TOO MUCH WORK.
SPEAKiNG OF, WE HAVE A DRAFT BiLL TO PASS. iT WOULD BE GOOD TO SORT iT OUT TONiGHT.
URGENT

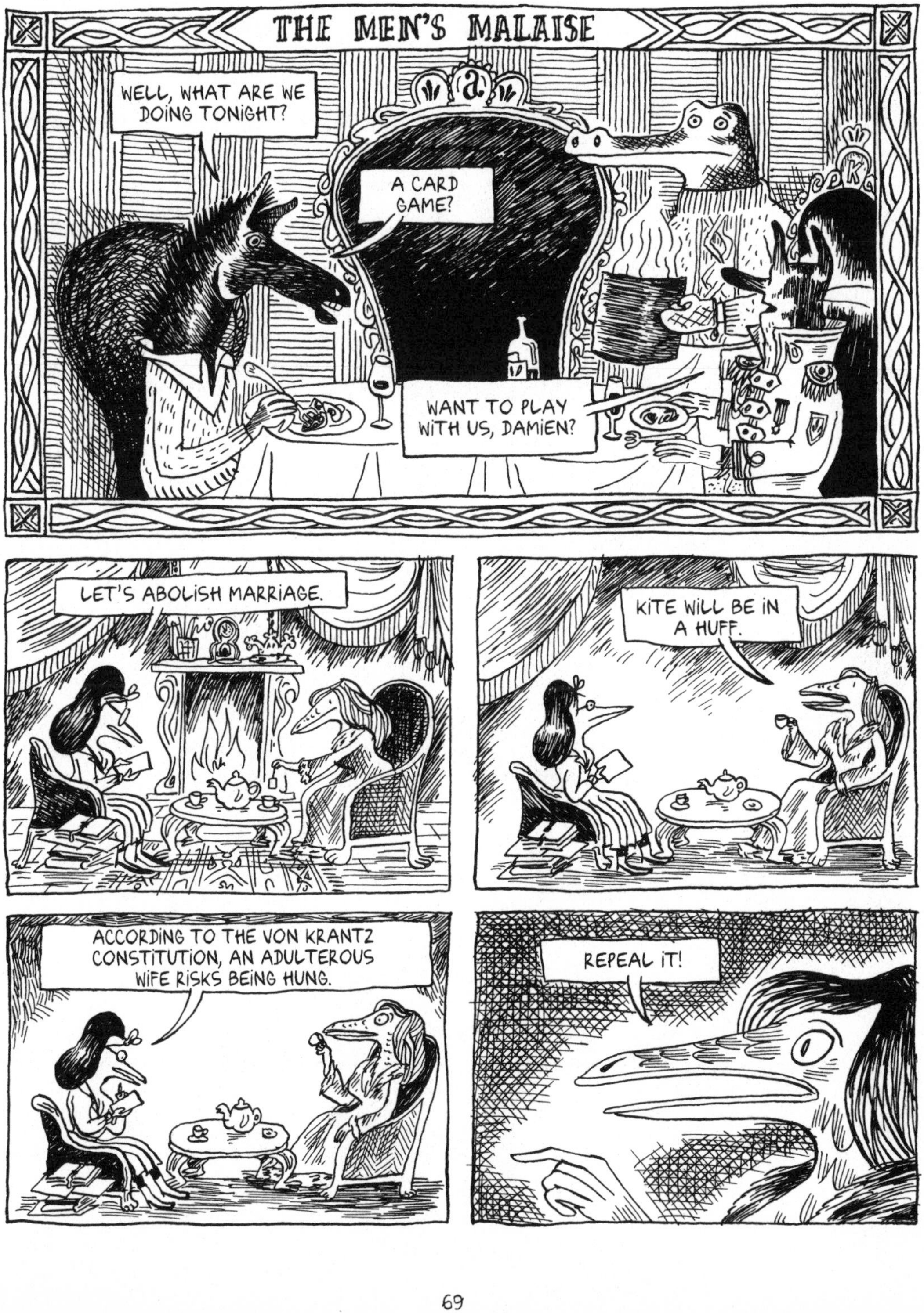
THE MEN'S MALAISE
WELL, WHAT ARE WE DOING TONIGHT?
A CARD GAME?
WANT TO PLAY WITH US, DAMIEN?
LET'S ABOLISH MARRIAGE.
KITE WILL BE IN A HUFF.
ACCORDING TO THE VON KRANTZ CONSTITUTION, AN ADULTEROUS WIFE RISKS BEING HUNG.
REPEAL IT!

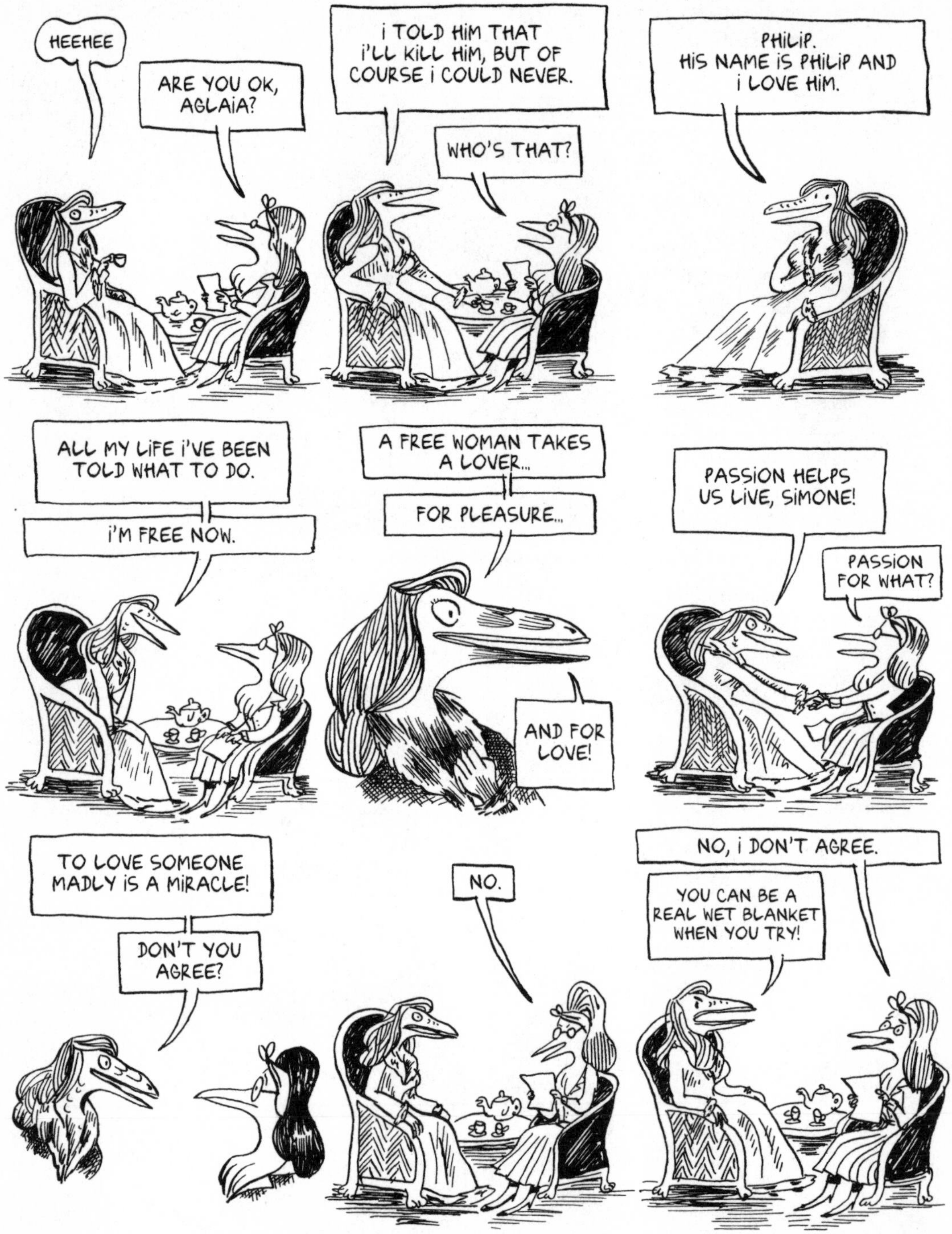
HEEHEE
ARE YOU OK, AGLAiA?
i TOLD HIM THAT i'LL KiLL HiM, BUT OF COURSE i COULD NEVER.
WHO'S THAT?
PHiLiP. HiS NAME iS PHiLiP AND i LOVE HiM.
ALL MY LiFE i'VE BEEN TOLD WHAT TO DO.
i'M FREE NOW.
A FREE WOMAN TAKES A LOVER...
FOR PLEASURE...
AND FOR LOVE!
PASSiON HELPS US LiVE, SiMONE!
PASSiON FOR WHAT?
TO LOVE SOMEONE MADLY iS A MiRACLE!
DON'T YOU AGREE?
NO.
NO, i DON'T AGREE.
YOU CAN BE A REAL WET BLANKET WHEN YOU TRY!

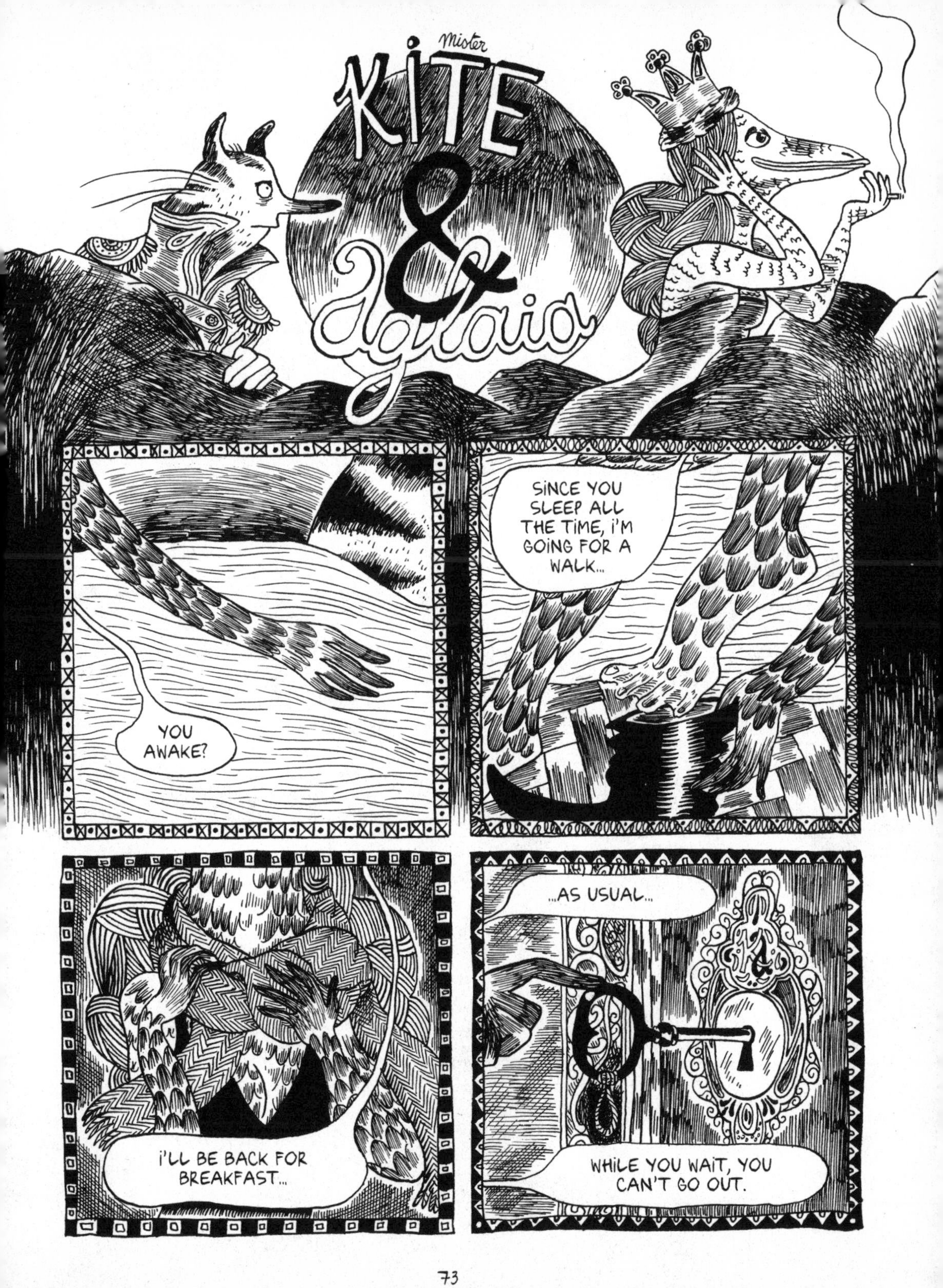

Mister
KITE
&
aglaia
YOU AWAKE?
SINCE YOU SLEEP ALL THE TIME, I'M GOING FOR A WALK...
I'LL BE BACK FOR BREAKFAST...
...AS USUAL...
WHILE YOU WAIT, YOU CAN'T GO OUT.

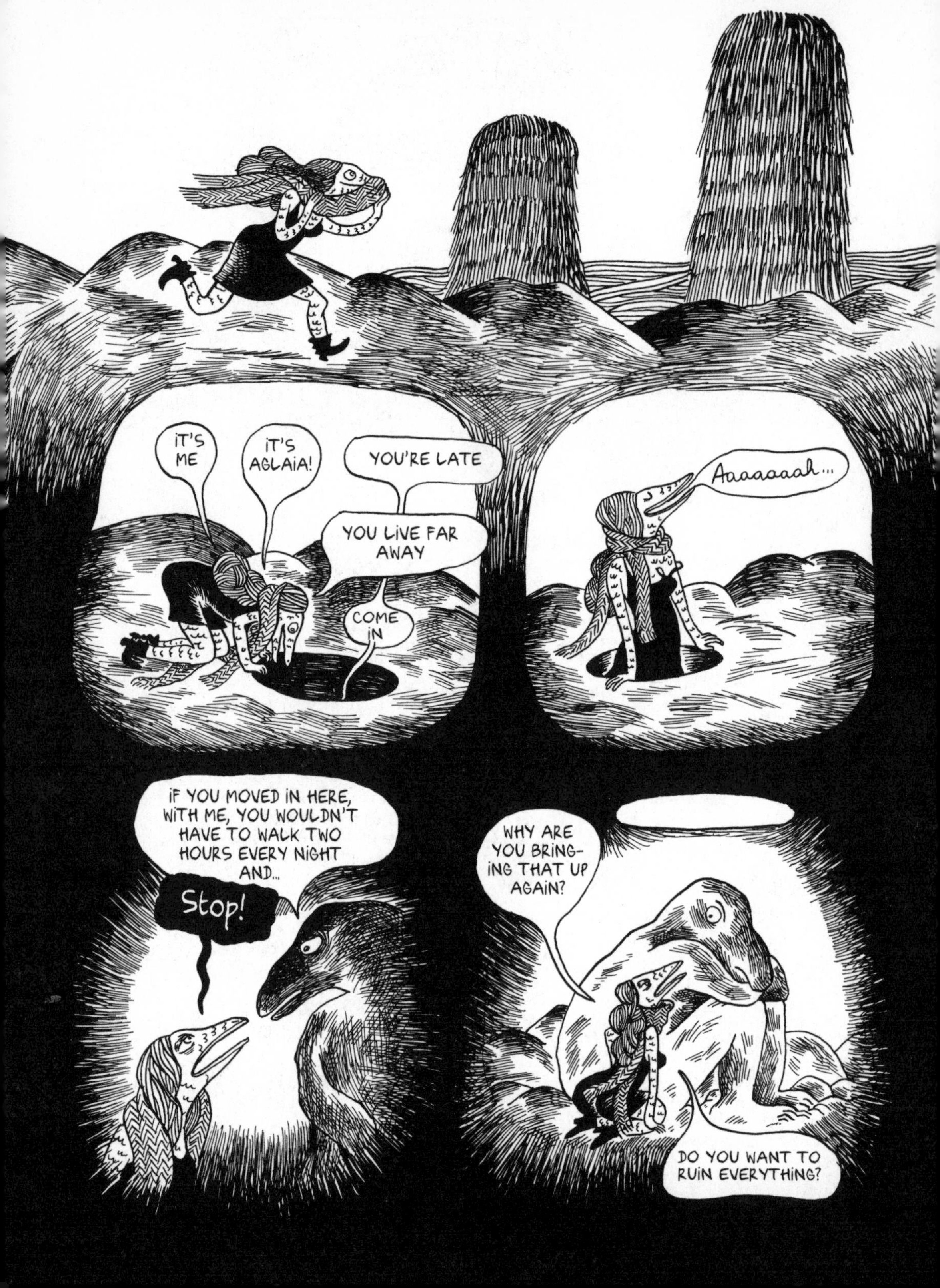
IT'S ME
IT'S AGLAIA!
YOU'RE LATE
YOU LIVE FAR AWAY
COME IN
Aaaaaaah...
IF YOU MOVED IN HERE, WITH ME, YOU WOULDN'T HAVE TO WALK TWO HOURS EVERY NIGHT AND...
Stop!
WHY ARE YOU BRING-ING THAT UP AGAIN?
DO YOU WANT TO RUIN EVERYTHING?

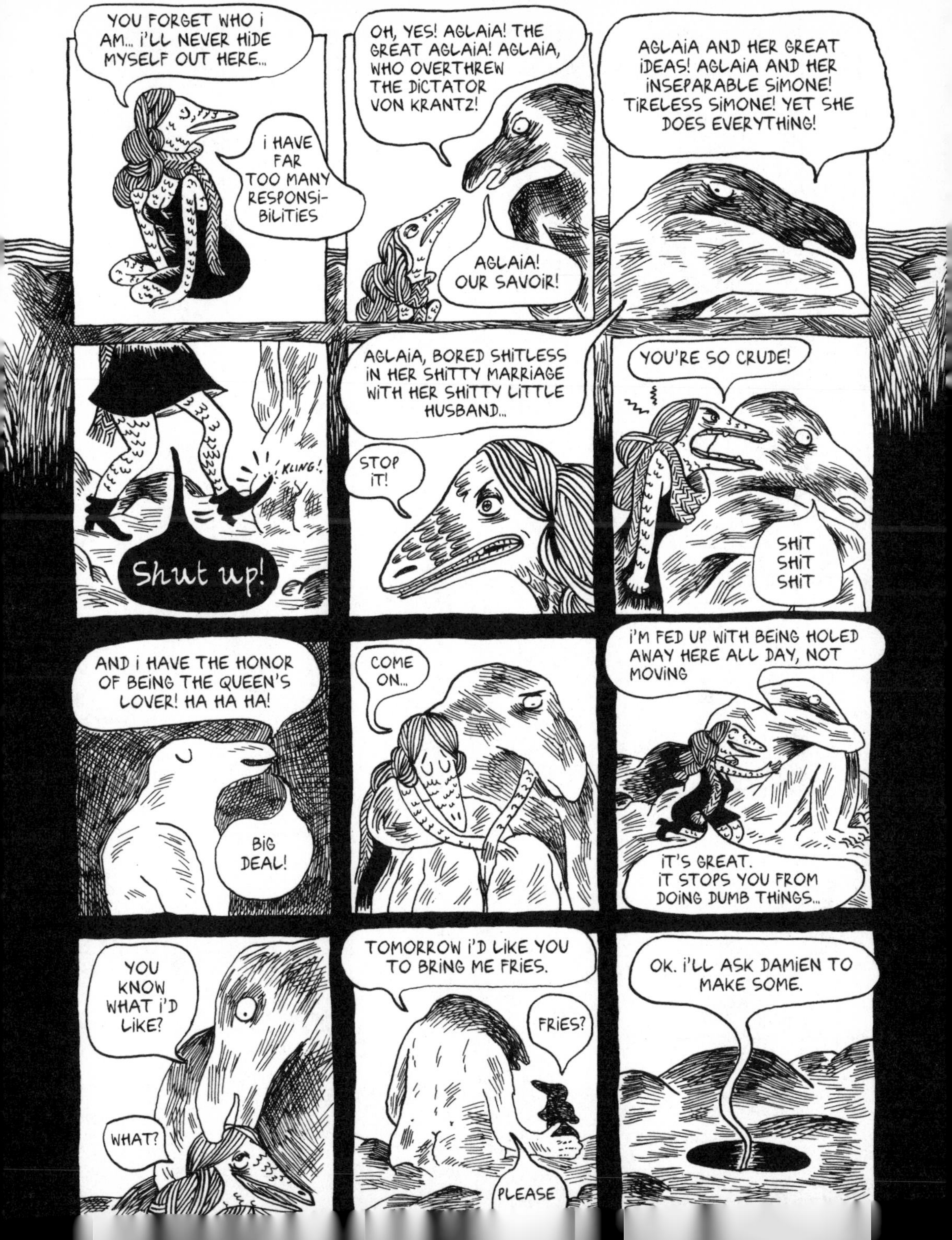
YOU FORGET WHO i AM... i'LL NEVER HIDE MYSELF OUT HERE...
i HAVE FAR TOO MANY RESPONSi-BiLiTiES
OH, YES! AGLAiA! THE GREAT AGLAiA! AGLAiA, WHO OVERTHREW THE DiCTATOR VON KRANTZ!
AGLAiA! OUR SAVOiR!
AGLAiA AND HER GREAT iDEAS! AGLAiA AND HER iNSEPARABLE SiMONE! TiRELESS SiMONE! YET SHE DOES EVERYTHiNG!
KLING!
Shut up!
AGLAiA, BORED SHiTLESS iN HER SHiTTY MARRiAGE WiTH HER SHiTTY LiTTLE HUSBAND...
STOP iT!
YOU'RE SO CRUDE!
SHiT SHiT SHiT
AND i HAVE THE HONOR OF BEiNG THE QUEEN'S LOVER! HA HA HA!
BiG DEAL!
COME ON...
i'M FED UP WiTH BEiNG HOLED AWAY HERE ALL DAY, NOT MOViNG
iT'S GREAT. iT STOPS YOU FROM DOiNG DUMB THiNGS...
YOU KNOW WHAT i'D LiKE?
WHAT?
TOMORROW i'D LiKE YOU TO BRiNG ME FRiES.
FRiES?
PLEASE
OK. i'LL ASK DAMiEN TO MAKE SOME.

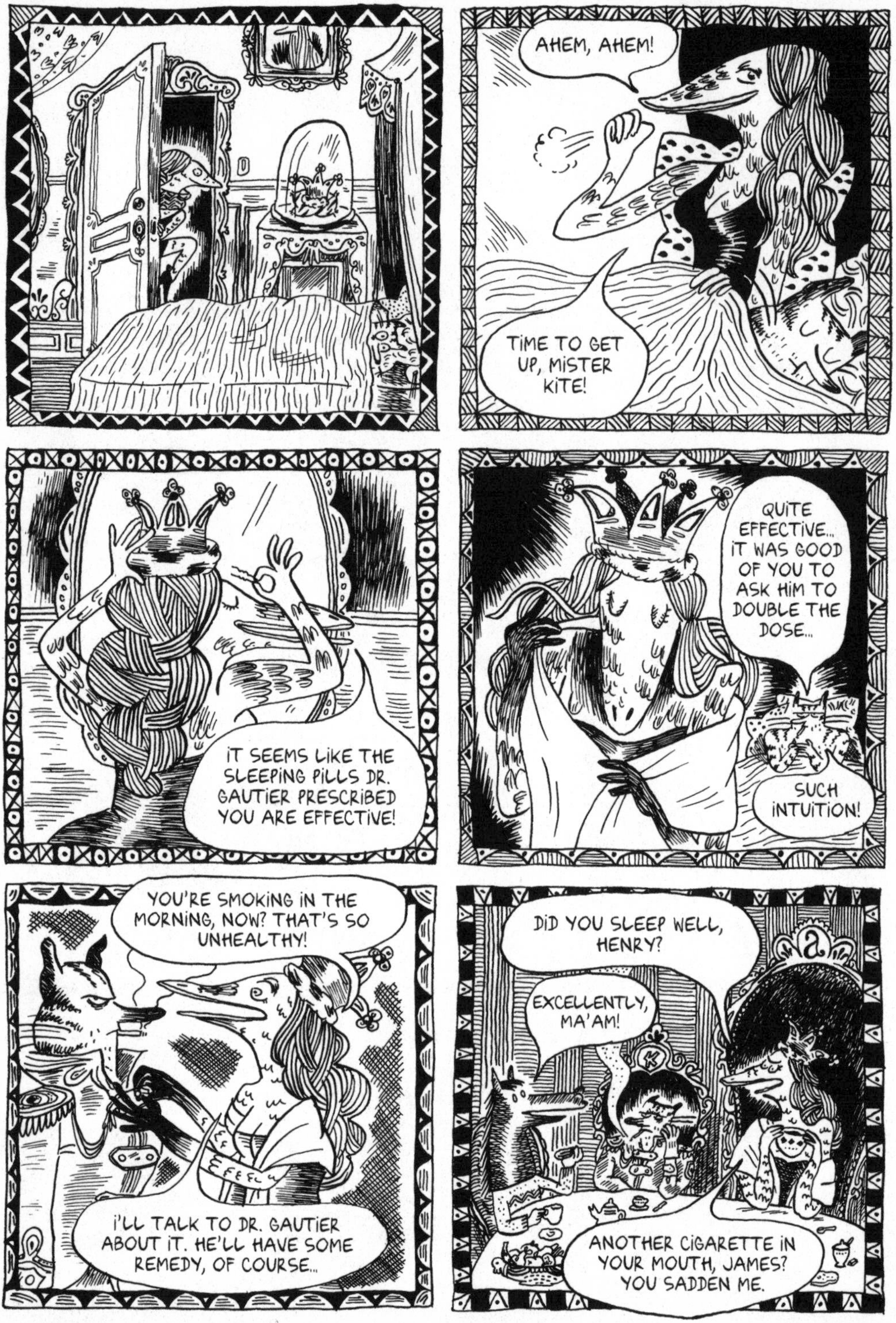
AHEM, AHEM!
TIME TO GET UP, MISTER KITE!
IT SEEMS LIKE THE SLEEPING PILLS DR. GAUTIER PRESCRIBED YOU ARE EFFECTIVE!
QUITE EFFECTIVE... IT WAS GOOD OF YOU TO ASK HIM TO DOUBLE THE DOSE...
SUCH INTUITION!
YOU'RE SMOKING IN THE MORNING, NOW? THAT'S SO UNHEALTHY!
I'LL TALK TO DR. GAUTIER ABOUT IT. HE'LL HAVE SOME REMEDY, OF COURSE...
DID YOU SLEEP WELL, HENRY?
EXCELLENTLY, MA'AM!
ANOTHER CIGARETTE IN YOUR MOUTH, JAMES? YOU SADDEN ME.

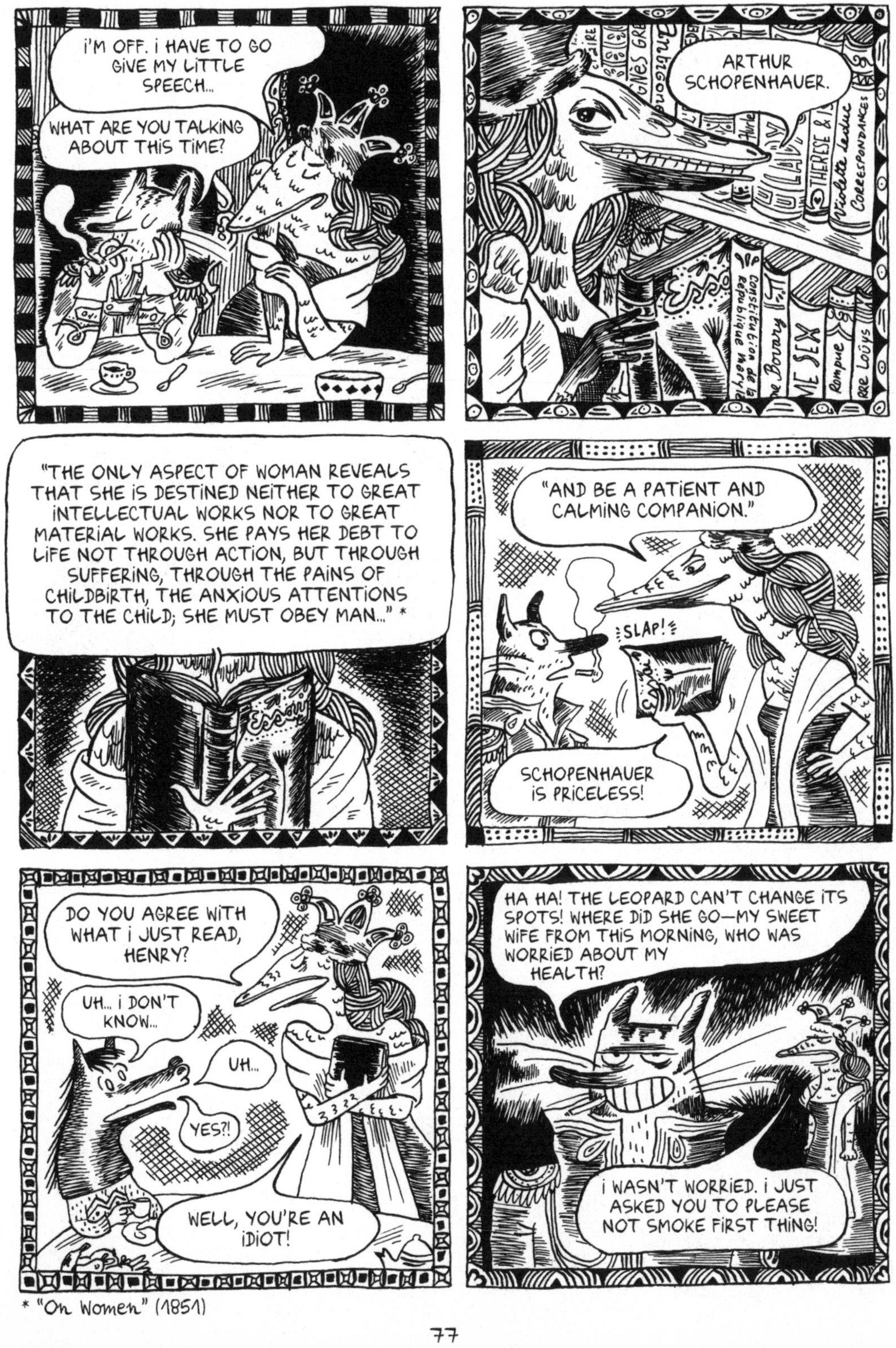
I'M OFF. I HAVE TO GO GIVE MY LITTLE SPEECH...
WHAT ARE YOU TALKING ABOUT THIS TIME?
ARTHUR SCHOPENHAUER.
"THE ONLY ASPECT OF WOMAN REVEALS THAT SHE IS DESTINED NEITHER TO GREAT INTELLECTUAL WORKS NOR TO GREAT MATERIAL WORKS. SHE PAYS HER DEBT TO LIFE NOT THROUGH ACTION, BUT THROUGH SUFFERING, THROUGH THE PAINS OF CHILDBIRTH, THE ANXIOUS ATTENTIONS TO THE CHILD; SHE MUST OBEY MAN..." *
"AND BE A PATIENT AND CALMING COMPANION."
SLAP!
SCHOPENHAUER IS PRICELESS!
DO YOU AGREE WITH WHAT I JUST READ, HENRY?
UH... I DON'T KNOW...
UH...
YES?!
WELL, YOU'RE AN IDIOT!
HA HA! THE LEOPARD CAN'T CHANGE ITS SPOTS! WHERE DID SHE GO—MY SWEET WIFE FROM THIS MORNING, WHO WAS WORRIED ABOUT MY HEALTH?
I WASN'T WORRIED. I JUST ASKED YOU TO PLEASE NOT SMOKE FIRST THING!

* "On Women" (1851)

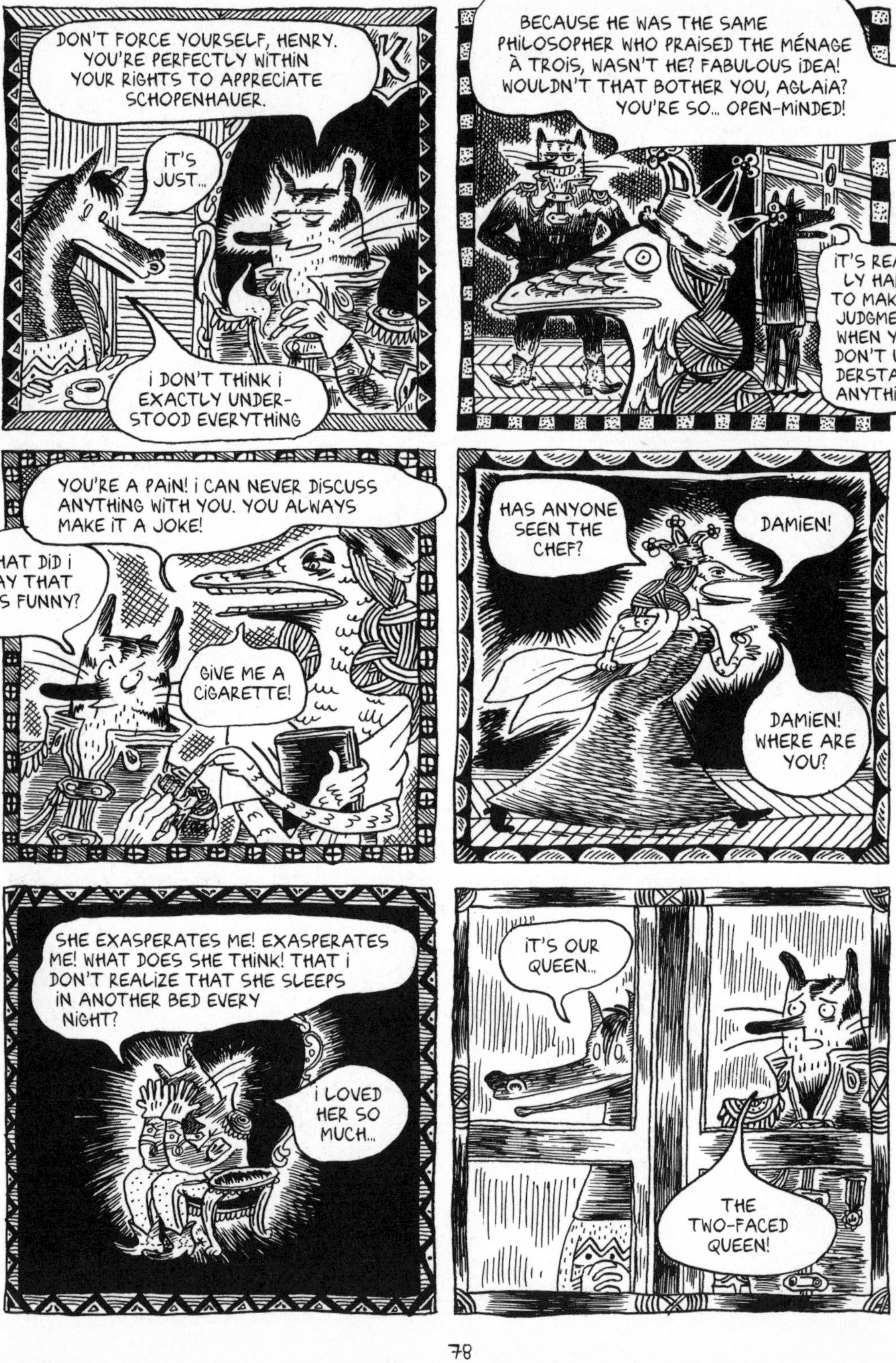
DON'T FORCE YOURSELF, HENRY. YOU'RE PERFECTLY WITHIN YOUR RIGHTS TO APPRECIATE SCHOPENHAUER.
IT'S JUST...
I DON'T THINK I EXACTLY UNDERSTOOD EVERYTHING
BECAUSE HE WAS THE SAME PHILOSOPHER WHO PRAISED THE MÉNAGE À TROIS, WASN'T HE? FABULOUS IDEA! WOULDN'T THAT BOTHER YOU, AGLAIA? YOU'RE SO... OPEN-MINDED!
IT'S REALLY HARD TO MAKE A JUDGMENT WHEN YOU DON'T UNDERSTAND ANYTHING.
YOU'RE A PAIN! I CAN NEVER DISCUSS ANYTHING WITH YOU. YOU ALWAYS MAKE IT A JOKE!
WHAT DID I SAY THAT WAS FUNNY?
GIVE ME A CIGARETTE!
HAS ANYONE SEEN THE CHEF?
DAMIEN!
DAMIEN! WHERE ARE YOU?
SHE EXASPERATES ME! EXASPERATES ME! WHAT DOES SHE THINK! THAT I DON'T REALIZE THAT SHE SLEEPS IN ANOTHER BED EVERY NIGHT?
I LOVED HER SO MUCH...
IT'S OUR QUEEN...
THE TWO-FACED QUEEN!

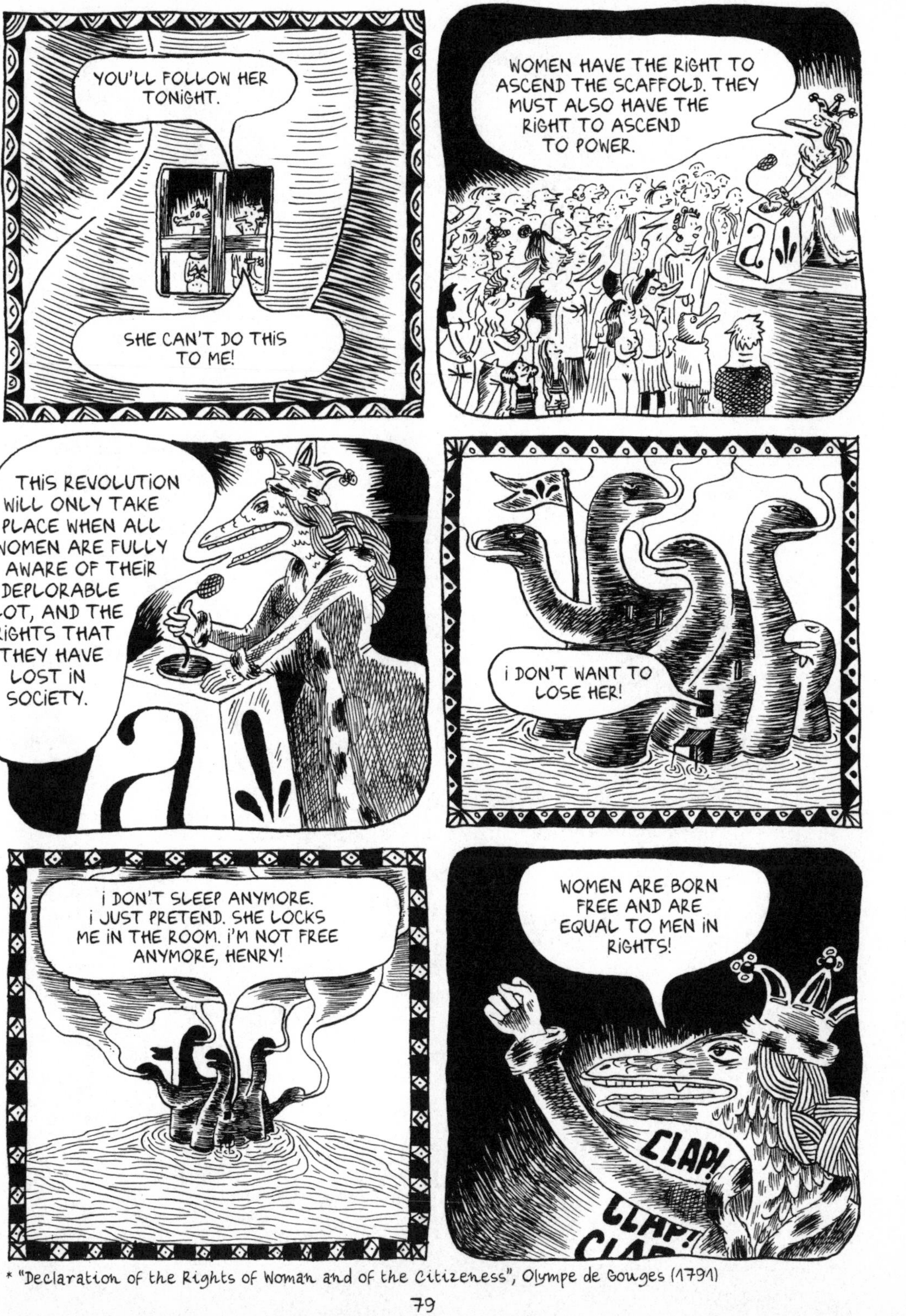

YOU'LL FOLLOW HER TONIGHT.
SHE CAN'T DO THIS TO ME!
WOMEN HAVE THE RIGHT TO ASCEND THE SCAFFOLD. THEY MUST ALSO HAVE THE RIGHT TO ASCEND TO POWER.
THIS REVOLUTION WILL ONLY TAKE PLACE WHEN ALL WOMEN ARE FULLY AWARE OF THEIR DEPLORABLE LOT, AND THE RIGHTS THAT THEY HAVE LOST IN SOCIETY.
I DON'T WANT TO LOSE HER!
I DON'T SLEEP ANYMORE. I JUST PRETEND. SHE LOCKS ME IN THE ROOM. I'M NOT FREE ANYMORE, HENRY!
WOMEN ARE BORN FREE AND ARE EQUAL TO MEN IN RIGHTS!
CLAP!
CLAP!

* "Declaration of the Rights of Woman and of the Citizeness", Olympe de Gouges (1791)

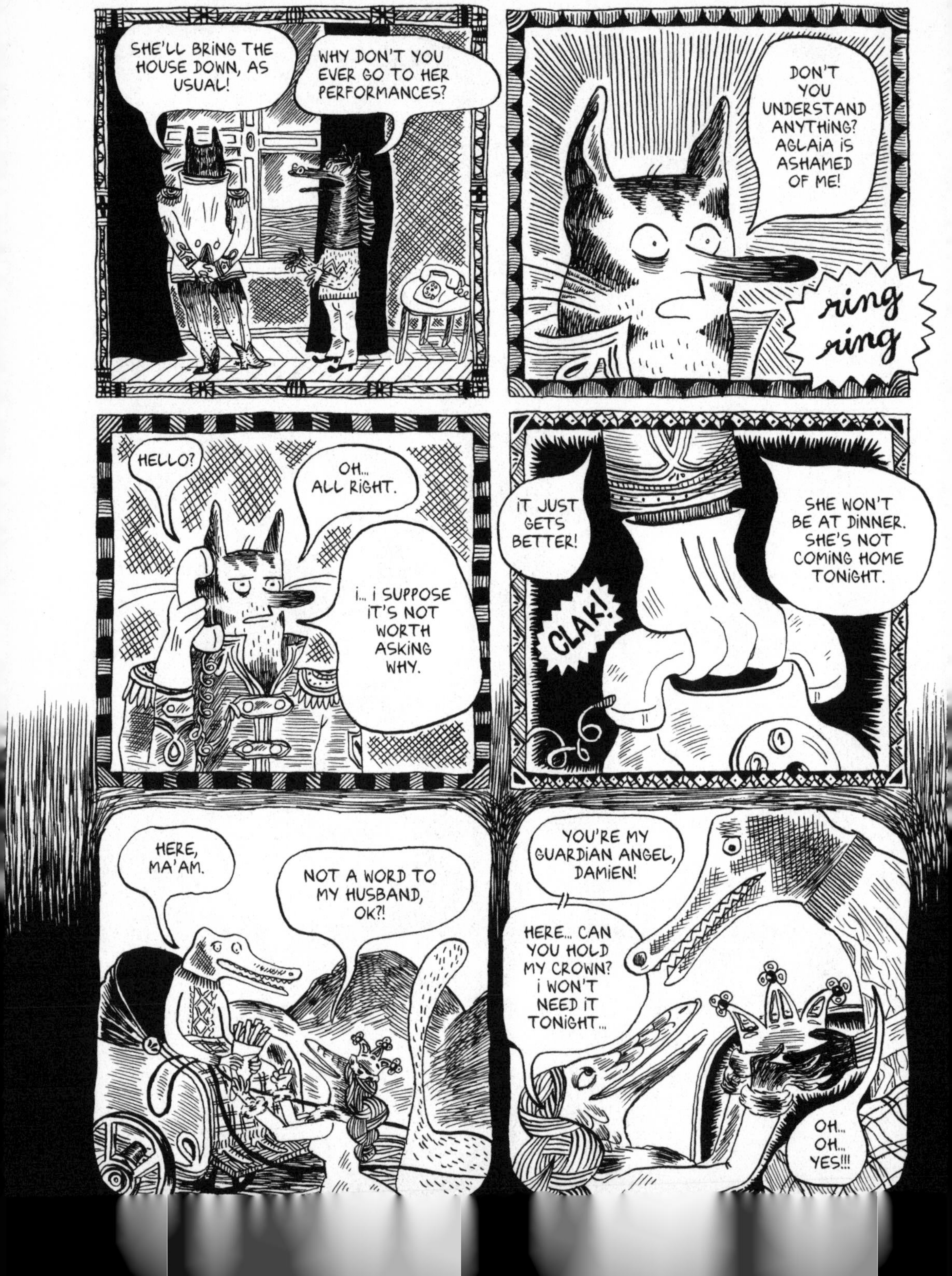
SHE'LL BRING THE HOUSE DOWN, AS USUAL!
WHY DON'T YOU EVER GO TO HER PERFORMANCES?
DON'T YOU UNDERSTAND ANYTHING? AGLAIA IS ASHAMED OF ME!
ring ring
HELLO?
OH... ALL RIGHT.
I... I SUPPOSE IT'S NOT WORTH ASKING WHY.
IT JUST GETS BETTER!
SHE WON'T BE AT DINNER. SHE'S NOT COMING HOME TONIGHT.
CLAK!
HERE, MA'AM.
NOT A WORD TO MY HUSBAND, OK?!
YOU'RE MY GUARDIAN ANGEL, DAMIEN!
HERE... CAN YOU HOLD MY CROWN? I WON'T NEED IT TONIGHT...
OH... OH... YES!!!

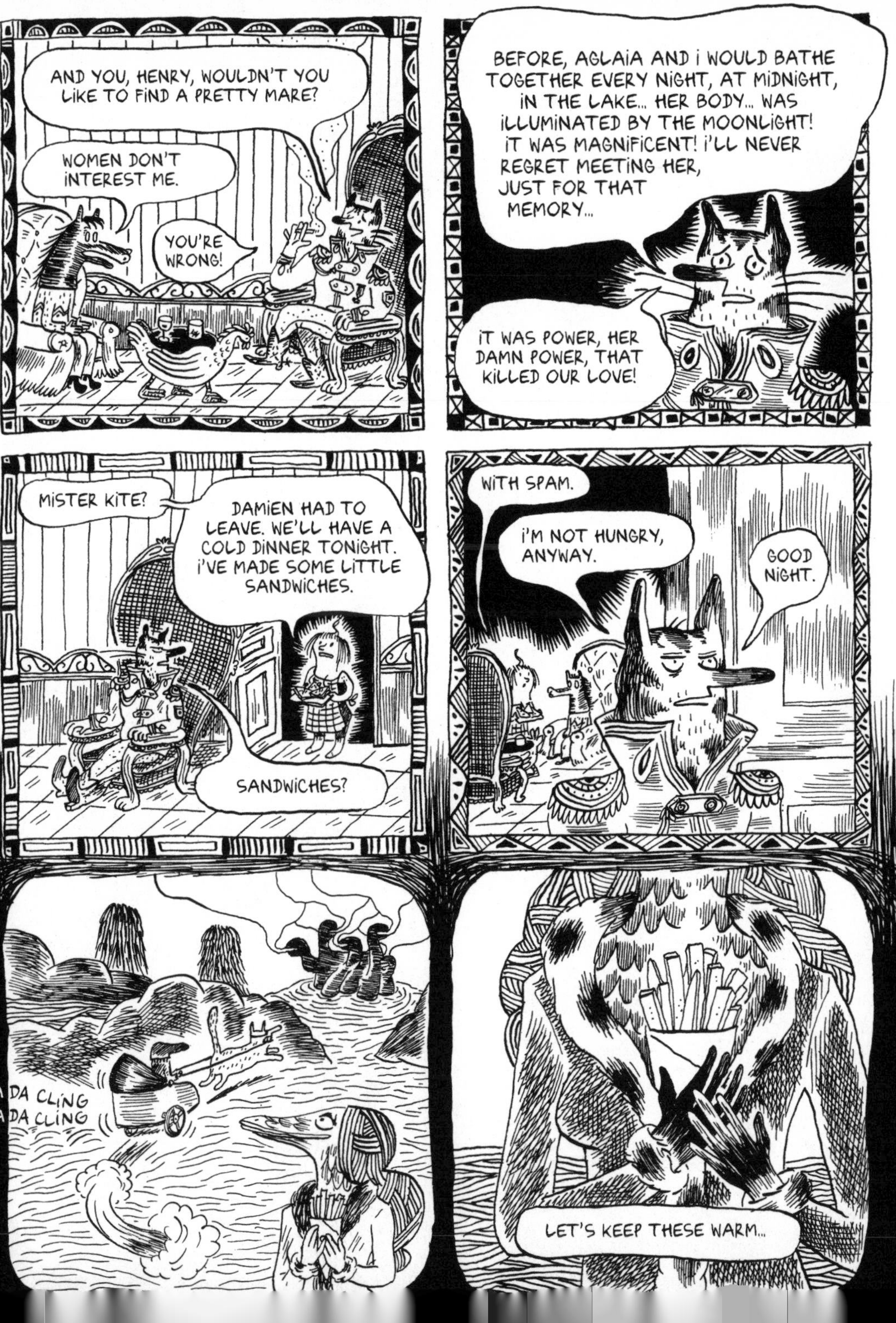

AND YOU, HENRY, WOULDN'T YOU LIKE TO FIND A PRETTY MARE?
WOMEN DON'T INTEREST ME.
YOU'RE WRONG!
BEFORE, AGLAIA AND I WOULD BATHE TOGETHER EVERY NIGHT, AT MIDNIGHT, IN THE LAKE... HER BODY... WAS ILLUMINATED BY THE MOONLIGHT! IT WAS MAGNIFICENT! I'LL NEVER REGRET MEETING HER, JUST FOR THAT MEMORY...
IT WAS POWER, HER DAMN POWER, THAT KILLED OUR LOVE!
MISTER KITE?
DAMIEN HAD TO LEAVE. WE'LL HAVE A COLD DINNER TONIGHT. I'VE MADE SOME LITTLE SANDWICHES.
SANDWICHES?
WITH SPAM.
I'M NOT HUNGRY, ANYWAY.
GOOD NIGHT.
BA DA CLING
BA DA CLING
LET'S KEEP THESE WARM...

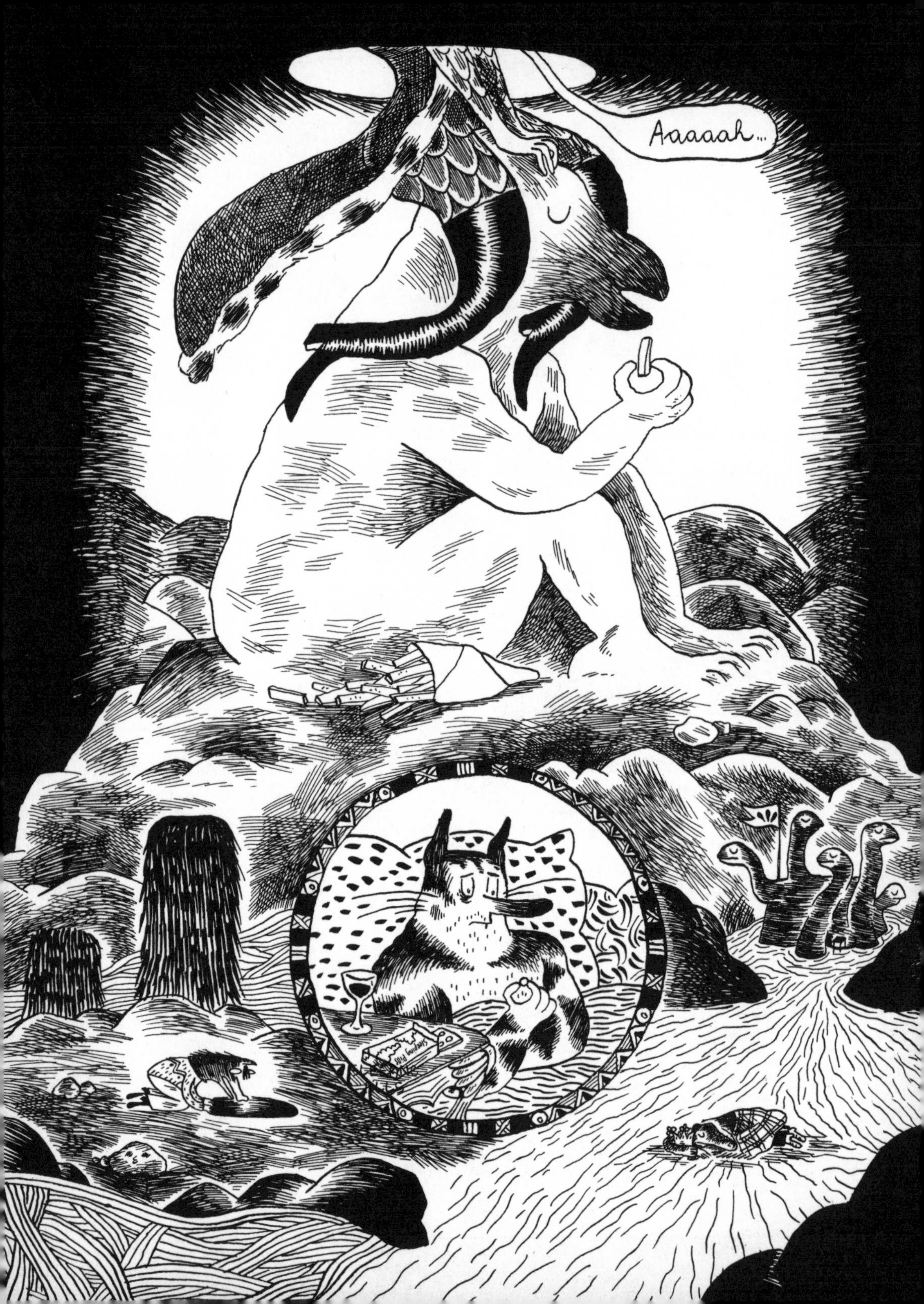
Aaaaah...
Sleeping Pills

THE CROWN

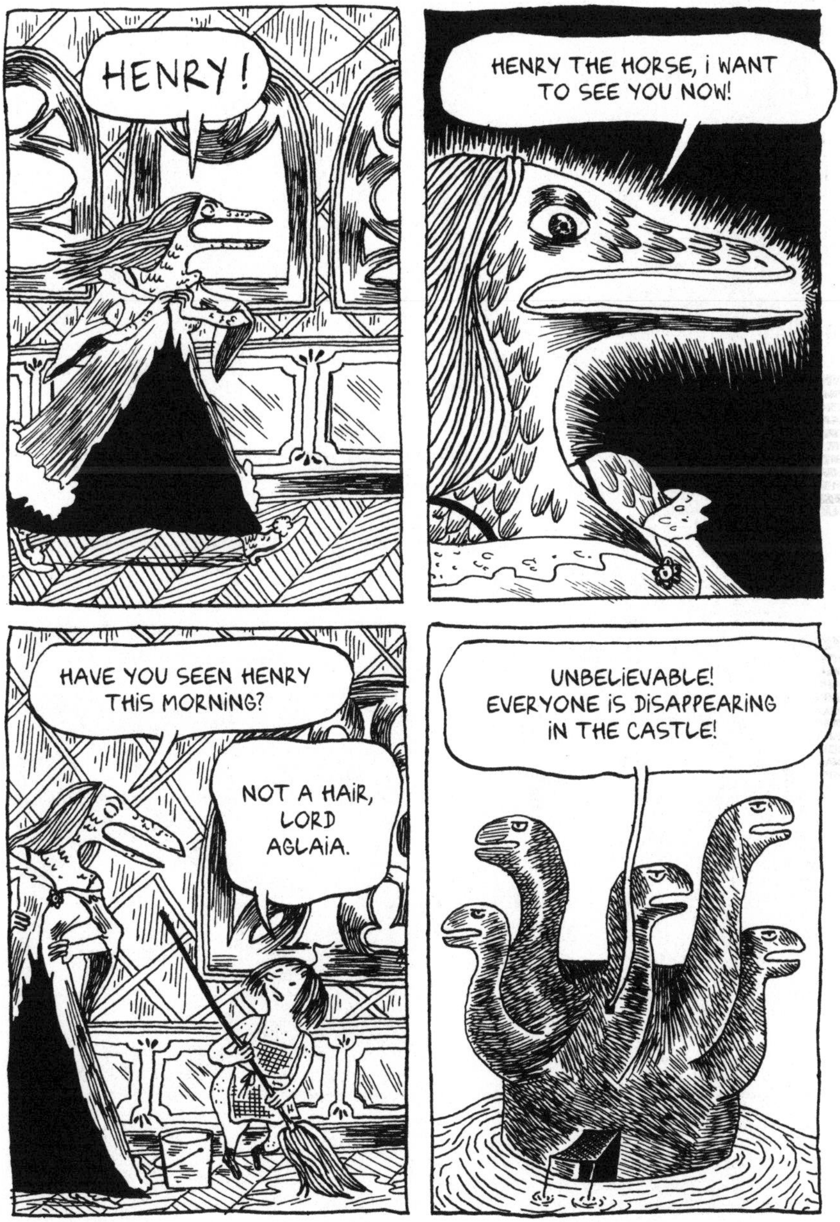
HENRY!
HENRY THE HORSE, I WANT TO SEE YOU NOW!
HAVE YOU SEEN HENRY THIS MORNING?
NOT A HAIR, LORD AGLAIA.
UNBELIEVABLE! EVERYONE IS DISAPPEARING IN THE CASTLE!

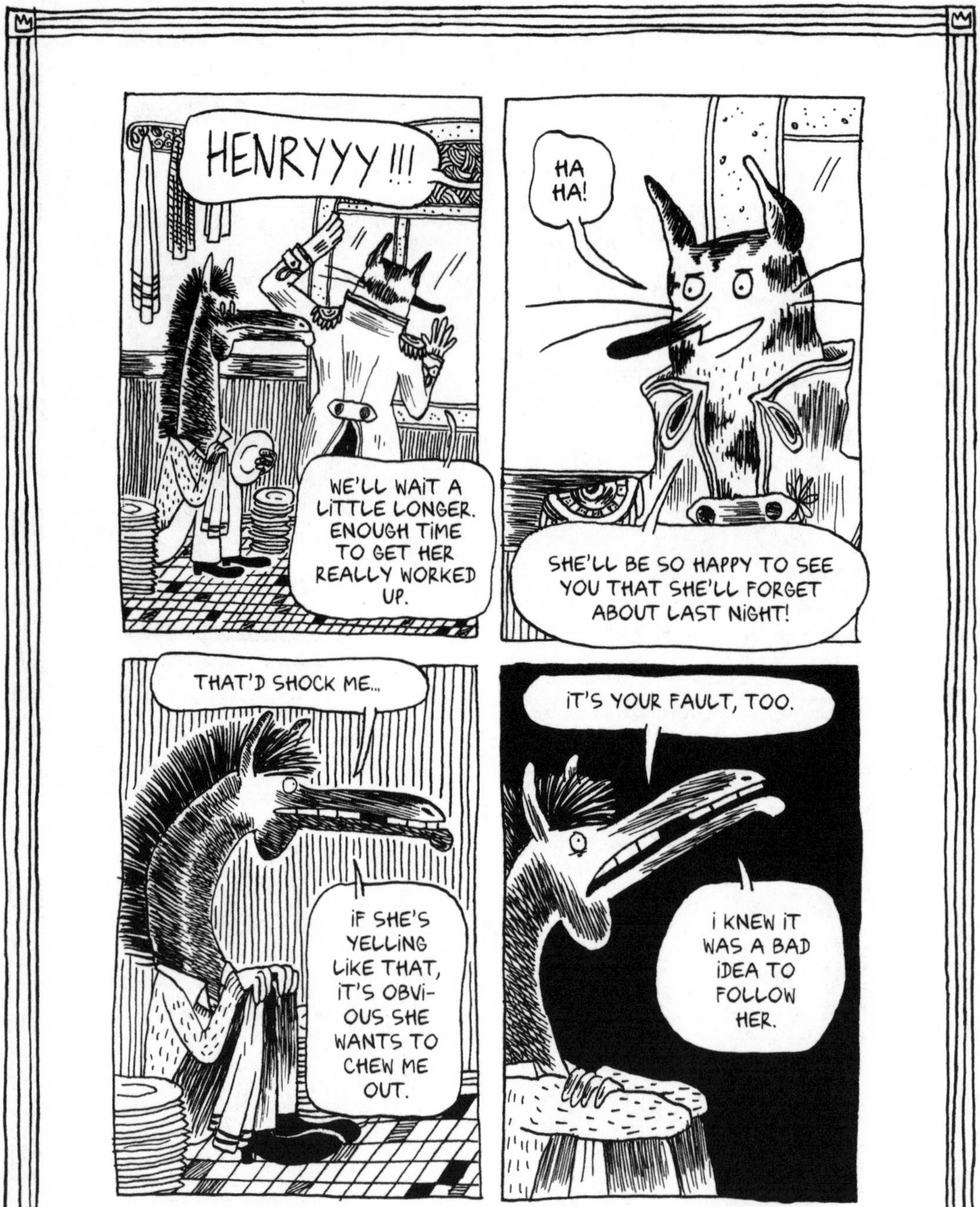
HENRYYY!!!
WE'LL WAIT A LITTLE LONGER. ENOUGH TIME TO GET HER REALLY WORKED UP.
HA HA!
SHE'LL BE SO HAPPY TO SEE YOU THAT SHE'LL FORGET ABOUT LAST NIGHT!
THAT'D SHOCK ME...
IF SHE'S YELLING LIKE THAT, IT'S OBVI-OUS SHE WANTS TO CHEW ME OUT.
IT'S YOUR FAULT, TOO.
I KNEW IT WAS A BAD IDEA TO FOLLOW HER.

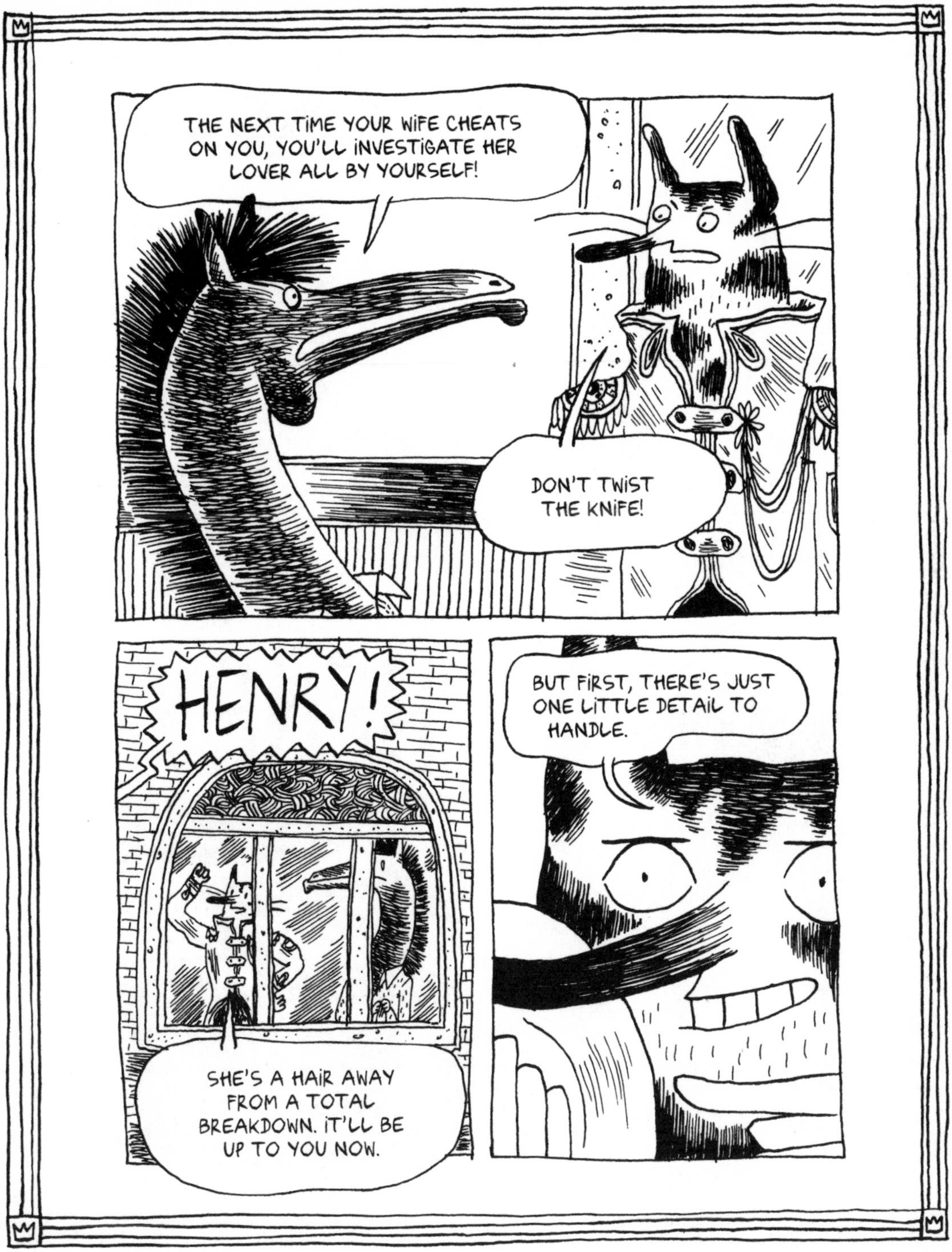
THE NEXT TIME YOUR WIFE CHEATS ON YOU, YOU'LL INVESTIGATE HER LOVER ALL BY YOURSELF!
DON'T TWIST THE KNIFE!
HENRY!
SHE'S A HAIR AWAY FROM A TOTAL BREAKDOWN. IT'LL BE UP TO YOU NOW.
BUT FIRST, THERE'S JUST ONE LITTLE DETAIL TO HANDLE.

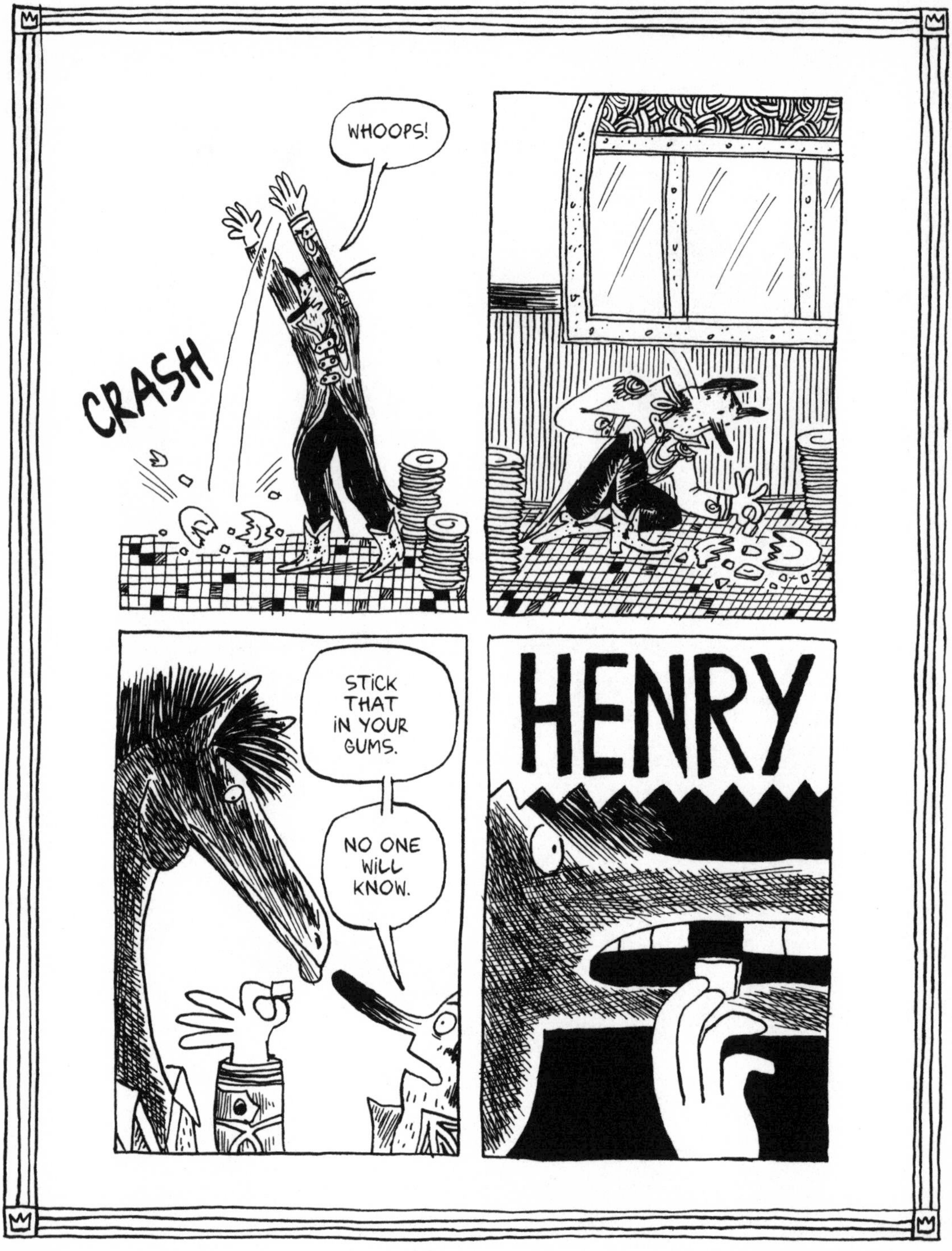
WHOOPS!
CRASH
STICK THAT IN YOUR GUMS.
NO ONE WILL KNOW.
HENRY

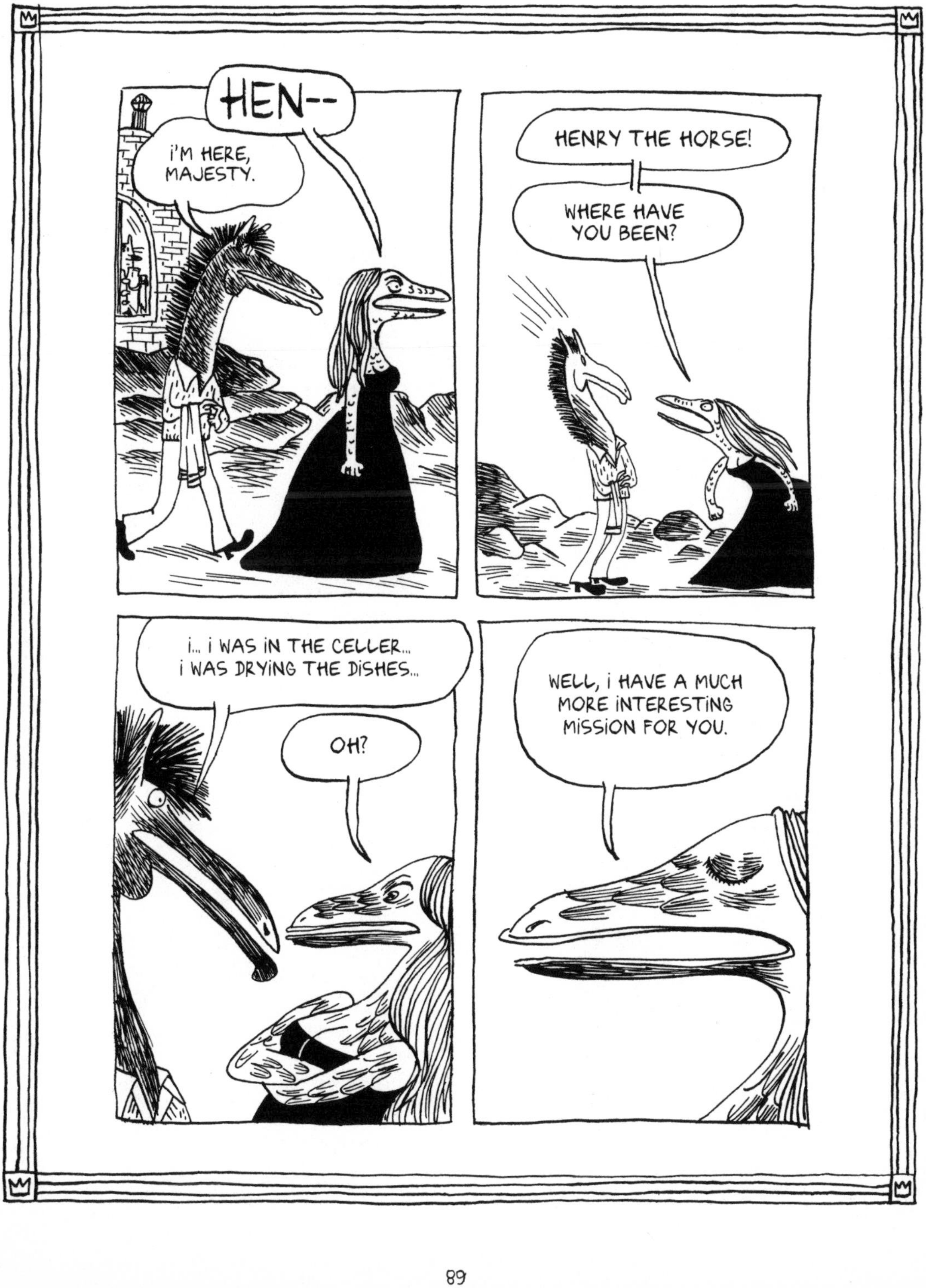
HEN--
I'M HERE, MAJESTY.
HENRY THE HORSE!
WHERE HAVE YOU BEEN?
I... I WAS IN THE CELLER... I WAS DRYING THE DISHES...
OH?
WELL, I HAVE A MUCH MORE INTERESTING MISSION FOR YOU.

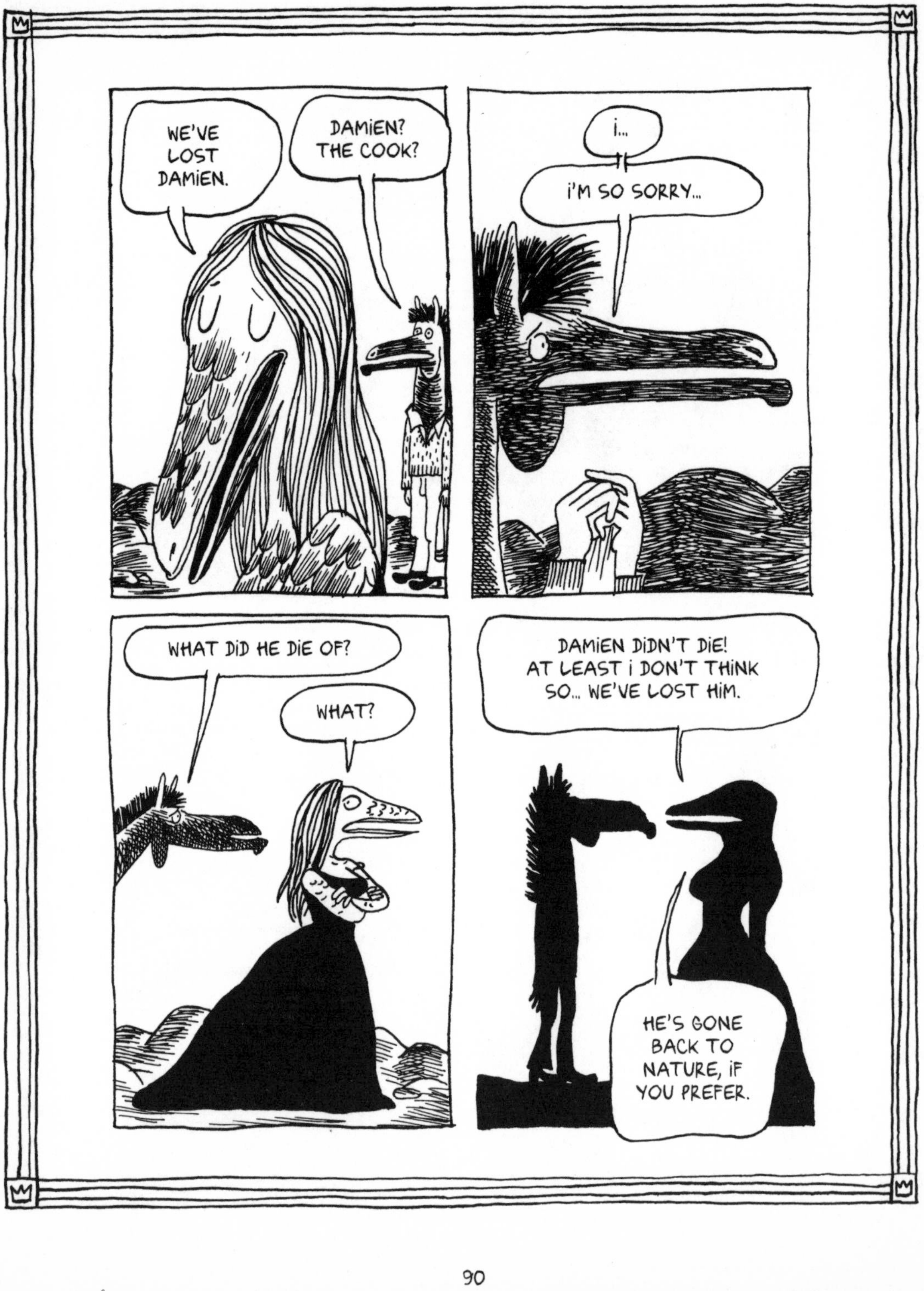

WE'VE LOST DAMIEN.
DAMIEN? THE COOK?
I...
I'M SO SORRY...
WHAT DID HE DIE OF?
WHAT?
DAMIEN DIDN'T DIE! AT LEAST I DON'T THINK SO... WE'VE LOST HIM.
HE'S GONE BACK TO NATURE, IF YOU PREFER.

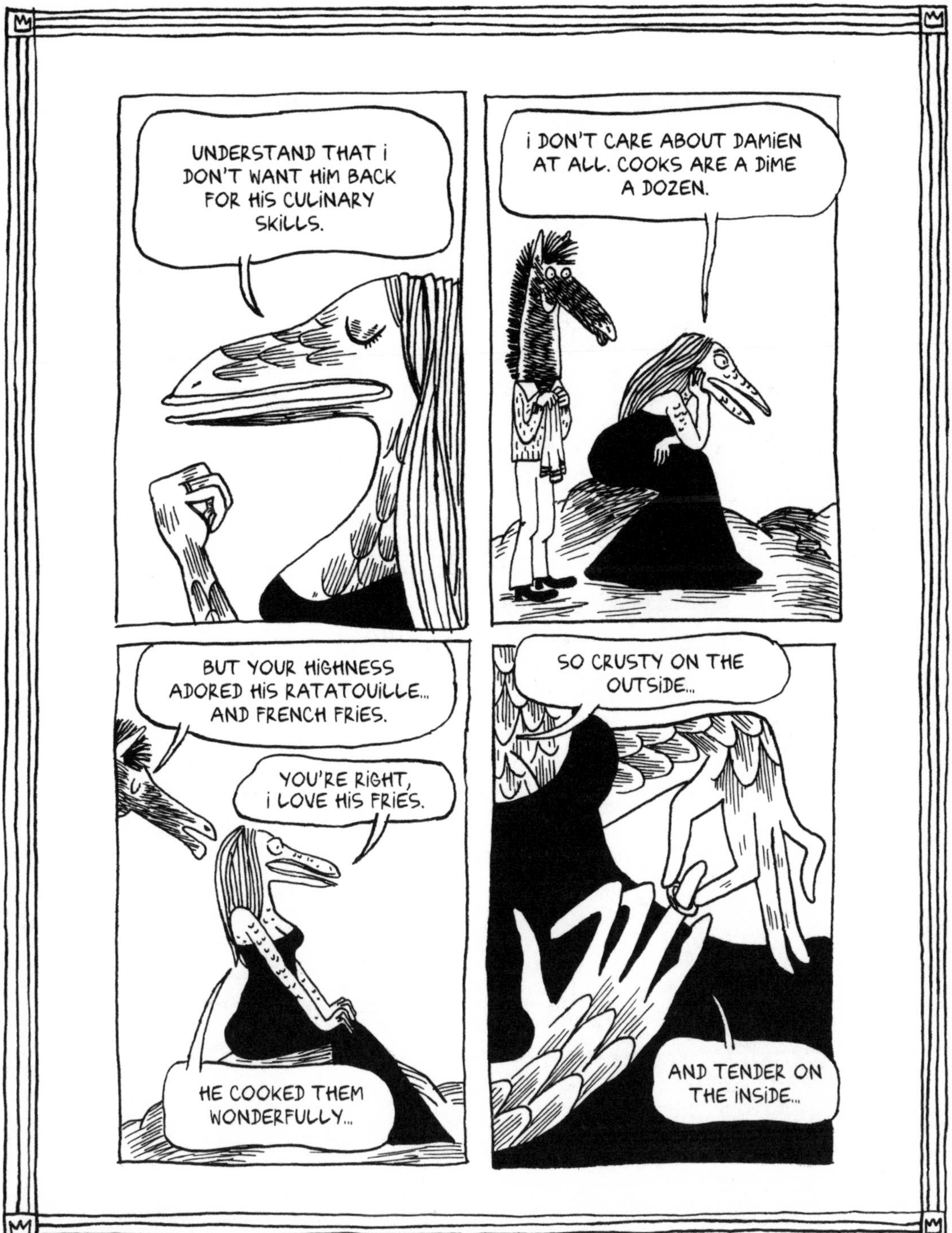
UNDERSTAND THAT I DON'T WANT HIM BACK FOR HIS CULINARY SKILLS.
I DON'T CARE ABOUT DAMIEN AT ALL. COOKS ARE A DIME A DOZEN.
BUT YOUR HIGHNESS ADORED HIS RATATOUILLE... AND FRENCH FRIES.
YOU'RE RIGHT, I LOVE HIS FRIES.
HE COOKED THEM WONDERFULLY...
SO CRUSTY ON THE OUTSIDE...
AND TENDER ON THE INSIDE...

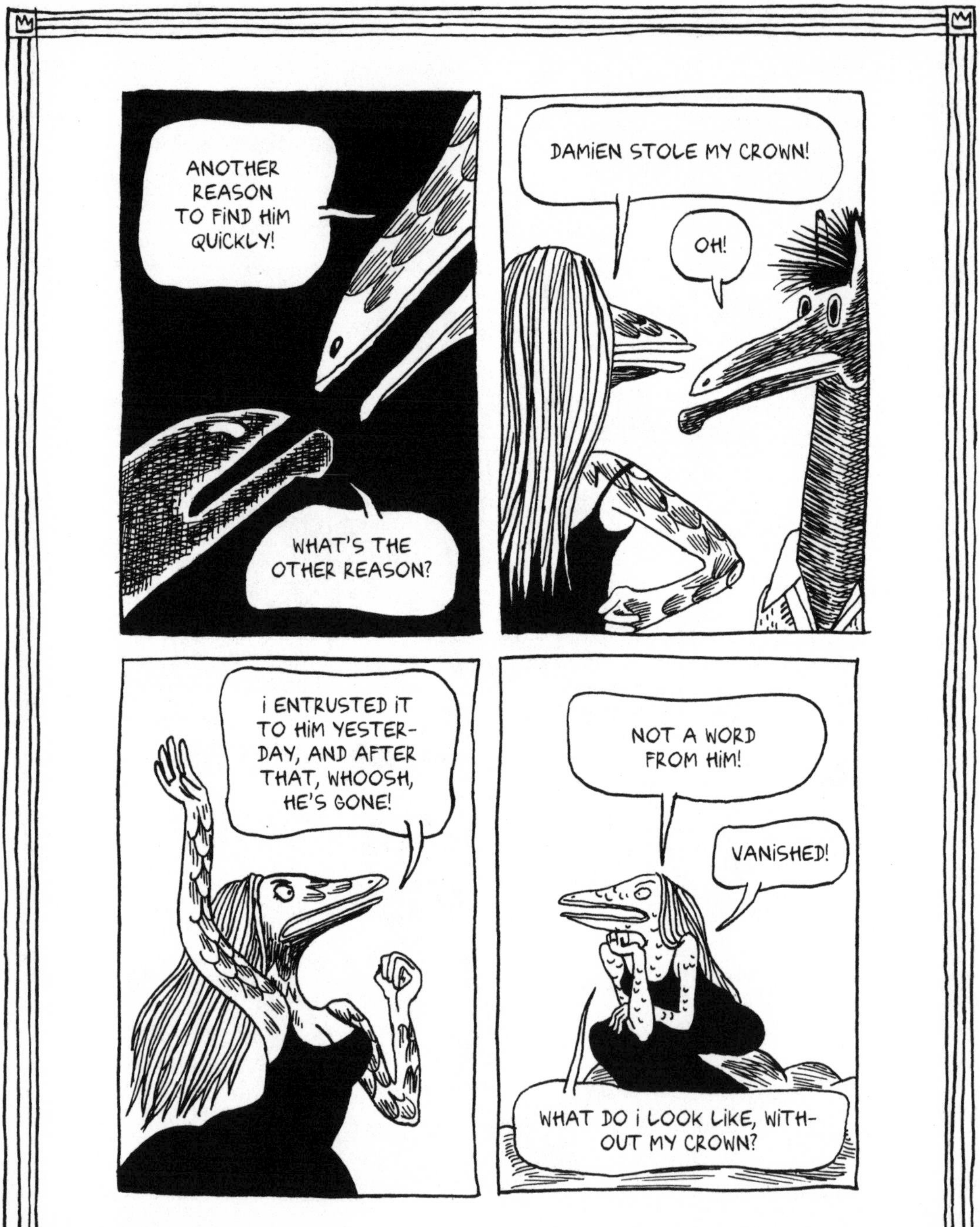
ANOTHER REASON TO FIND HIM QUICKLY!
WHAT'S THE OTHER REASON?
DAMIEN STOLE MY CROWN!
OH!
I ENTRUSTED IT TO HIM YESTER-DAY, AND AFTER THAT, WHOOSH, HE'S GONE!
NOT A WORD FROM HIM!
VANISHED!
WHAT DO I LOOK LIKE, WITH-OUT MY CROWN?

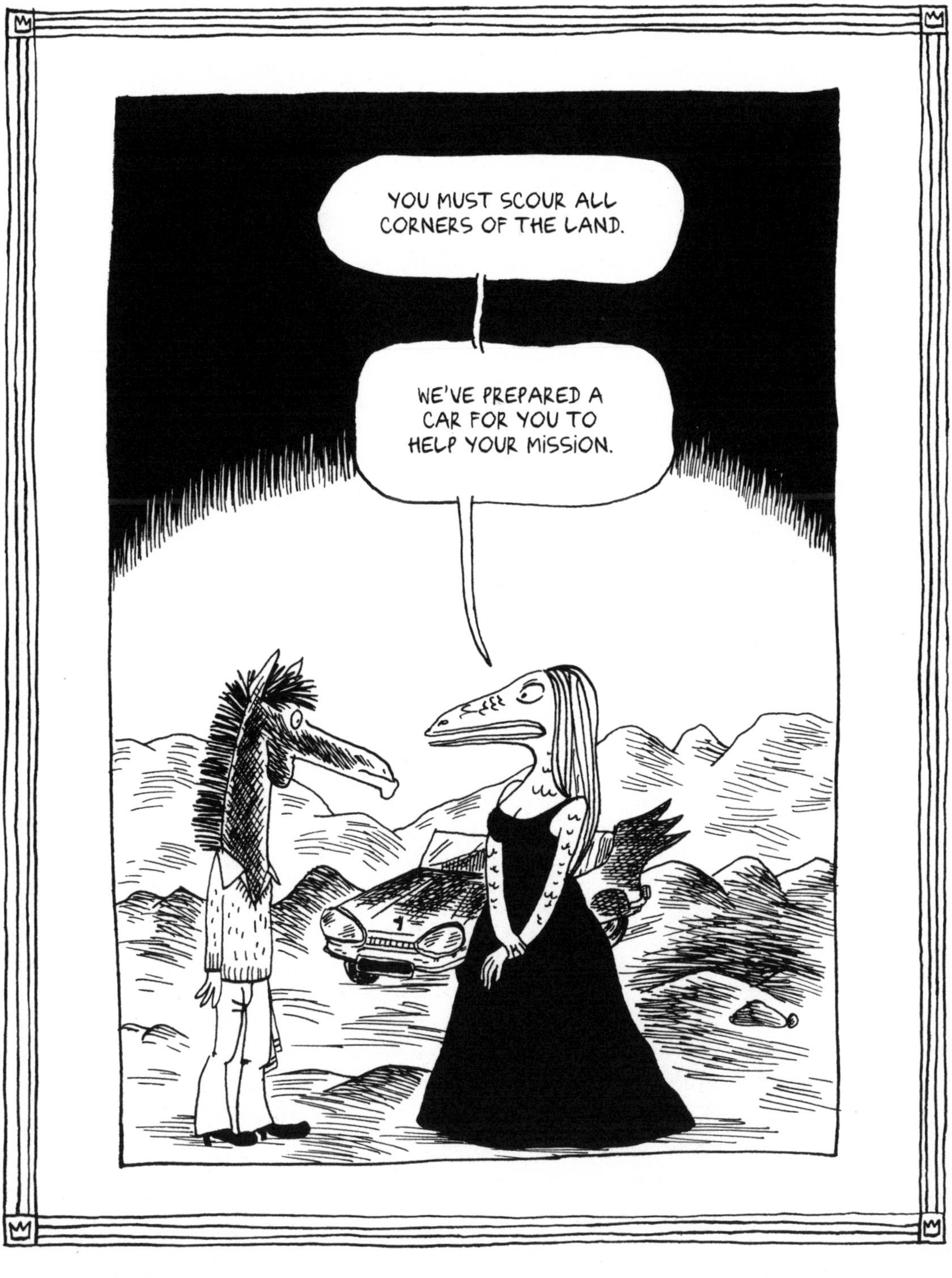
YOU MUST SCOUR ALL CORNERS OF THE LAND.
WE'VE PREPARED A CAR FOR YOU TO HELP YOUR MISSION.

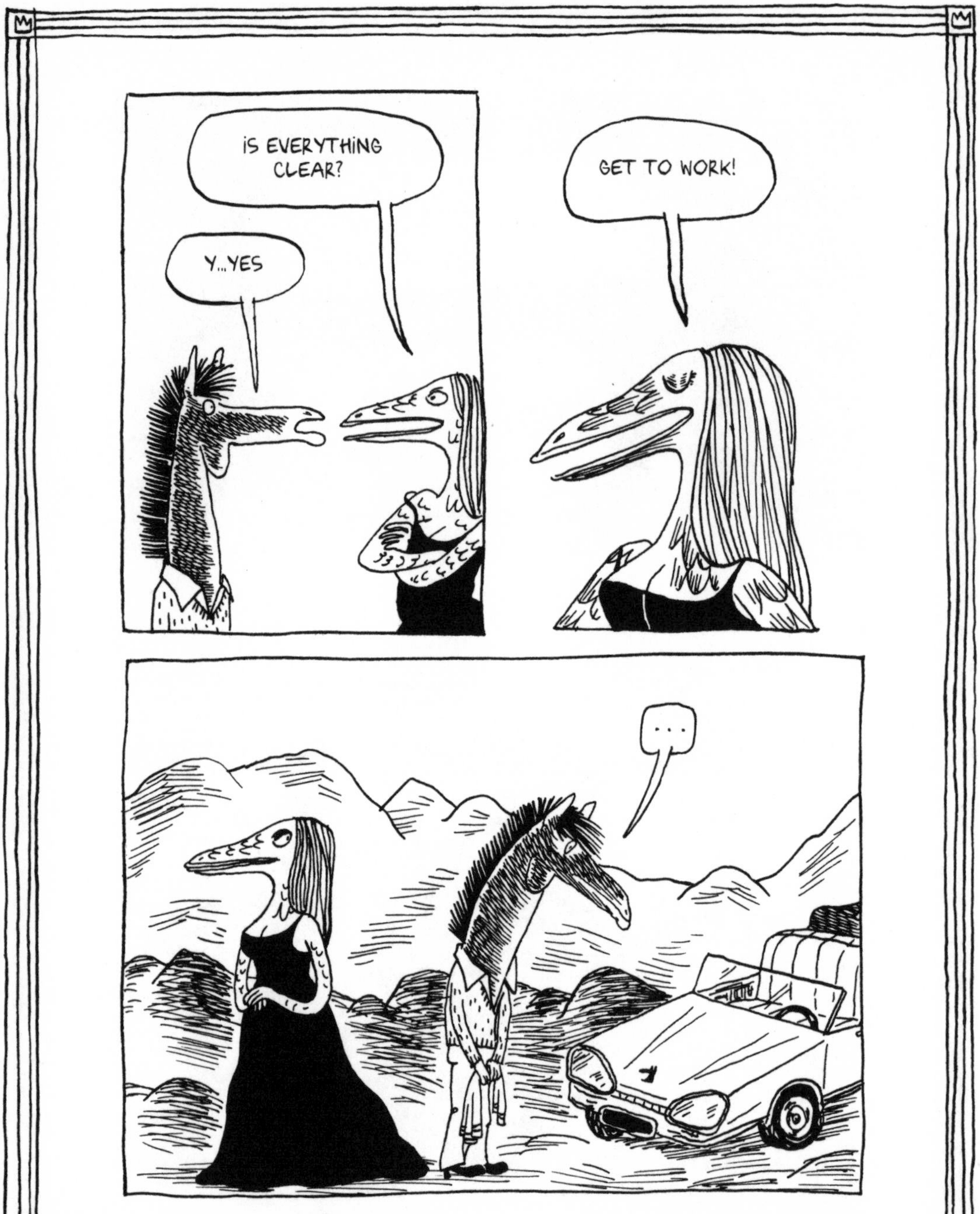
IS EVERYTHING CLEAR?
Y...YES
GET TO WORK!
. . .

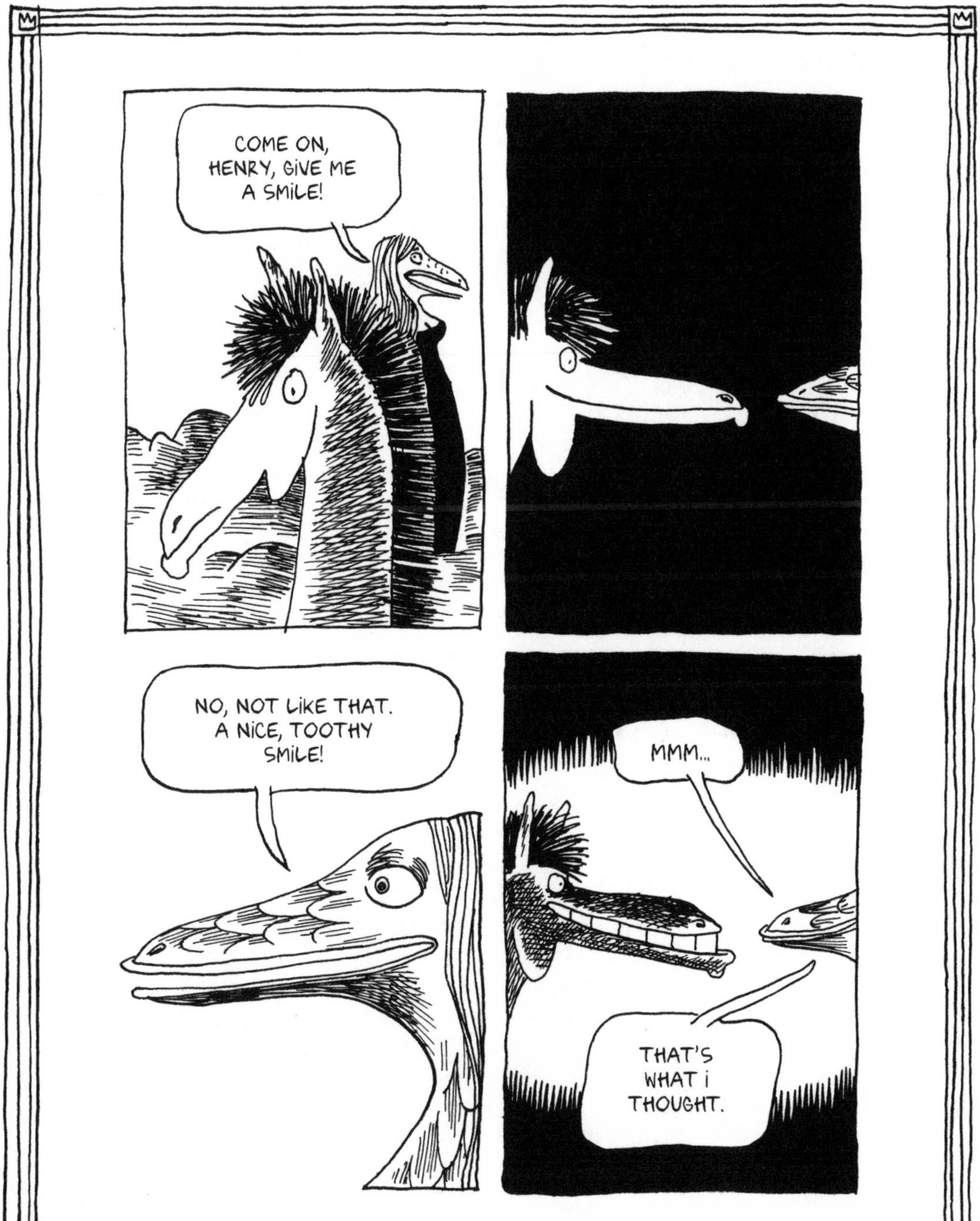
COME ON, HENRY, GiVE ME A SMiLE!
NO, NOT LiKE THAT. A NiCE, TOOTHY SMiLE!
MMM...
THAT'S WHAT i THOUGHT.

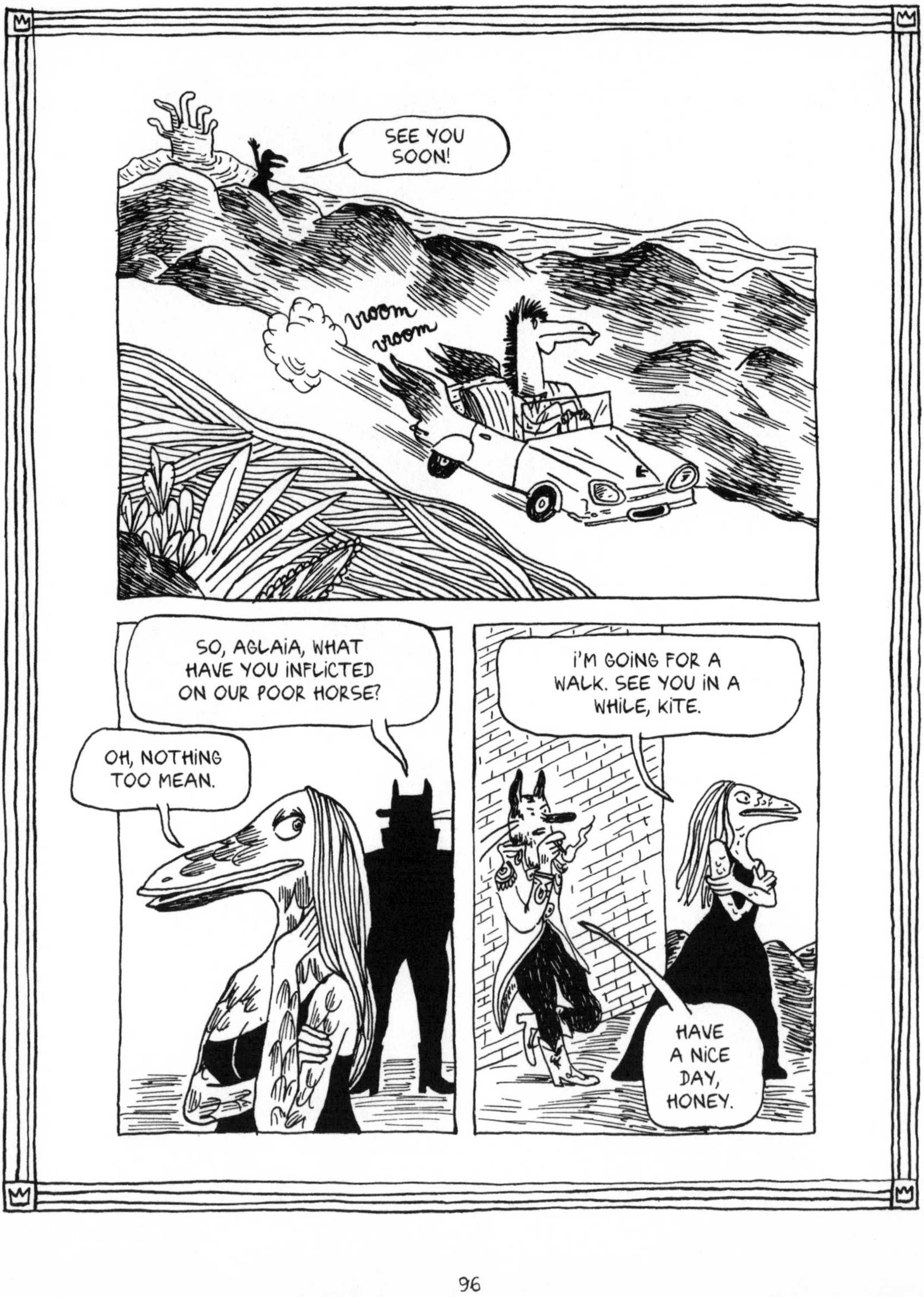
SEE YOU SOON!
vroom vroom
SO, AGLAIA, WHAT HAVE YOU INFLICTED ON OUR POOR HORSE?
OH, NOTHING TOO MEAN.
I'M GOING FOR A WALK. SEE YOU IN A WHILE, KITE.
HAVE A NICE DAY, HONEY.

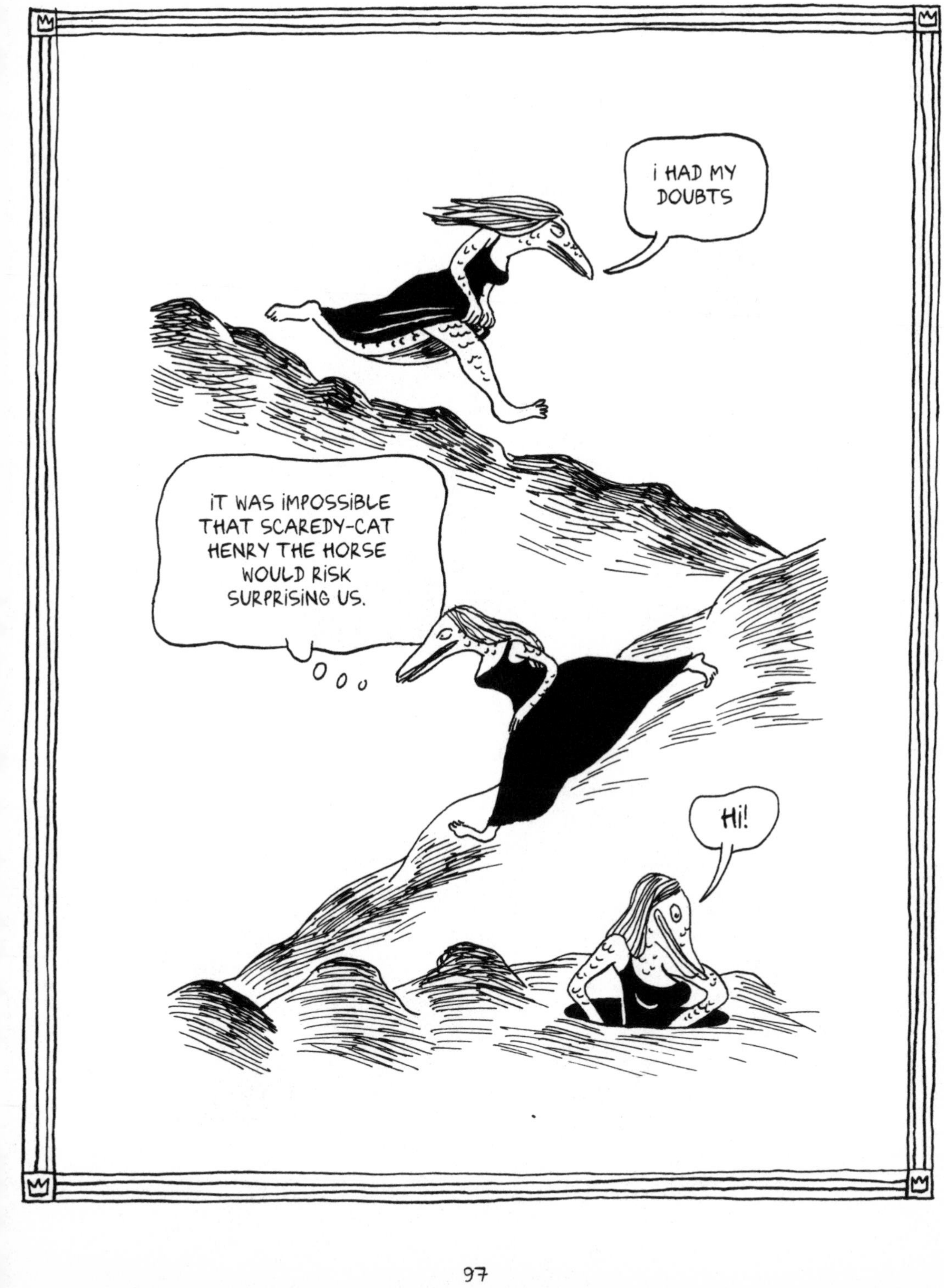
I HAD MY DOUBTS
IT WAS IMPOSSIBLE THAT SCAREDY-CAT HENRY THE HORSE WOULD RISK SURPRISING US.
HI!

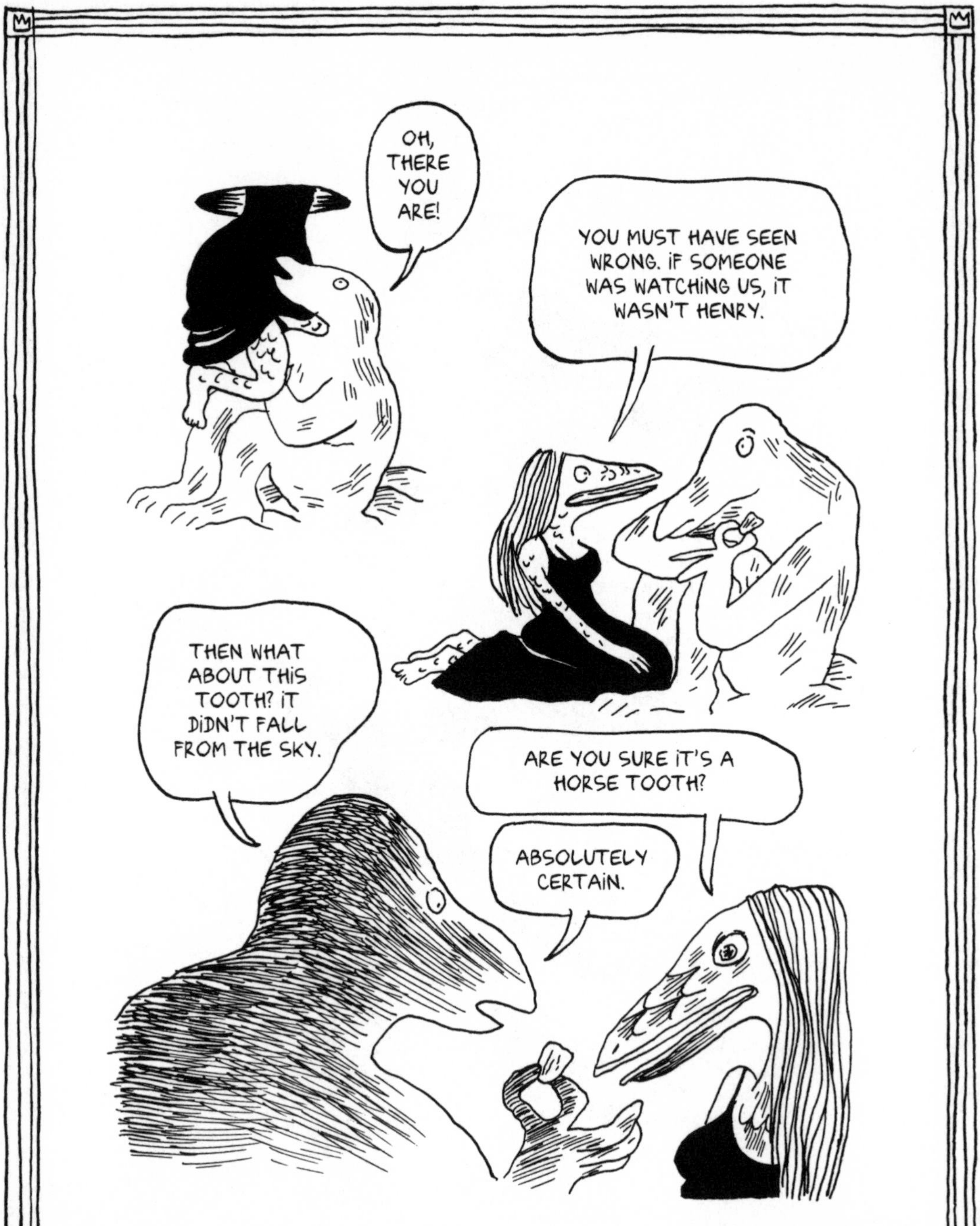
OH, THERE YOU ARE!
YOU MUST HAVE SEEN WRONG. IF SOMEONE WAS WATCHING US, IT WASN'T HENRY.
THEN WHAT ABOUT THIS TOOTH? IT DIDN'T FALL FROM THE SKY.
ARE YOU SURE IT'S A HORSE TOOTH?
ABSOLUTELY CERTAIN.

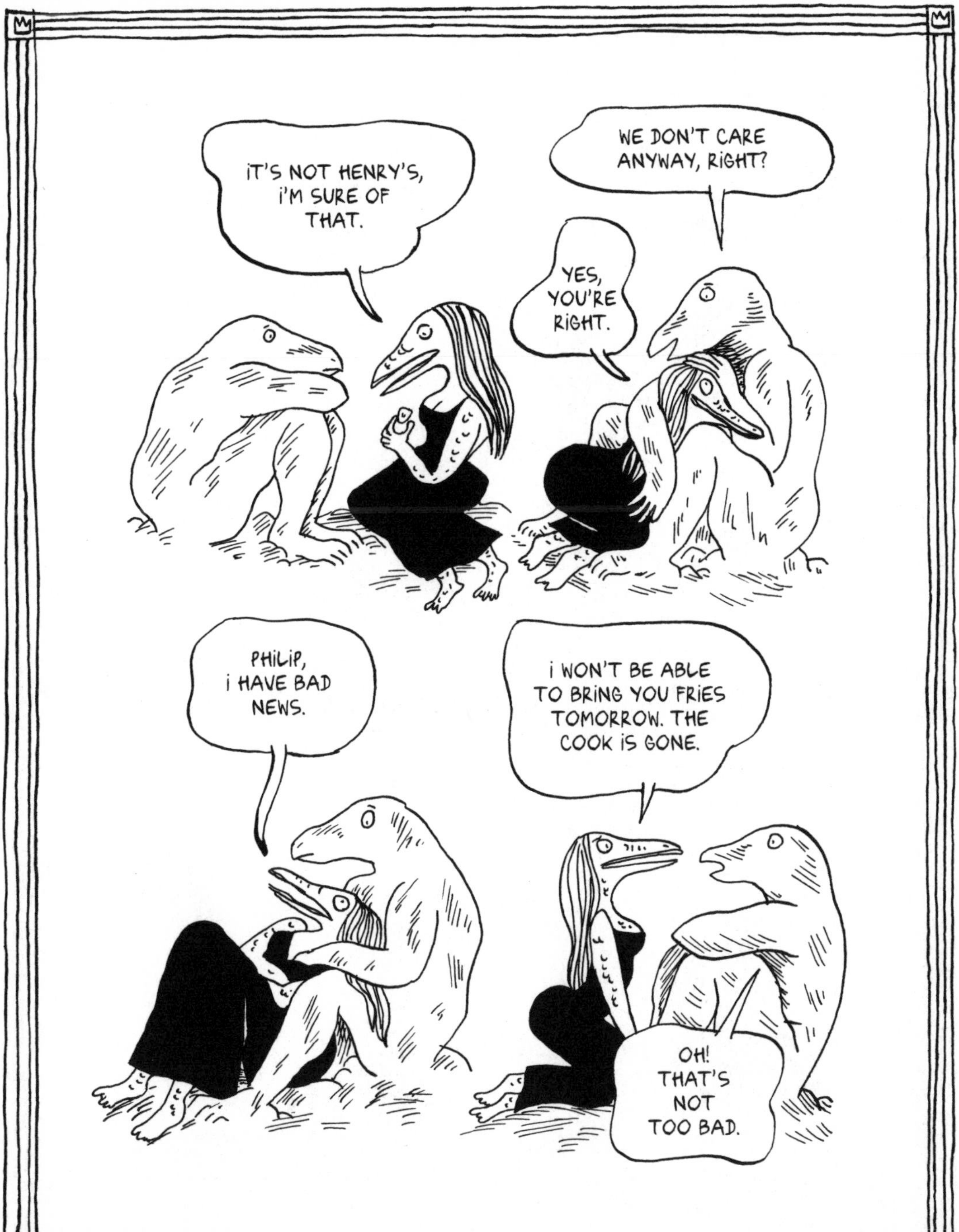
IT'S NOT HENRY'S, I'M SURE OF THAT.
WE DON'T CARE ANYWAY, RIGHT?
YES, YOU'RE RIGHT.
PHILIP, I HAVE BAD NEWS.
I WON'T BE ABLE TO BRING YOU FRIES TOMORROW. THE COOK IS GONE.
OH! THAT'S NOT TOO BAD.

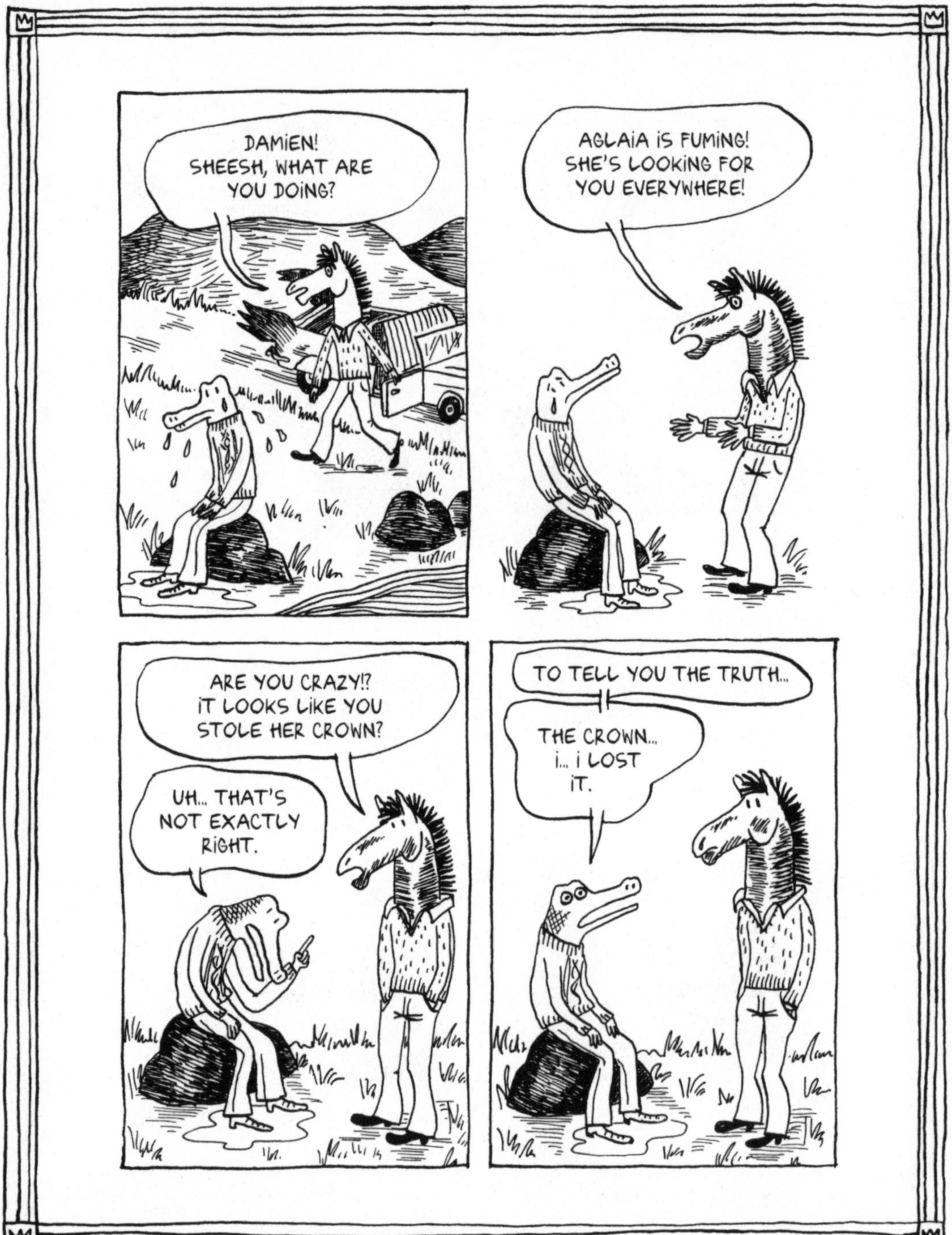

DAMIEN! SHEESH, WHAT ARE YOU DOING?
AGLAIA IS FUMING! SHE'S LOOKING FOR YOU EVERYWHERE!
ARE YOU CRAZY!? IT LOOKS LIKE YOU STOLE HER CROWN?
UH... THAT'S NOT EXACTLY RIGHT.
TO TELL YOU THE TRUTH...
THE CROWN... I... I LOST IT.

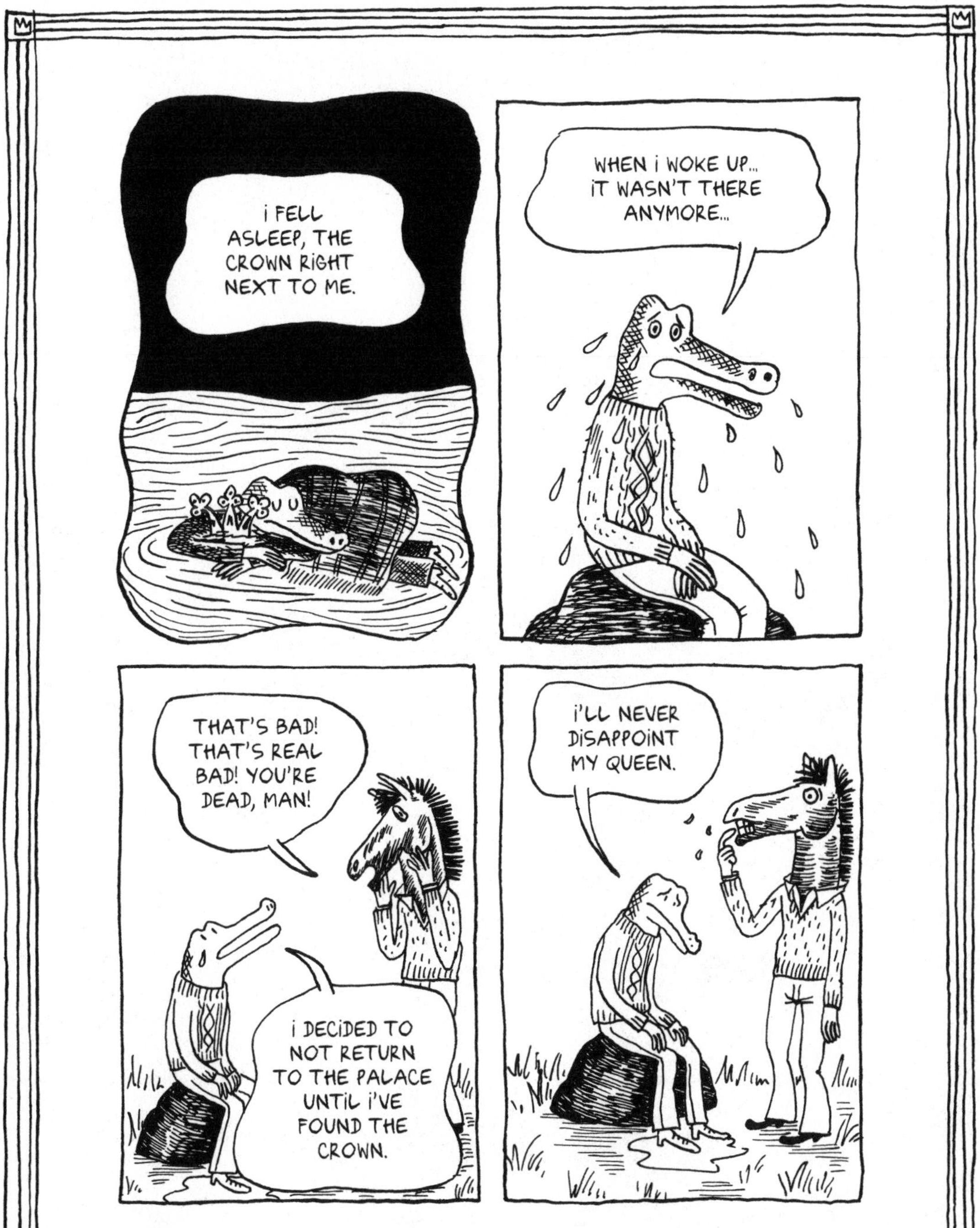
I FELL ASLEEP, THE CROWN RIGHT NEXT TO ME.
WHEN I WOKE UP... IT WASN'T THERE ANYMORE...
THAT'S BAD! THAT'S REAL BAD! YOU'RE DEAD, MAN!
I DECIDED TO NOT RETURN TO THE PALACE UNTIL I'VE FOUND THE CROWN.
I'LL NEVER DISAPPOINT MY QUEEN.

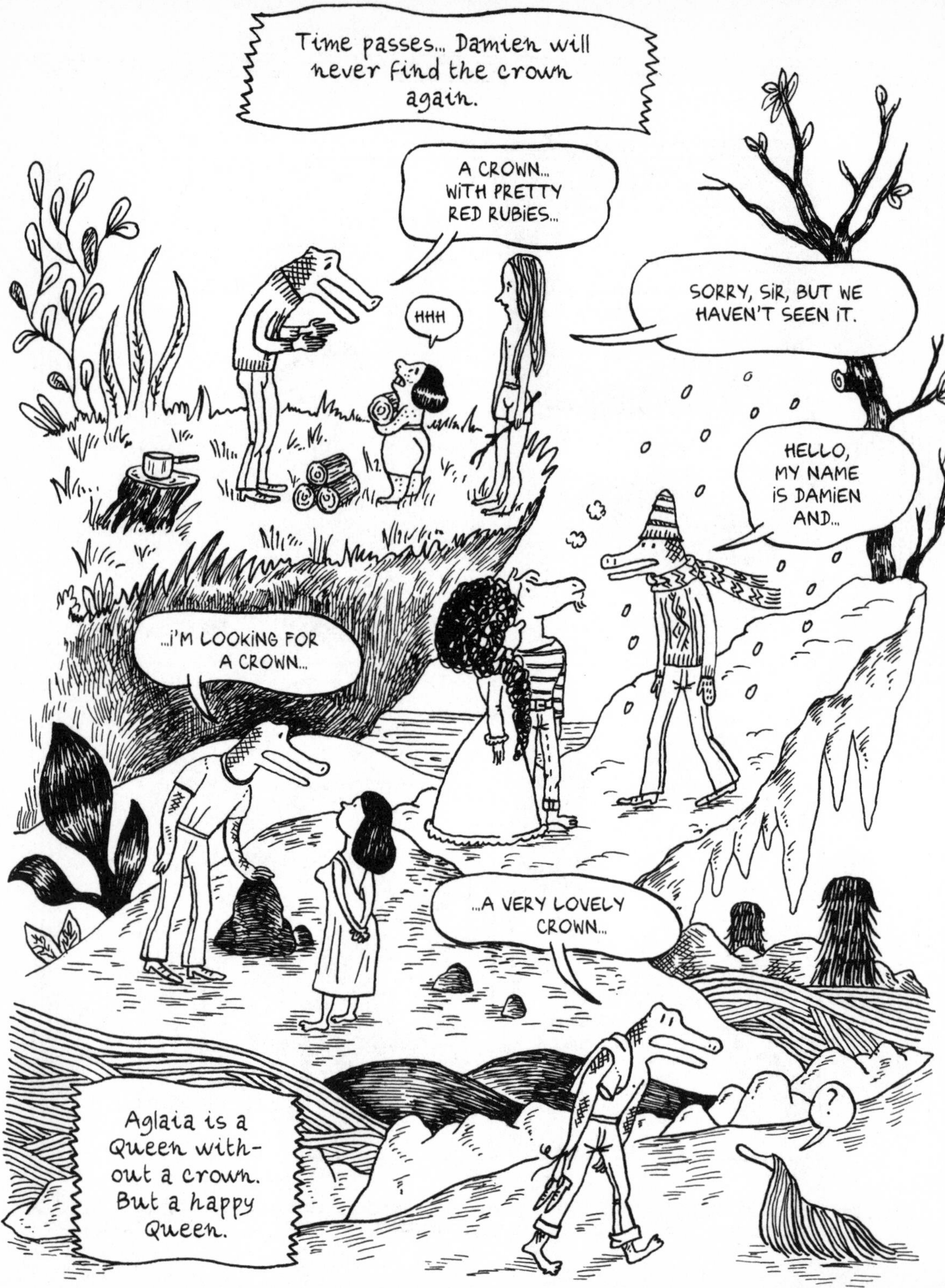

Time passes... Damien will never find the crown again.
A CROWN... WITH PRETTY RED RUBIES...
HHH
SORRY, SIR, BUT WE HAVEN'T SEEN IT.
HELLO, MY NAME IS DAMIEN AND...
...I'M LOOKING FOR A CROWN...
...A VERY LOVELY CROWN...
?
Aglaia is a Queen without a crown. But a happy Queen.

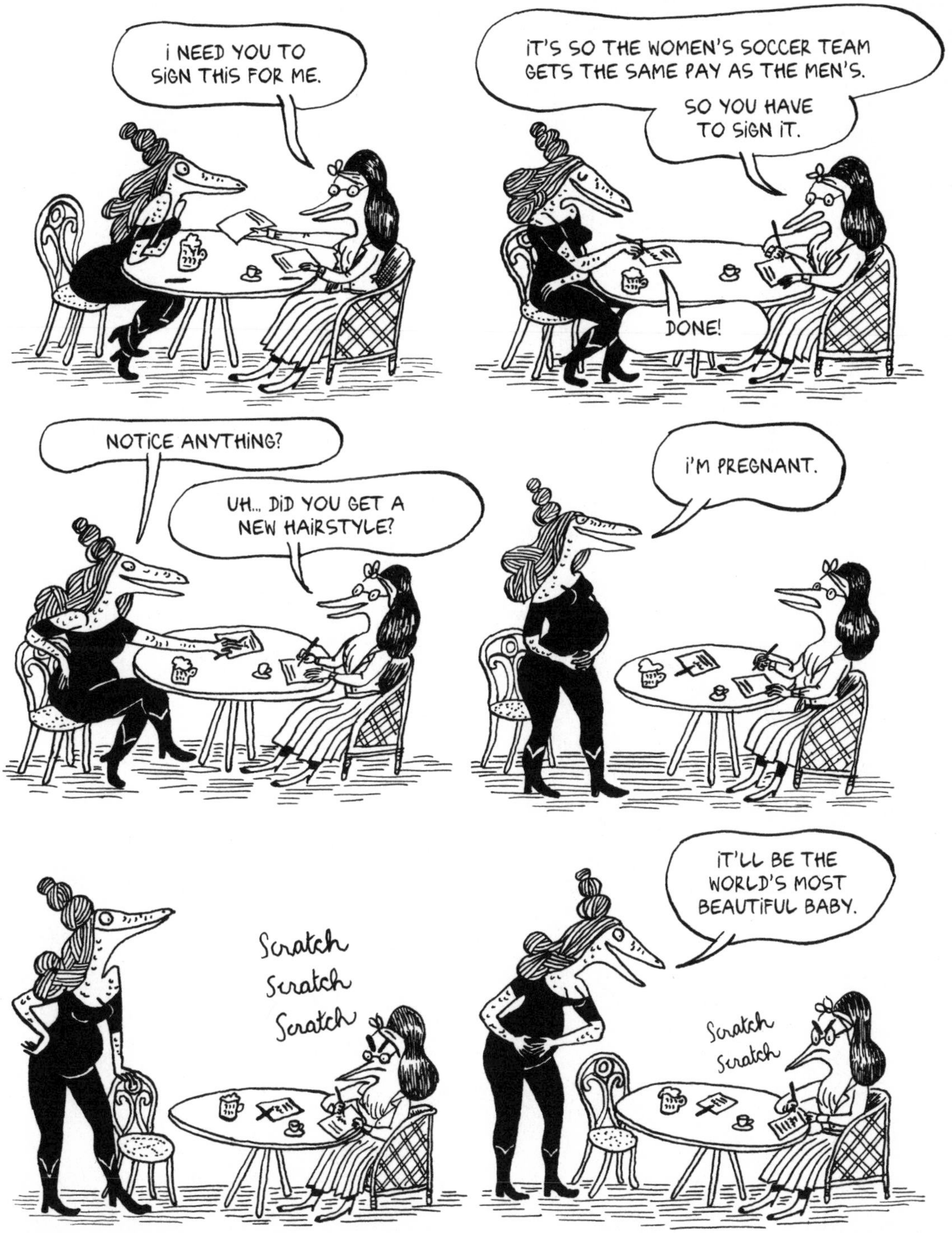
I NEED YOU TO SIGN THIS FOR ME.
IT'S SO THE WOMEN'S SOCCER TEAM GETS THE SAME PAY AS THE MEN'S.
SO YOU HAVE TO SIGN IT.
DONE!
NOTICE ANYTHING?
UH... DID YOU GET A NEW HAIRSTYLE?
I'M PREGNANT.
Scratch Scratch Scratch
IT'LL BE THE WORLD'S MOST BEAUTIFUL BABY.
Scratch Scratch

INTERLUDE FOR SIMONE, PRIME MINISTER

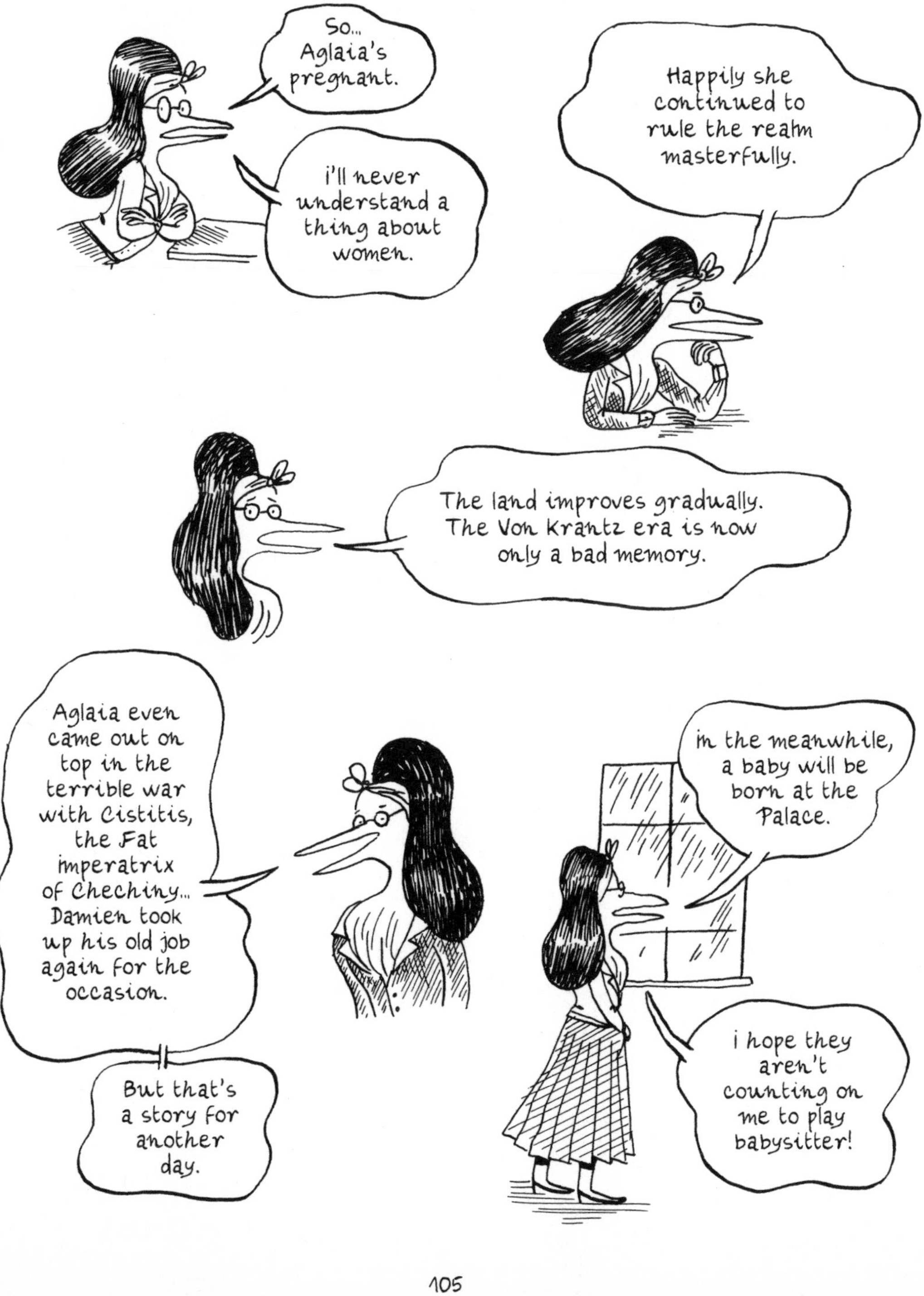

So... Aglaia's pregnant.
I'll never understand a thing about women.
Happily she continued to rule the realm masterfully.
The land improves gradually. The Von Krantz era is now only a bad memory.
Aglaia even came out on top in the terrible war with Cistitis, the Fat imperatrix of Chechiny... Damien took up his old job again for the occasion.
But that's a story for another day.
In the meanwhile, a baby will be born at the Palace.
I hope they aren't counting on me to play babysitter!

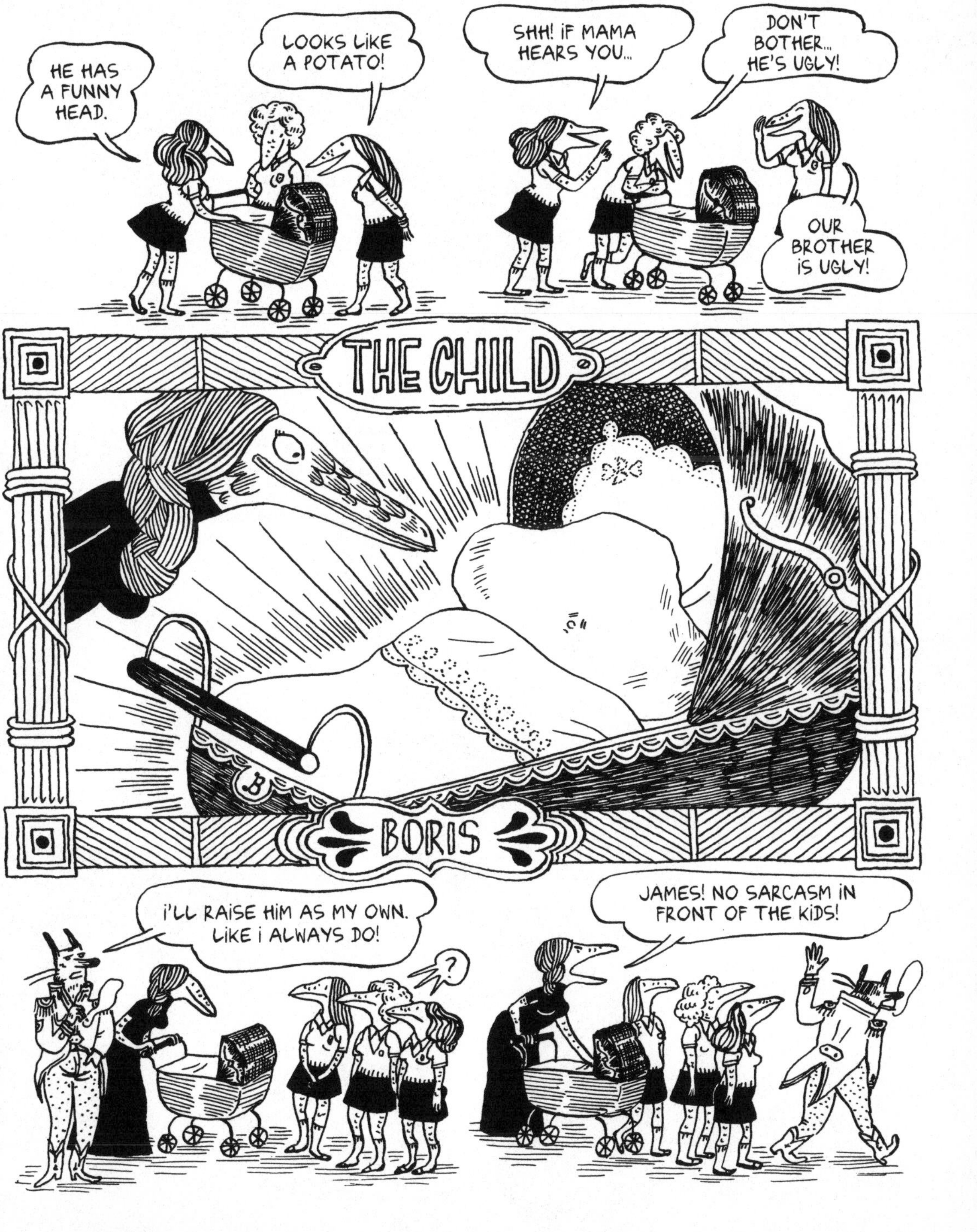
HE HAS A FUNNY HEAD.
LOOKS LIKE A POTATO!
SHH! IF MAMA HEARS YOU...
DON'T BOTHER... HE'S UGLY!
OUR BROTHER IS UGLY!
THE CHILD
BORIS
I'LL RAISE HIM AS MY OWN. LIKE I ALWAYS DO!
?
JAMES! NO SARCASM IN FRONT OF THE KIDS!

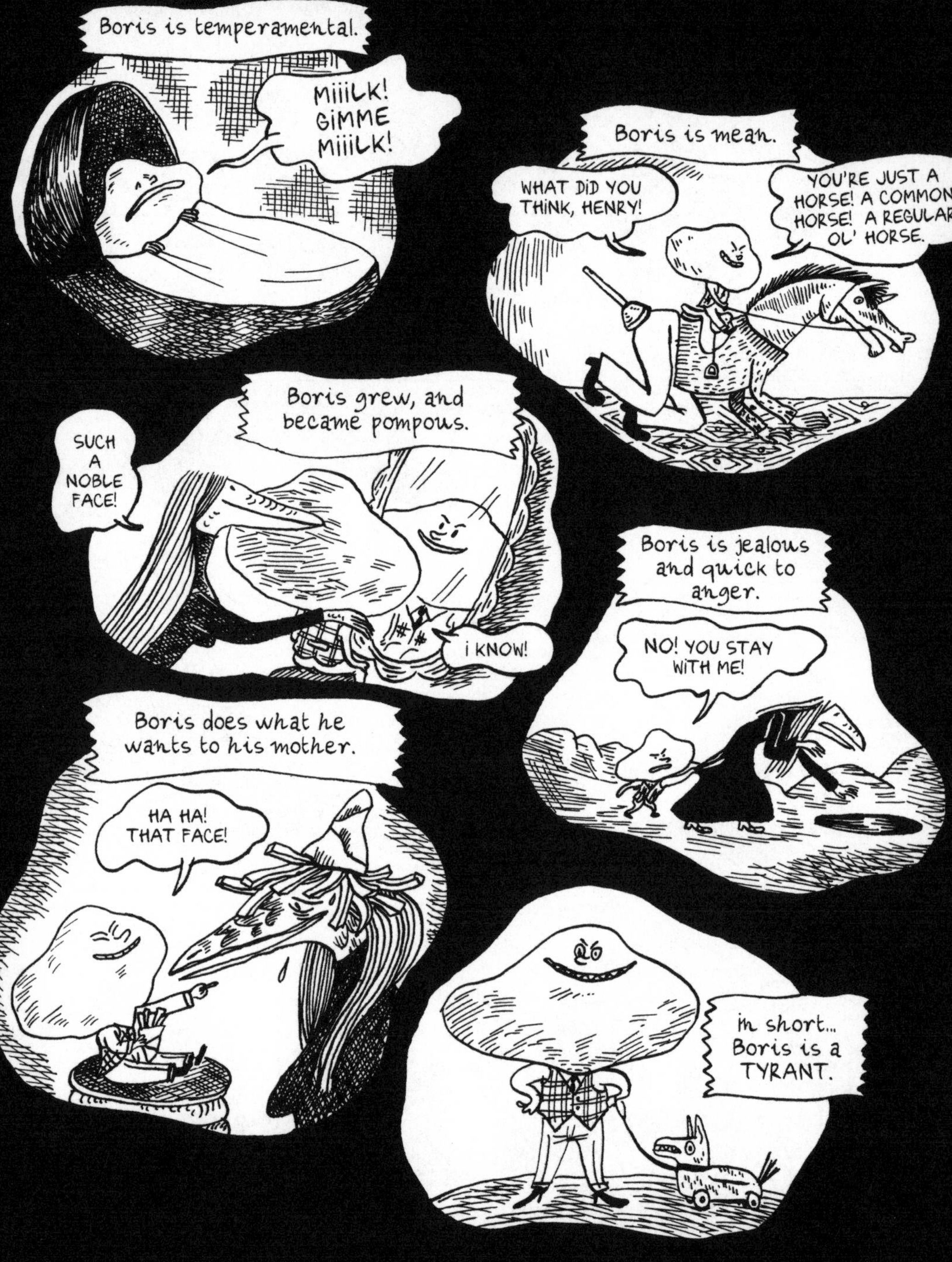
Boris is temperamental.
MiiiLK! GiMME MiiiLK!
Boris is mean.
WHAT DiD YOU THiNK, HENRY!
YOU'RE JUST A HORSE! A COMMON HORSE! A REGULAR OL' HORSE.
Boris grew, and became pompous.
SUCH A NOBLE FACE!
i KNOW!
Boris is jealous and quick to anger.
NO! YOU STAY WiTH ME!
Boris does what he wants to his mother.
HA HA! THAT FACE!
in short... Boris is a TYRANT.

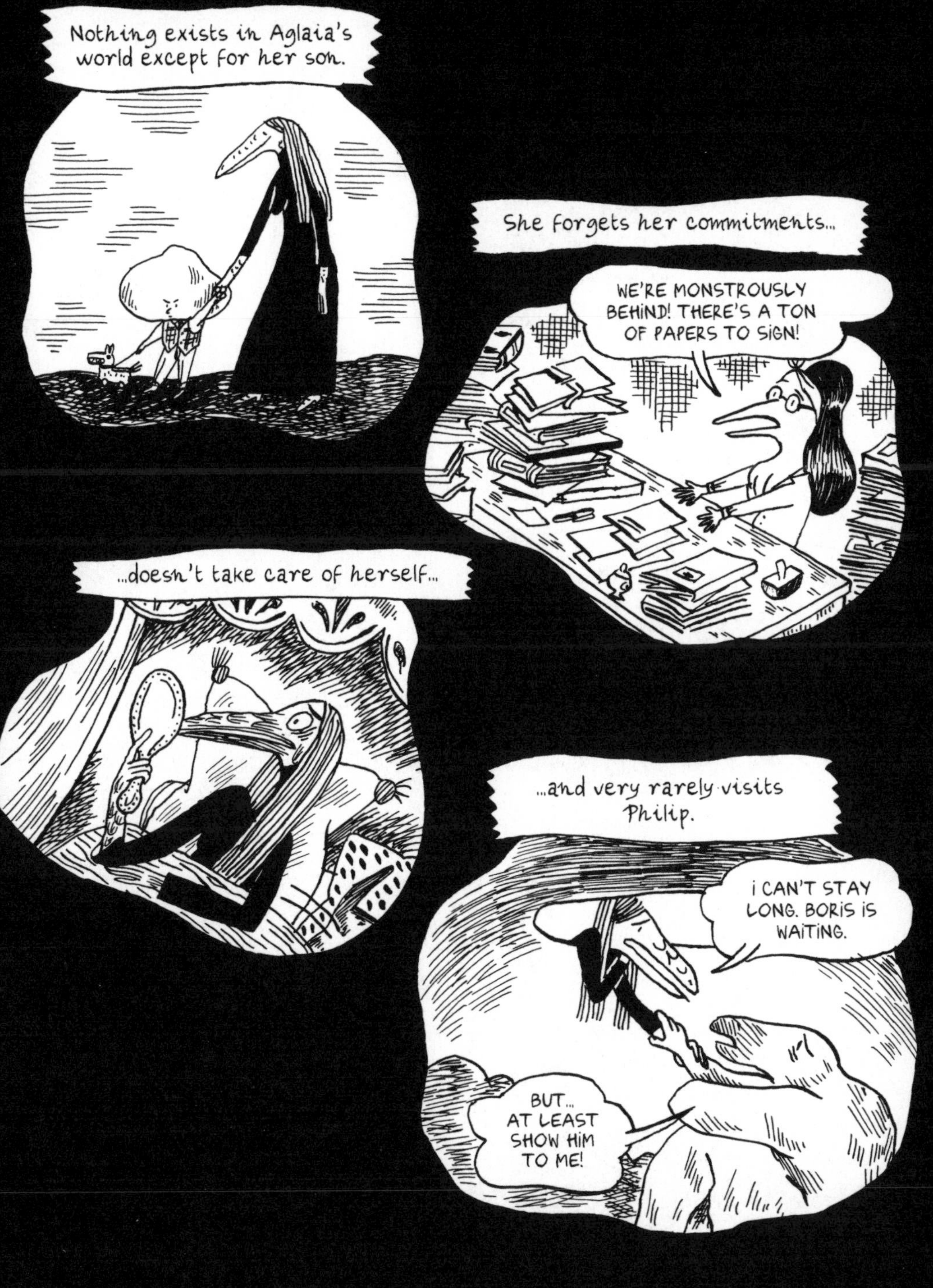
Nothing exists in Aglaia's world except for her son.
She forgets her commitments...
WE'RE MONSTROUSLY BEHIND! THERE'S A TON OF PAPERS TO SIGN!
...doesn't take care of herself...
...and very rarely visits Philip.
I CAN'T STAY LONG. BORIS IS WAITING.
BUT... AT LEAST SHOW HIM TO ME!

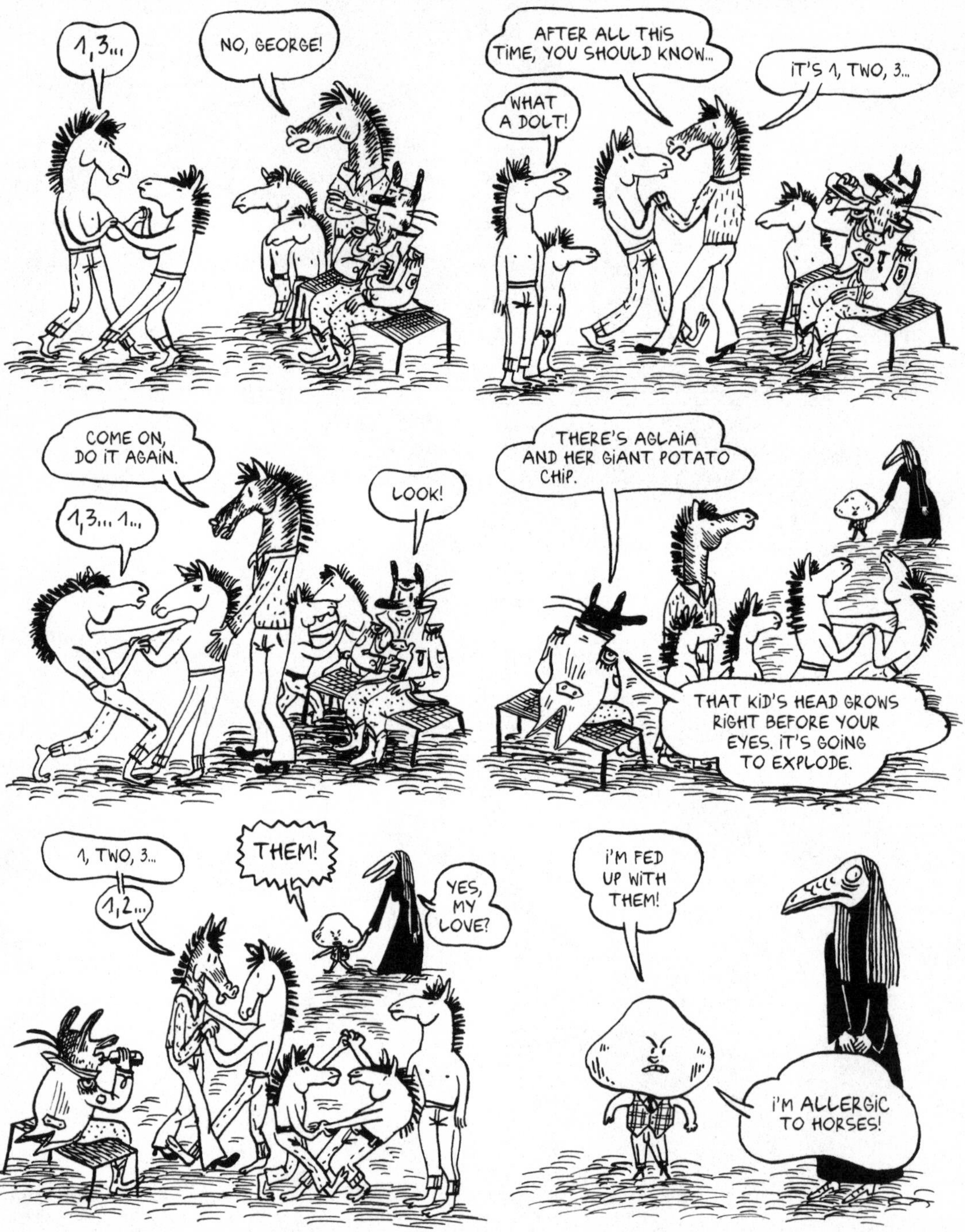
1,3...
NO, GEORGE!
AFTER ALL THIS TIME, YOU SHOULD KNOW...
WHAT A DOLT!
IT'S 1, TWO, 3...
COME ON, DO IT AGAIN.
1,3... 1...
LOOK!
THERE'S AGLAIA AND HER GIANT POTATO CHIP.
THAT KID'S HEAD GROWS RIGHT BEFORE YOUR EYES. IT'S GOING TO EXPLODE.
1, TWO, 3...
1,2...
THEM!
YES, MY LOVE?
I'M FED UP WITH THEM!
I'M ALLERGIC TO HORSES!

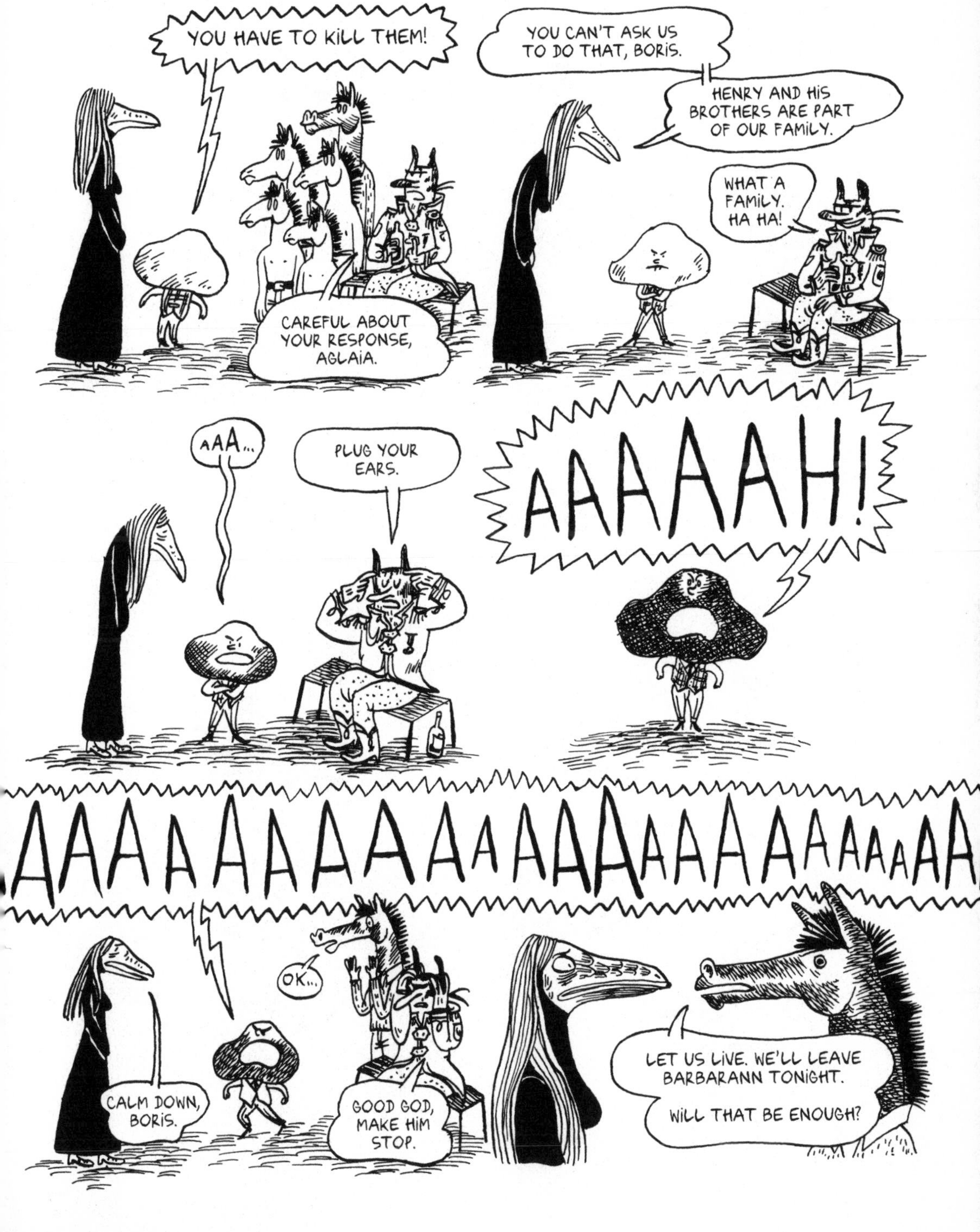
YOU HAVE TO KiLL THEM!
CAREFUL ABOUT YOUR RESPONSE, AGLAiA.
YOU CAN'T ASK US TO DO THAT, BORiS.
HENRY AND HiS BROTHERS ARE PART OF OUR FAMiLY.
WHAT A FAMiLY. HA HA!
AAA...
PLUG YOUR EARS.
AAAAAH!
AAAAAAAAAAAAAAAAAAAA
CALM DOWN, BORiS.
OK...
GOOD GOD, MAKE HiM STOP.
LET US LiVE. WE'LL LEAVE BARBARANN TONiGHT.
WiLL THAT BE ENOUGH?

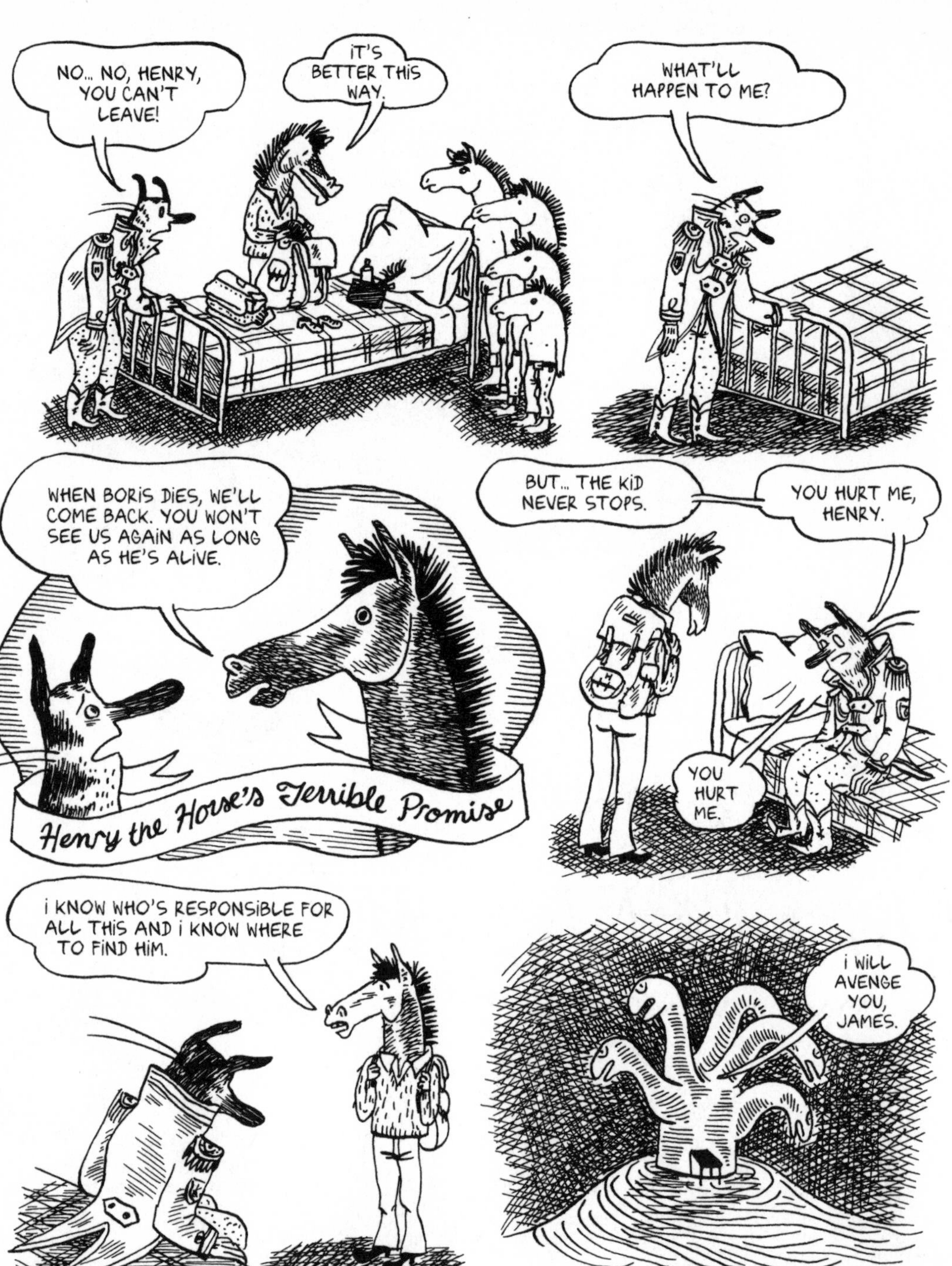
NO... NO, HENRY, YOU CAN'T LEAVE!
IT'S BETTER THIS WAY.
WHAT'LL HAPPEN TO ME?
WHEN BORIS DIES, WE'LL COME BACK. YOU WON'T SEE US AGAIN AS LONG AS HE'S ALIVE.
Henry the Horse's Terrible Promise
BUT... THE KID NEVER STOPS.
YOU HURT ME, HENRY.
YOU HURT ME.
I KNOW WHO'S RESPONSIBLE FOR ALL THIS AND I KNOW WHERE TO FIND HIM.
I WILL AVENGE YOU, JAMES.

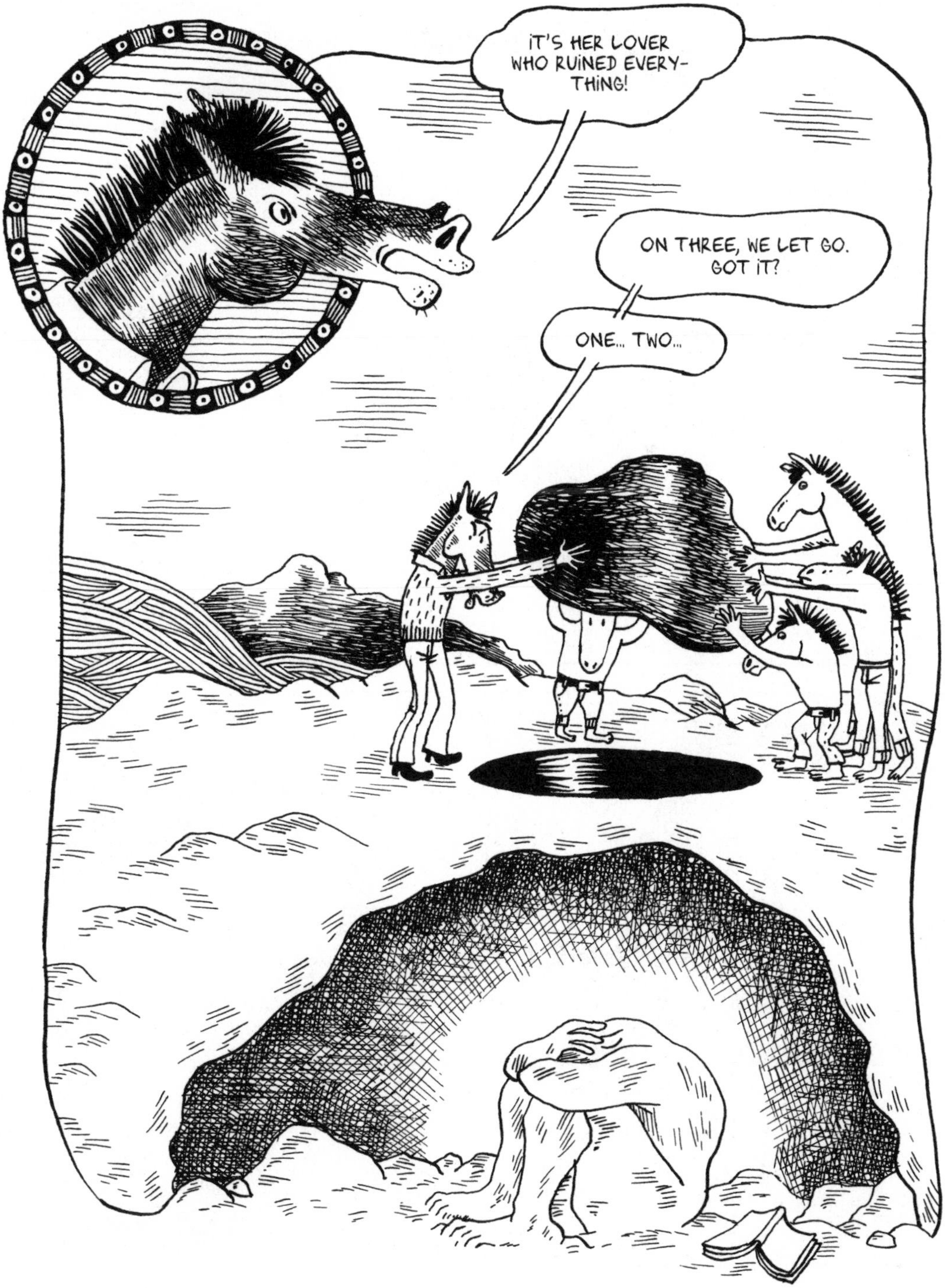
IT'S HER LOVER WHO RUINED EVERY-THING!
ON THREE, WE LET GO. GOT IT?
ONE... TWO...

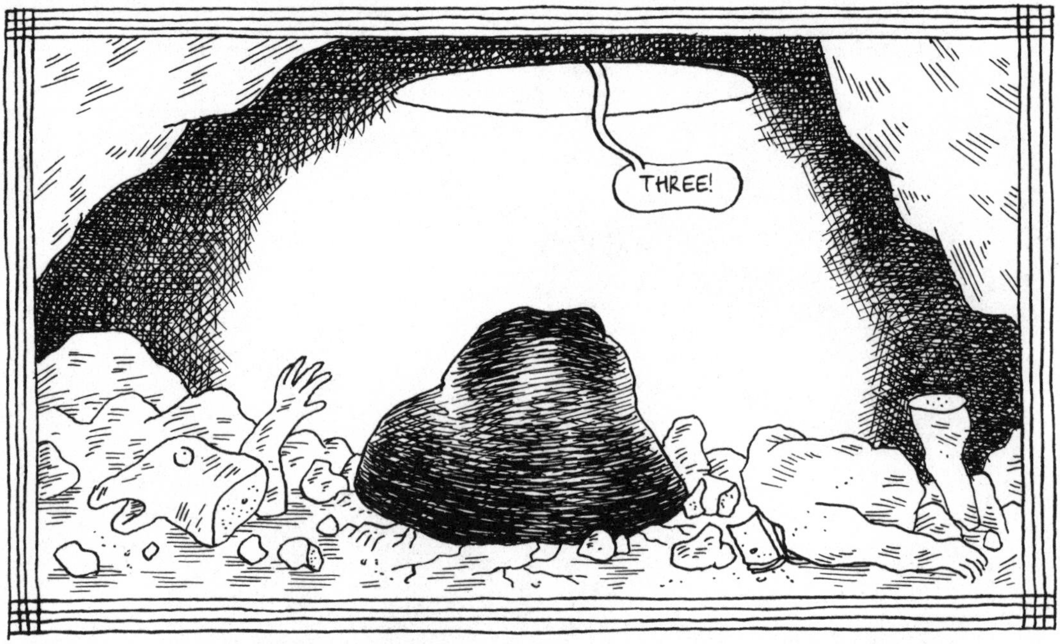
THREE!

Two men had loved Aglaia madly. She lost them both on the same day.

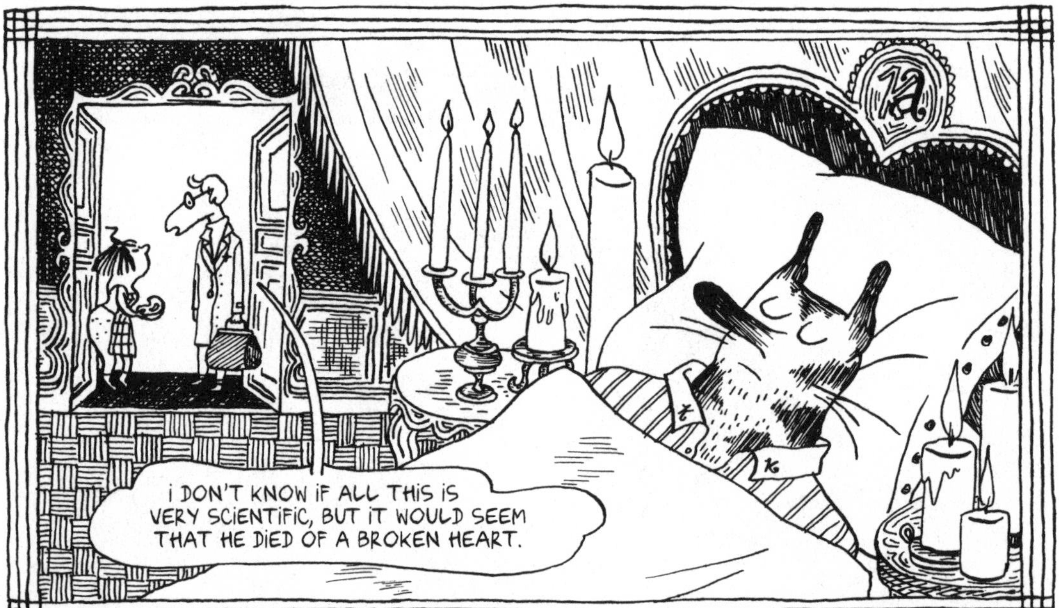
I DON'T KNOW IF ALL THIS IS VERY SCIENTIFIC, BUT IT WOULD SEEM THAT HE DIED OF A BROKEN HEART.

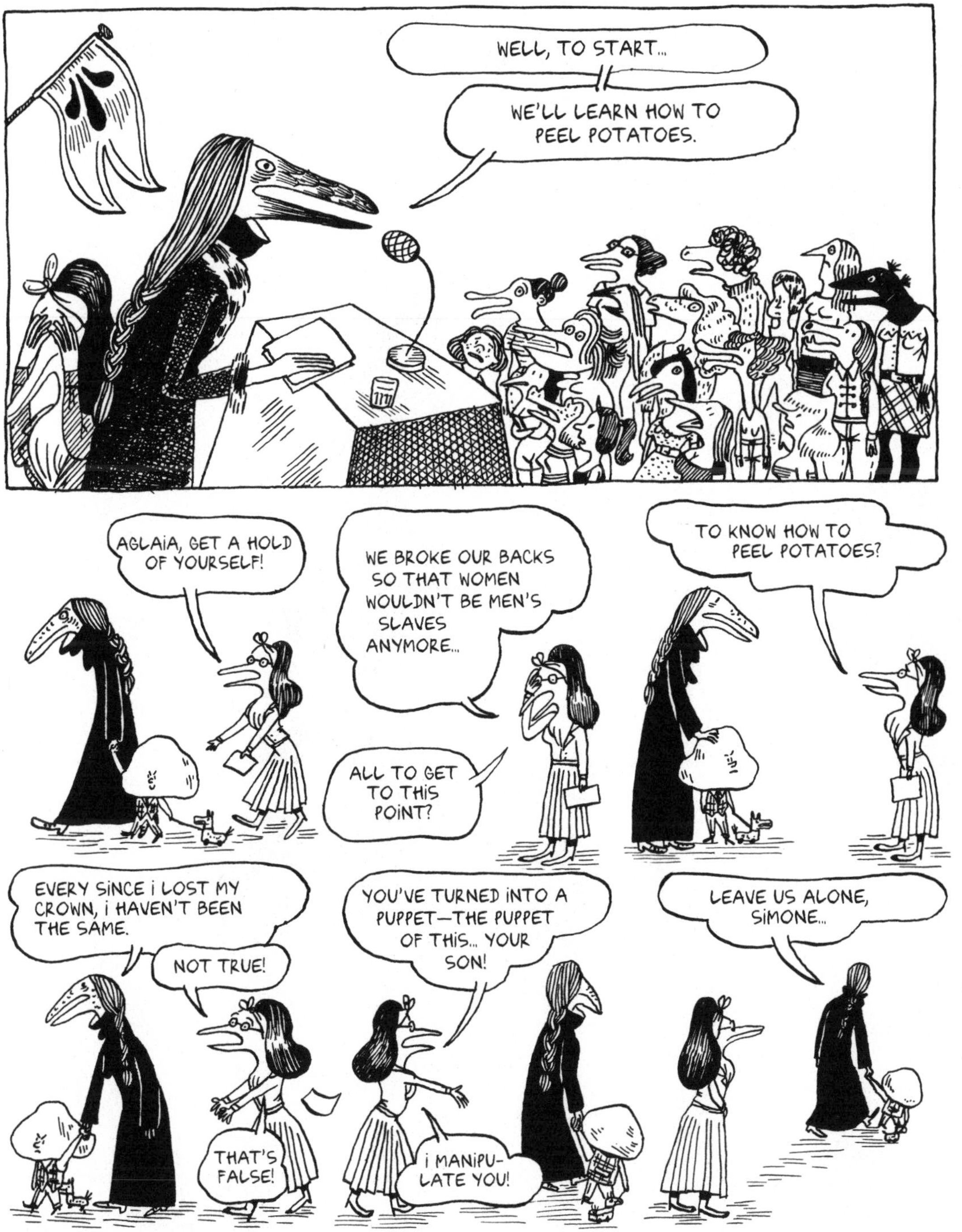
WELL, TO START...
WE'LL LEARN HOW TO PEEL POTATOES.
AGLAIA, GET A HOLD OF YOURSELF!
WE BROKE OUR BACKS SO THAT WOMEN WOULDN'T BE MEN'S SLAVES ANYMORE...
ALL TO GET TO THIS POINT?
TO KNOW HOW TO PEEL POTATOES?
EVERY SINCE I LOST MY CROWN, I HAVEN'T BEEN THE SAME.
NOT TRUE!
THAT'S FALSE!
YOU'VE TURNED INTO A PUPPET—THE PUPPET OF THIS... YOUR SON!
I MANIPU-LATE YOU!
LEAVE US ALONE, SIMONE...

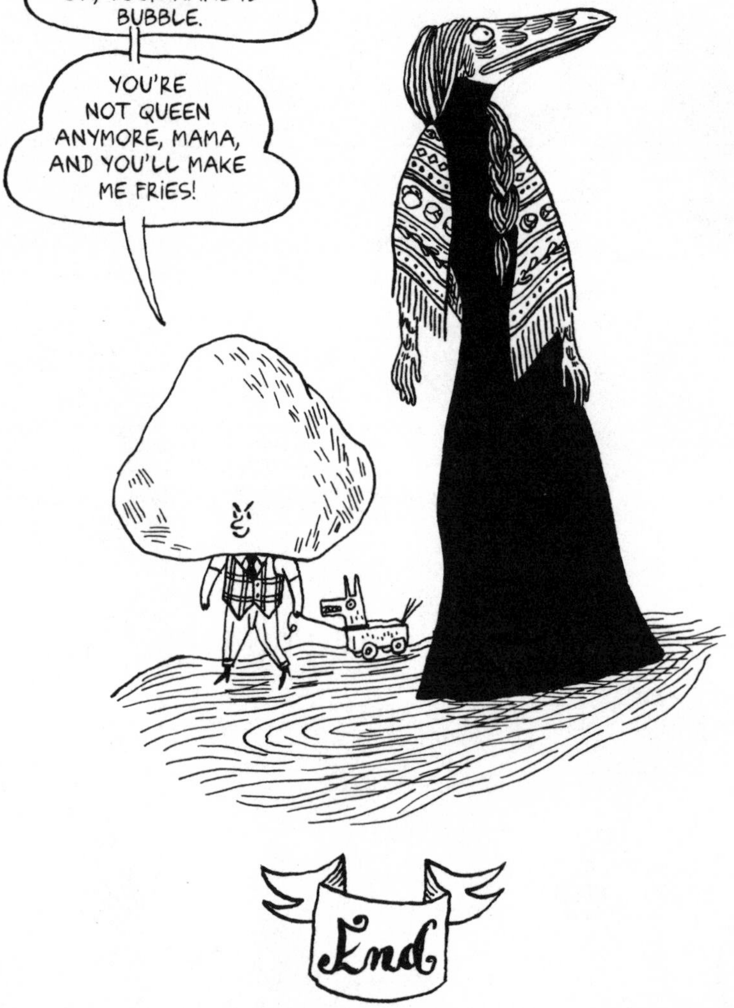
WE'LL GIVE YOU A NEW NAME.
FROM NOW ON, YOUR NAME IS BUBBLE.
YOU'RE NOT QUEEN ANYMORE, MAMA, AND YOU'LL MAKE ME FRIES!
End

EPILOGUE

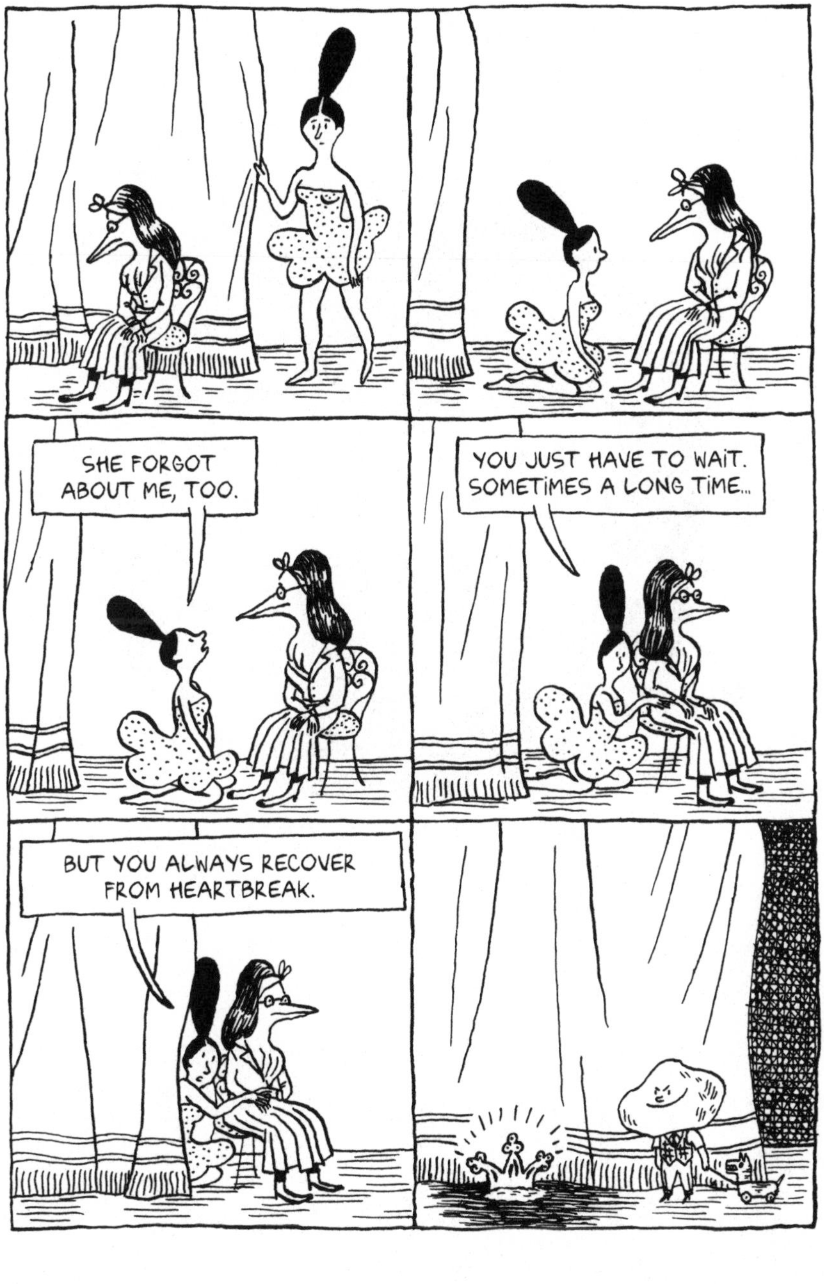

SHE FORGOT ABOUT ME, TOO.
YOU JUST HAVE TO WAIT. SOMETIMES A LONG TIME...
BUT YOU ALWAYS RECOVER FROM HEARTBREAK.